S0-BEZ-069

FEB 2 3 2017

Praise for *Found*

"*Found* portrays a multi-faceted heroine who fights to keep her nursing patients alive, yet is afraid to live fully. Through her travels across the globe, Natalie learns to stop running from her demons, both imagined and very real, and allow love to catch her."

—ELIZABETH HEIN,
author of *How To Climb The Eiffel Tower*

WITHDRAWN
DOWNERS GROVE PUBLIC LIBRARY

"*Found* is an enrapturing story intertwining self-discovery with romance, adventure, and mystery. Not only will the descriptions of multiple countries make you want to travel and explore, but this novel will especially resonate with those who work in the medical field—in so many ways, it is their story."

—DIANE GAGE LOFGREN, MS,
Chief Marketing Officer of a major health care organization,
and the author of *Women I Want To Grow Old With*
and *Get Published: Top Editors Tell You How*

"Full of adventures to exciting and exotic places with colorful characters and sexy men, *Found* is a fast-paced debut novel with unexpected twists and turns."

—ELENA MIKALSEN, PH.D. CLINICAL PSYCHOLOGIST,
member of Women's Fiction Writers Association

FEB 2 3 2017

WITHDRAWN
DOWNERS GROVE PUBLIC LIBRARY

# FOUND

# FOUND

A Novel

## Emily Brett

SparkPress, a BookSparks imprint
A Division of SparkPoint Studio, LLC

Copyright © 2016 Emily Brett

All rights reserved, including the right to reproduce this book
or portions thereof in any form whatsoever.

Published by SparkPress, a BookSparks imprint,
A division of SparkPoint Studio, LLC
Tempe, Arizona, USA, 85281
www.gosparkpress.com

Published 2016

Printed in the United States of America

ISBN: 978-1-940716-80-0 (pbk)
ISBN: 978-1-940716-81-7 (e-bk)
Library of Congress Control Number: 2016940082

Cover design © Julie Metz, Ltd./metzdesign.com
Author photo © Jeff Noble
Formatting by Katherine Lloyd/theDESKonline.com

All company and/or product names may be trade names,
logos, trademarks, and/or registered trademarks and are the
property of their respective owners.

THIS IS A WORK OF FICTION. NAMES, CHARACTERS,
PLACES, AND INCIDENTS EITHER ARE THE PRODUCT OF THE
AUTHOR'S IMAGINATION OR ARE USED FICTITIOUSLY.
ANY RESEMBLANCE TO ACTUAL PERSONS, LIVING OR DEAD,
IS ENTIRELY COINCIDENTAL.

*For Glenn,*

*the love of my life*

# 1

et the crash cart, I'm calling a code!" I slammed the bright
blue button. Mr. Watson's life hung in the balance. Nurses,
respiratory therapists, and doctors rushed into room 2211. I
snapped open my patient's gown and attached defibrillator pads
to his chest, hoping to shock him back to life. It didn't matter that I hadn't had my coffee yet because nothing beats the
adrenaline rush of performing a code first thing in the morning.
*Come on, Natalie. You've done this a thousand times. Save his ass!* I
adjusted the monitors, blew away the stubborn curl that always
fell into my eyes, and got ready to shock.

Something hadn't looked right the minute I entered the
room. The patient, a sixty-four-year-old recovering from a heart
attack, appeared pale and plastic. His eyes were rolled to the
back of his head and his mouth gaped wide open, lips dry and
cracked. I walked around the bed to check on Mr. Watson and
almost slipped right on my ass. A massive puddle of bright red
blood had begun to coagulate on the white linoleum floor. A
steady trickle dripped from his pinky finger. The arterial line,
like an IV but placed in an artery to continuously monitor blood
pressure, dangled by a thin piece of tape.

Dr. Lyken rushed into the room in response to the overhead
emergency page.

"What's going on, Natalie?"

"He's bleeding out!" I yelled "Clear!" and delivered two hundred kilojoules of electricity to my patient's heart. The smell of singed hair reached my nostrils. *Do not die on me. Come on!*

Doctors and nurses watched the monitors, waiting for the rhythmic blips to move across the screen, while one nurse straddled the patient and performed CPR. Another nurse began applying mounds of gauze to the open artery, hoping to stop the hemorrhage. Only the crack of a rib could be heard with each chest compression. My heart raced and I bit down on my bottom lip. Paddles in hand, I hovered over the patient, ready to shock again. *Come on, Watson. Fucking live!*

"What else?" Dr. Lyken asked. "Another round of epinephrine, please." Gloves were flying on and off as medical staff ran in and out, barking orders to nurses and technicians.

"He came in with a heart attack and is supposed to go the OR later this afternoon." I quickly changed the EKG paper on the heart monitor, hoping with a fresh strip we'd see a blip of life. "His wife is Betty Watson, the RN who works here. He's lost a lot of blood."

The doctor peered down at the blood-soaked gauze on the man's arm, where the line had been connected. The bleeding had stopped but unfortunately, so had his heart. "More lidocaine and continue with CPR," he said.

Another doctor popped his head into the room. "Anything I can do to help here?" he asked.

"We've got it covered. Thanks," Dr. Lyken said.

I looked back at Dr. Lyken. "His wife visited him early this morning, stayed a few minutes, and left right at the seven o'clock shift change. We were still going over reports when she walked out. Shortly after that, his oxygen dropped and his blood pressure plummeted." I got ready to deliver yet another shock. More smells of burning hair. The steady tone of the flatline EKG and the hum and beeps of the IV pumps filled the room as we all anxiously stared at the heart monitor.

"Anybody else come in the room before you got here?" asked the doctor. Only authorized visitors were allowed in and out of the ICU, under the supervision of the patient's nurse.

"The night nurse, I assume, or his wife." Two respiratory techs squeezed oxygen into the mask secured over Mr. Watson's face. *Breathe, damn it!*

Another two rounds of medication and electric shocks. Nothing. I placed my stethoscope on Mr. Watson's chest. *Damn.* I shook my head at Dr. Lyken. Trash lay everywhere. Gauze, catheters, IV bags were strewn all over the room. At 7:42 a.m., the doctor ordered everyone to stop and called out the time of death. *Fuck! I failed.*

Walking out of the room, I peeled off the pieces of my disposable protective gear and slammed them into the biohazard bin. I went to the sink to wash my hands. My purple clogs were splashed with bodily fluids and stuck to the carpet as I walked the hallway. God only knew what kinds of filth these shoes had accumulated. After drying my hands, I pulled out the disinfectant wipes and cleaned my clogs. This was the third code we'd run this week, but unlike the previous two this one did not have a happy ending. My energy nose-dived from the adrenaline rush, but I still had almost my whole shift to get through.

Working in this environment for the past seven years had left me a bit immune to the sadness of death. Saving lives allows me to feel strong and important, but I know I can't save them all, or dwell on the ones I didn't. But it still sucks. Seasoned ICU nurses, like myself, know they must recover quickly and then move on.

I not only wanted to move on to my next patient, but I felt a strong desire to move on to another hospital, another city, another world. I loved being an ICU nurse but Porter was an old city hospital and slow to make any changes. The administration, equipment, and even the staff were stale. Other hospitals were bringing in electronic charting, tuition reimbursement, and nursing education incentives. I needed a change. I feared if I didn't do something soon, I might run out of time.

For the past several months, travel nurse companies had been contacting me. I'd agreed to let one send me more information. I loved the challenge of taking on a new adventure and I knew travel nursing could be my ticket out of here. Moving around from place to place would allow me to be free and independent. I could make a name for myself, not one that preceded "the renowned surgeon's daughter." God, I hated that. I wished people would respect me for how I do my job, not because of my last name. Mom had even told me to "go color the world." I wasn't sure how much time I had left, anyway. And if I could get paid as a nurse to travel, even better!

I returned to Mr. Watson's room and began the postmortem care. The charge nurse, Judy, came in to help, carrying a gray body bag. We began pulling Mr. Watson's tubes, including the urine catheter and both IVs. I wet washcloths and started to clean Mr. Watson's naked body. The gel from the defibrillator pads stuck to his burnt, gray chest hair and his arms were bloodstained. I taped up holes where the tubes had been and rolled him to his right side so that the charge nurse could slip the body bag underneath. Moving him on his left, we pulled the other half of the bag out, placing his body completely on top of it. Judy tucked his arms and legs into the large plastic sack. With one last wipe of the washcloth to his face, I leaned into his ear and whispered, *"You can go now; it's okay."*

"Why do you always do that?" asked Judy.

"What?"

"Whisper in a patient's ear. I've seen you do it several times. What do you say to them?"

"I give them permission to go. The hospice nurses did it with my mom. They told me that when you give someone approval to go, they seem more at peace. I think it helps. It's like their own little send-off."

"I like that, Natalie." She gave me a warm smile.

I pulled up the zipper, encasing his body in the bag, gently wrapping him in his cocoon. I left the head of the bag open for a brief minute and sighed. This part of the job never seemed easy, no matter who had died. By closing the bag, his inexistence became final. The patient would be off to whatever awaited him on the other side—like stuffing an envelope and then sending it off in the mail, never to be seen again. Two security guards came into the room and with one final zip, my patient, now a tagged 185-pound bag, headed to the morgue.

"Wait!" a female voice yelled. Betty Watson sauntered over to her dead husband. She shifted the pink motorcycle helmet under her arm and opened the body bag. Her nails were stained yellow from too many cigarettes.

"Betty, hi. Um . . . I'm sorry." Fumbling for words, I wiped my forehead with the back of my hand and looked down at the body, then peeled off my gloves.

Betty took Mr. Watson's cold hand and slid his gold wedding ring off his finger. She appeared to be . . . smirking? Next, she went for the ruby on his pinky. She placed both pieces of jewelry in her pocket and zipped him back up. "Thank you," she said before walking away. The ice in her Russian accent could freeze a country. *She didn't just do that?*

Judy and I exchanged glances. "Weird," Judy said, signaling the security guards to wheel Mr. Watson away.

"Should I go after her?" I started biting my nails. Ever since

I'd told Betty I didn't want to be friends anymore, I had avoided her at all costs.

"Nah. Leave her alone. She's a good nurse, but a bit crazy. You'll only open the door again to something you don't want. Let her go. Come on, we've got patients waiting for beds."

I sat down at the nurse's station to finish charting. Thirty minutes later, I had received two new patients: an elderly, dying woman sent in from a nursing home with skin wounds and a young woman fresh out of surgery after a mastectomy from breast cancer. These were easy admissions and I welcomed a couple of low-stress assignments. Fortunately, caring for two new patients distracted me from the morning chaos. I could focus on them now, not on Mr. Watson's death.

Lunch came as a welcome break and I decided to eat with a few of my closest nurse friends. I met Karen and Elizabeth in the lounge since the recent snowfall had made it too cold to eat outside. We placed our Styrofoam containers on the table and I started spreading dressing over my salad.

Karen is a single mother of two with a scumbag for an ex-husband who, for the longest time, paid her no child support. A petite, pretty Italian woman, she put herself through nursing school and usually worked the bonus shifts to make extra money. For someone so small, she sure didn't take any shit. She once told me she had hired a private investigator to track down her deadbeat ex. The detective helped her find out where he lived, worked, and how much money he had. A few weeks later, payments poured in.

"We heard what happened this morning, Nat. That sucks!" Karen said. "I'm sorry you walked into that first thing. Have you seen Betty?"

"Yeah. She came by as we were sending him to the morgue. Didn't say much, just took his rings. It creeped me out."

"You were always so nice to her," Elizabeth said. "If she did to me what she did to you, I would've taken her outside and shown her a thing or two. Calling you at all hours of the night to talk about her love life? Showing up at your house? That would piss me off." Elizabeth took a bite of pizza. A tall blonde with bright blue eyes, she'd been a nurse for ten years and had become a bit jaded. She was one of the good ones still left at Porter, but if you crossed her or did something to piss her off, she wouldn't hesitate to report you. She's great to have on your side, one of the best nurses I know, but if the day comes when you mess up, pray that she's not working with you.

"She's so weird. I told you that," Karen said, wrinkling her nose. "She gets too clingy with people and then won't leave them alone. And didn't she marry that guy three weeks after meeting him? And now he's dead. What's up with that?"

"She seemed normal when we first met. It's only been lately that something seems like it's snapped."

"Crazy woman." Elizabeth said, playing with the jeweled lanyard around her neck. I could see she had pasted a fresh picture of her young daughter to the badge dangling at her busty chest. "Natalie, you're staring off. You okay?"

I snapped out of my thoughts. "Listen, guys. I've been thinking about . . . leaving."

Karen pulled back her thick curls and formed a bun on top of her head, securing it with a pen. "What do you mean?"

"I feel . . . stuck. Like I need a fresh start. Maybe it's time for me to move on." I bit the inside of my cheek and moved the fork around in my food.

"Is this about that jackoff from the other day?" Elizabeth asked. "Forget him. You'll bounce back from that piece of shit; you always do."

"It's everything lately. I don't know . . . "

"Natalie, are you thinking about leaving Porter?" Karen asked.

"Yeah, like maybe . . . traveling." I couldn't look her in the eye.

"You mean, like a travel nurse? Going to different hospitals and working in different places all the time? I don't know, Nat." We sat eating in silence for several seconds, and Karen kept her eyes on me the entire time. "So tell me about the jackoff."

"There's not much to tell. Another blind date. A friend from college kept bugging me to meet this cop who worked with her husband. After a few phone calls, he asked me to lunch. During the last phone conversation, he asked me, if I looked like a movie star, who would it be?" Karen raised her eyebrows and Elizabeth giggled.

I rolled my eyes and kept talking. "Not really thinking about it, I decided on Minnie Driver. You know, from her first movie, *Circle of Friends*: roundish face with long, frizzy, curly hair. It was the only answer I could come up with on the spot. He must've liked my response because we made a date."

"Okay. Go on," Karen said.

I pushed my lunch away, my appetite gone. "When I opened the door—shit, you should've seen his face. Utter disappointment. His shoulders slumped and I knew he didn't want to go through with it."

"Don't be ridiculous, Nat. Come on."

"I'm not done, Karen. It gets worse. We got in his truck and started driving. After about ten minutes of very, very small talk, he made a U-turn and headed back toward my apartment."

"He brought you back home? Why?"

I folded my arms across my chest and leaned back in the chair. "Good question. I asked him that and he said, 'Um, I just remembered something I've got to take care of at a friend's house. You know, water plants, check the doors. I totally spaced

it and really need to go. Do you mind if we do this another time?'
Nice, huh?"

"No! Really? I don't get it." Karen reached for my arm.

"Karen, even though I wanted to get out of the car and be
thankful that I didn't spend another second with this guy, I fucking went upstairs and cried. He didn't like the way I looked.
Period. As if he was anything special."

"That's total bullshit," Elizabeth chimed in.

"I agree but I'm so tired of the dating game. How many
more of these shitheads do I need to go through? It's like I'm
attracting shit. Either they become a one-night stand or they're
shit. I'm twenty-seven years old. I don't have time for this crap."

"And this is the reason you want to quit your job and leave?
Natalie, you're a beautiful person. So it wasn't meant to be. There
are a lot of nice guys out there. You'll find one."

"Not really interested." Nobody said anything. Breaking the
silence, I continued. "That's not the only reason. I feel I'd better
do something before it's too late." Karen reached for my hand
and placed hers on top of mine. "Sorry to ruin lunch with all my
crap. I just—"

"Hey, I need help!" a nurse yelled from one of the rooms
down the hallway.

The three of us jumped up and ran to where Pat, a very tiny,
older nurse, struggled under the weight of a four hundred-pound
man. We walked into a smell so foul that I almost brought up
my lunch. This man, who'd been admitted for alcohol intoxi-
cation, had had a bowel movement in his bed with the room
serving as his toilet. He had tried to get up, but being drunk, his
grossly obese, naked body got stuck in the bedrails, along with
all his shit. The sheets, the floor, and the patient were covered in
feces. The room stank like sewage. Pat just stood there shaking
her head while the patient laughed.

Elizabeth went over to his large body, tattooed with swastikas and skulls, and asked, "You think this is funny?" The man laughed harder. I reached over and pulled the pleated curtain shut so that others outside of the room wouldn't have to witness the disgusting mess.

The man's head looked like a watermelon with a filthy mustache. His eyes were cold and dark, and he kept laughing at us, jiggling the fat rolls stuck between the bed rails. Clenching my back teeth and trying not to breathe, I went to get washcloths, a basin of soapy water, and a fresh, extra-large gown. Karen and I, lucky us, lifted the patient from his filthy bed to a chair. We struggled under his weight and the smell. He said with a sinister smile, "Make sure you don't miss any spots!" I almost intentionally dropped him on his ass. *I've really got to get out of here.*

Thirty minutes later the room sparkled and so did the patient. Only the smell of peppermint oil and disinfectant filled the ICU. I didn't think the day could get any worse. I put my critical care reference books and coffee mug into my messenger bag, anxious to get home to take a very long shower. I needed to put this day behind me.

# 2

I poured myself a glass of wine and collapsed on the couch. Swallowing a sip of the rich, acidic alcohol, I relaxed. I sat in silence, playing with a swimming medal that had fallen from my trophy shelf above and thinking about what had happened earlier that morning.

Something bothered me about what I'd walked into. The bandage that was supposed to keep Mr. Watson's line in place had looked as if it had been perfectly peeled off his skin, without a rip. If the line had fallen out on its own, the stress from the dangling catheter would've ripped the dressing. It looked as if someone had purposely taken off the gauze and tape very gently, keeping the whole contraption intact. I didn't remember hearing the alarms go off. Had they been muted? That could only be done two ways: on the monitor from within the room, or sometimes—when on a phone call or talking to someone at the nurse's station and the alarms went off—after making sure it was not urgent, a nurse could mute the alarm on the main monitor for thirty seconds. But only trained staff knew that. Maybe Mr. Watson hadn't just bled out. Maybe someone sabotaged him. I leaned my head against the back of the couch and closed my eyes. Poor Betty; bad luck seemed to follow her everywhere. *Maybe I should call to check on her. Then again, why did I ever befriend her?*

"Hi, Betty? It's Natalie." I bit the nail clean off my right thumb.

"Yes? What do you want? Last time we talked you told me to lose your number. I assumed you would've done the same." Her words cut through the phone.

I sighed deeply. "I know. I just wanted to tell you I-I'm sorry we couldn't save your husband. I tried to tell you when you came to see him this morning."

"Yeah, well, such is life." She smacked her gum and I heard ice clinking around a glass.

"Um, okay. I . . ." I cleared my throat.

"Look, Natalie. You were done with me. I make a mistake or two and that's it for you. We're no longer friends. You said it yourself. So fine, that's it. Piss off."

I closed my eyes and inhaled the fermented grapes from my wine. "I'm sorry I blew you off." Silence. *This is a shitty idea, Natalie.* "Look, I feel awful that your husband died on my watch. I feel like it could've been prevented and I want you to know that . . ."

"What do you mean, prevented? Accidents can be prevented. You calling this an accident?"

"N-No, I'm not saying that . . . I just . . ." I shook my head. *Oh, forget it.* "Look, I'm sorry for your loss. That's all I wanted to say."

"Well, I don't need your 'sorry.' Bad stuff happens to me all the time. You wouldn't get that, being Daddy's little girl. Go back to your perfect life and don't worry about me. I'll be fine. I. Always. Survive." Her words resounded low and hard.

Dial tone. The bitch had hung up on me. Judy was right; I should've left Betty alone. She'd caused me so much trouble already.

I had been assigned relief charge nurse one day with Betty as one of my staff nurses. Sometimes staff nurses get put in charge when the lead nurses call in sick, so I filled in. Charge nurses act as supervisors of the floor. They make the nursing assignments, rove around the unit helping any nurse who needs it, and put out any fires. I was watching Betty's patient while she went to lunch when the shit hit the fan. Betty had told me she'd just hung the last IV antibiotic for her stable pneumonia patient. She had been off the unit less than five minutes when her patient's call bell went off. I walked in and glanced at the monitor. Her heart rate and blood pressure were running way too high. What the hell? Had Betty not just given me a stable report? I checked on Mrs. Lewis, the patient, and asked her if she felt okay.

"My chest hurts and I can't breathe," she said, beads of sweat clustering upon her forehead, her eyes open wide and her cheeks bright red with heat.

"Were you feeling this way before now?" I frantically surveyed her body for answers.

"I felt fine. Then the nurse came in. Told me she started giving me the antibiotic. Then, the pain started." She grabbed her chest and shot straight up in bed. "Help me, please!"

I took the IV bag in my hands and turned it over to check the label. *Fuck me!* Betty had hung the wrong medication! Damn it! I stopped the IV pump and opened the normal saline bag to flush out Mrs. Lewis's veins. Betty had infused a medication used to increase a patient's blood pressure when it got too low. Mrs. Lewis had been admitted a few days earlier with low blood pressure and pneumonia. The ER had started her on meds, but according to her chart, over the last few days she had stabilized. The blood pressure drug had not been removed from her med list and there must have been a bag left in her medicine drawer. Both bags looked identical. Dipshit had grabbed the wrong bag!

I stayed with the patient and watched her heart rate begin to decrease and her blood pressure normalize. The medication appeared to be out of her system and I felt confident she'd be okay. I didn't explain to Mrs. Lewis the details of what had happened. I swiftly removed the IV bag Betty had hung and emptied it in the sink. Checking again that the saline flowed freely into her arm, I reassured her that she would start to feel better soon. Betty could do all the explaining to her patient later. Sure that the patient would recover without any issues, I went to go find Betty. I found her eating alone, as usual, in the lunchroom.

"We need to talk," I said, sitting down next to her and slamming the empty medication bag on the table. "You hung the wrong med on your patient, not the antibiotic."

"What? No, I hung the antibiotic, like I told you when I went to lunch." Betty kept shoving her salad into her mouth.

I leaned in closer. "No, Betty, you didn't. You hung dopamine. She could've had a heart attack. That's a big deal," I told her, my voice rising.

Betty's hand holding the fork now made a fist, with the tongs pointing toward my hand. Her knuckles went white and she started to shake. "Natalie. Please. Do not report this. I can't afford another write-up. I'll be suspended. I'm on probation as it is. I won't be able to feed my kid."

I glanced at the fork. *This chick is crazy.* Slowly, I moved my hand to my lap and out of Betty's reach. "What do you want me to do, Betty? Ignore it? I can't do that. I won't do that. You almost killed your patient."

She put down the fork. "Natalie, I'm begging you. The patient is okay now, right? What did you tell her?"

"I haven't told her anything. I went in and shut off the IV as soon as I saw it. Her heart rate and blood pressure came down within a few minutes. She doesn't have a clue what happened."

Betty leaned back in her chair and tilted her head as a slow sneer came across her face. "Okay, then. Let's just pretend it didn't happen. I cannot lose this job, Natalie." Then, her long nails reached across the table and sank into my arm.

My stomach turned rock hard and I stood up from the table. I narrowed my eyes on Betty. "Don't let it happen again." I had to get out of there.

I don't know why I listened to Betty's pleading. I can't explain it. Fear? Pity? Whatever. I tossed aside my integrity and agreed to cover up her error, not saying a word about it again. Each day that has gone by since, I've regretted my decision. But if I were to say anything now, it'd turn into a whole big deal. Betty's stupidity would make me look bad and the fact that I covered it up, even worse! Why did I have to be charge nurse that day? It tore at my gut. And yet, I still remained closed-mouthed.

Then there was Mr. Petronoff. Betty had been assigned to him one morning. I had the two patients next door. When Betty introduced herself, Mr. Petronoff began screaming in Russian: "*Eezverg! Eezverg!*"

I ran into his room to see if I could help and saw Betty leaning over Mr. Petronoff, whispering in his ear, her hands on both of his shoulders, and his knees pulled up to his chest. I couldn't make out her words. His face appeared ashen and his lips trembled.

"What's going on here?" I barked.

Betty slowly let go of her patient's shoulders and stood up, one vertebra at a time. She turned toward me, slunk over to where I stood and whispered into my ear, "He's crazy." I watched Betty leave and then went over to Mr. Petronoff.

"Are you okay, sir?" I fumbled with his sheets, trying to comfort him. His pupils filled up his eyes.

Mr. Petronoff gripped my hand. "Please, please, nurse. I don't want her taking care of me. Please."

"What happened?"

"No. No." He rolled on his side, turning his back to me.

Touching his shoulder, I reassured him. "Okay. Let me go see what's going on. Don't worry, okay? I'll be right back." Leaving the room, I could still hear him muttering, "*Eezverg, eezverg.*" I went to the nurse's station where Betty stood with the charge nurse.

"Natalie, do you mind switching patients with Betty? She knows Mr. Petronoff and feels it would be a conflict of interest. She's not comfortable taking care of him." Betty stood up very tall and coldness banked in her eyes.

*Fuck this. I'm done with her.* Confused about what I had witnessed in the room and what Mr. Petronoff kept repeating to me, I naïvely accepted the change. Grabbing Betty's arm as she walked by me, I wanted to know what had happened prior to my coming into the room.

"Nothing. The guy's crazy," she said with a flat tone. "I know him from way back. He's a crazy Russian." Before I could ask more, Betty pulled away from me and walked off.

Relieved when I told him I would be his nurse, Mr. Petronoff relaxed and his mutterings stopped. I had started examining him when the charge nurse poked her head into the room, asking me if his wife could come in.

"Sure, bring her back."

"She can explain to you," he said, nodding his head. I took the stethoscope out of my ears. Mr. Petronoff looked toward the curtain.

"Explain what to me, Mr. Petronoff?" I straightened his blankets.

"Good morning. Hello," his wife said, nodding in my direction and kissing her husband on the forehead. Mr. Petronoff spoke in Russian to his wife. She then whirled her head around and squinted at me. "What is going on here? My husband is frightened." She squeezed his hand.

This was getting too weird. "Um, I'm sorry. I don't understand . . . let me introduce myself. I'm—"

"That other woman who came in here. What is her name?"

"The nurse? There was another nurse in here. Her name is Betty. It's all good now. I'm his nurse."

Mrs. Petronoff quickly shoved open the curtains and looked around the unit. I came up behind her and asked that she come back in the room. Her eyes were fixed on Betty, who was across the hall. Mrs. Petronoff quickly spun around and walked back into the room.

"Do you know who that woman is?" she said in her thick accent, her finger wagging at me.

Sighing, I explained. "Look, I'm your husband's nurse. I'm Natalie."

"Do you know what the word '*eezverg*' means, Nurse Natalie?" Her eyes narrowed.

"No, I don't."

"The word mean *monster*."

"Okay . . . Betty's a monster?" *They're all fucking nuts!*

"She used to be involved . . . What you call it? Mob?"

"The mob?" My voice raised several octaves. Mrs. Petronoff crossed her arms in front of her chest. She didn't look happy with me. I cleared my throat. "I'm sorry, but Betty's been a nurse here for a while."

"Do you know where she came from? What she was?"

"She came from Russia. I assume she was a nurse there."

Mrs. Petronoff threw her finger in front of my face. "Ha! You don't know anything about her! Just wait . . . you'll see."

Before Mrs. Petronoff could finish, I heard the code bell go off next door and I ran out of the room to help. Mr. Petronoff got transferred out of the ICU before his wife had finished her story.

I didn't want to think too much about Betty. She annoyed

the crap out of me with her endless phone calls after work about a guy she'd met online, or how hot and heavy sex got with this doctor or that doctor. I didn't want to hear any more. I finally stopped answering her calls. Why did I feel the need to help everybody? Like I'm some kind of savior or something?

Right. I couldn't even save my own mother.

I definitely needed to get away from Porter for a while. To clear my head, I walked down to the mailbox and retrieved three days' worth of mail. I separated junk and bills, then came across a thick envelope that caught my attention. The writing on the front said, "The Traveling Nurse: An International Organization— Doing what you love, wherever your heart takes you." It was the company I had given my address to, requesting more information.

*Follow the signs, Natalie. Follow the signs.*

I opened the envelope and started reading about how the international organization sent nurses to different countries. A stipend and room and board were included. They wanted a time commitment ranging anywhere from two weeks to two years. The current featured country: Belize. *Where the hell's Belize?* On the brochure, a woman snorkled amidst a rainbow of tropical fish, another woman relaxed in a hammock hanging between two coconut trees with a view of the Caribbean Sea, and a man waterskied in clear blue waters.

*This could be my chance,* I thought. Being able to be a nurse in a place straight out of a Corona commercial, getting paid for it and having benefits? *What the hell am I waiting for?*

After a much-needed good night's sleep, I felt happy to be off work for two days and wanted to go to the pool for a quick workout. Swimming always cleared my head.

The pool at Foxwood Fitness Center reminded me of my swimming days. What I wouldn't give to go back to the days of racing. Before Mom . . . I closed my eyes and dove in. The water was always a cool seventy-four degrees, and even though you could see several areas of rust and broken tiles, I loved it. Stroke after stroke, I let the bubbles out through my nose and felt exhilarated. I realized that I looked forward to investigating this travel nurse thing.

After swimming two miles, I climbed out of the pool, wrapped my towel around my waist, and got in the car, leaving a wet mark on my seat. Pool bathrooms don't exactly win cleanliness awards. I always wear my towel home and change in the privacy of my own room. Back at my apartment, I took a deep breath and made my weekly phone call to my dad.

"Hello? Natalie?" I could hear Willie Nelson playing in the background.

"Hi, Dad. How are you?" I asked, with little inflection. I spit out a piece of cuticle I had bitten off.

"Okay. You?" He turned the music down and I thought I heard him shush someone.

"I'm fine. Have you talked to Jennifer lately?" I picked up a picture of my mother and held it to my chest. *Why is it so hard to talk to him? Help me, Mom.*

"I see her around the hospital. We had lunch the other day. Your sister has become a very good physician. I'm proud of her." He cleared his throat.

I closed my eyes and shook my head. "Well, tell her hi for me next time you see her."

Jennifer has always been my dad's favorite. She became the doctor, she married and gave him a grandkid, and she always sees him at work. I, on the other hand, captured my mom's heart in a special way and I'm happy I did.

"Will do." A woman giggled in the background.

*Damn him.* "Um, real quick, Dad. I've been thinking about applying for a job as a travel nurse."

"I see." He cleared his throat again. "I'm not sure I like the idea of you traveling alone, Natalie."

"I'll be fine. I don't need a man to travel. Or, to do anything else. I'm perfectly capable of being on my own. In fact, I'm used to it."

"That's not what I meant. Look, I—"

"Dad, I appreciate your concern but I'm not asking for approval. I'm trying to keep you informed of what is going on in my life."

He let out a sigh and again hushed whoever occupied his bed. *Oh god, Dad, not another one.*

"Well, consider me informed. Let me know when you leave, please." His words were sharp.

I laughed bitterly under my breath. After several seconds of silently listening to each other breathe, hurt and anger took over. "I'll see what I can do. Oh, and make sure you tell your newest flavor of the week in the background there, to shut the hell up when you're on the phone with your daughter!" I hung up and placed my mother's picture back on the mantel. *I miss you, Mom. More than you can ever know.*

The next morning I completed all the applications, added my résumé, and contacted all my references. Everything was ready to go. I walked to the mailbox thinking it would be a good time to let my boss know that I'd applied to this organization. I had two weeks of paid time off that I could use for taking the trip, so I wasn't worried about losing pay. I telephoned Judy. I looked up to her as my mentor and friend, and everything I had learned to do well in the ICU she had taught me.

"Hey, Judy, it's Natalie," I said, twirling my hair through my fingers.

"Hi. What's up?"

"I'm thinking of going overseas as part of a travel nurse assignment. I may be needing two weeks' vacation time soon. I'll let you know when I'm leaving if I get accepted."

"Why not just take a vacation?"

"I'd rather get paid for it . . .and I'm thinking of a change, anyway. I want out of here. I feel stuck. I keep running into obstacles and I need to do something with my life. I've been thinking about this a lot."

"Natalie, is everything all right? I don't want to lose you."

"Yeah, I just need to do this, Judy. Trust me, please? I'll talk to you when I'm at work tomorrow. There's something else that's been bothering me." I stared out the window.

"Go ahead."

"Nah, it can wait." I didn't want to go over the death of Mr. Watson again but I wanted to tell her my theory. "I'll see you later."

The following day, I walked into Judy's office. "Got a sec?" I asked.

"Sure, Natalie. Come on in." Judy pushed a chair toward me. Pictures of her three beautiful daughters decorated her bulletin board. One had just graduated nursing school and would soon be on the unit with us.

I described the scene in Mr. Watson's room and Judy looked bewildered. "You sure about this? The line, the bandage, the monitor alarms? You think someone purposefully disconnected it, causing him to bleed out? It does seem strange, him crashing suddenly."

"I keep wondering why the tape securing the arterial line wasn't ripped. If the hub had come out of the catheter or the line had accidentally fallen out, there would have been some kind of tear. The OR techs secure that line so well that I highly doubt it just fell off. It had to have been *taken* off. It appeared completely intact!"

"Natalie, this is serious stuff. Would you be willing to write a statement? I'll have to talk to security and maybe the police if the security tapes show anything."

"I think you should. And one more thing, remember when Betty came to get her husband's belongings as we finished up the postmortem care?"

"Yes . . . That whole thing seemed a bit weird."

"Well, I think a lot of that had to do with the tension between us." Wringing my hands, I filled her in on my history with Betty, confessing my guilt. I felt like I had failed Judy by covering for Betty.

"You don't think Betty had anything to do with her husband's death, do you?" Judy looked directly into my eyes. "I mean, she's a good nurse. I know she doesn't get along with a lot of people, but her nursing skills are solid."

"No! I'm not saying she did it. No . . . " I looked at the floor. I hadn't thought about that but now that Judy mentioned it . . . could it be . . . ? "No, Judy. I don't think so. I wanted to get that shit off my chest, that's all."

"Okay. Well, thanks for telling me. What's done is done, Natalie. You're an excellent and very conscientious nurse. I know you care very much about all your patients. Let it go. As for Mr. Petronoff, well . . . I don't know what to make of that. Seems like Betty has a dark cloud over her, doesn't it?"

"Yeah. I've had enough darkness myself. I'm ready for some sunshine."

Judy leaned over to hug me. For a brief second, I pretended to be hugging my mother.

I clocked out for the day and heard several nurses talking about Betty Watson. The rumors going around were that Mr.

Watson had had a heart attack after an apparent struggle with Betty's daughter. The two had been home alone and Betty's daughter claimed that he came at her, propositioning her for sex. Watson went to grab her as she came at him with a frying pan. That's when he collapsed and had a heart attack. So the guy happened to be a scumbag. Aren't they all? Maybe someone did want him dead. Maybe he deserved it.

Shaking my head clear, I got in the car feeling a bit liberated, as if a 5'6", 110-pound Russian weight had been lifted off my chest.

A few weeks later, while I was deep breathing in my down-ward-facing dog position, the phone rang. I almost didn't answer it, but then I saw the caller ID: The Traveling Nurse. I jumped up and grabbed the phone, almost tripping over my yoga mat.

"Hello?"

"My name is Peggy and I'm calling about travel nursing. Is there a Natalie Ulster available?"

"I'm Natalie."

"Are you still interested in our program?"

"Yes. You received my application?" I stood still.

"I need to ask you a few questions. Consider this your interview."

"Okay, shoot."

After twenty minutes of basic interview questions—why are you choosing to leave your current workplace, where do you see yourself in five years, what are your strengths, yadda, yadda, yadda—Peggy made her decision. "We'd love for you to join us. We have availability in Belize. Would that work for you? Sorry to seem rushed, but I'm desperate for quality nurses."

Dancing around my tiny apartment, I thrust my fist into the air. "Absolutely. What do I need to do?"

"I'll e-mail you some forms to fill out and we need to do a background check. Please make sure your immunizations are all up to date. We'd like to have you there in two weeks. Does that give you enough time?"

"Of course. I've got some time saved up at work and I already have my passport."

"Excellent!" Peggy exclaimed in a sharp British accent. "I'm sending you three documents. Review the contract, sign it, and e-mail it back. I'll phone you once I receive everything. Then you'll get all the information regarding transport, room and board, and your flight itinerary. We take care of everything. Bring your nursing experience and your sense of adventure. Cheers!"

"Thank you so much for this opportunity, Peggy!"

I'd opened a door. My life soon would take a different direction. Now I needed to start reading about Belize. I didn't sleep at all that night, but instead sat at the computer looking up everything I could find on the small country. My eyes dashed across the screen. Belize was in Central America, bordered by Guatemala and Mexico with the Caribbean Sea to the east. It had the largest cave system in the West and bursted with jungles, wildlife reserves, tropical plants, and animals. Lucky for me, English and Spanish were the native tongues and the average weather stayed around eighty-four degrees. Perfect for swimming! Perfect for escaping. My burning eyes told me I had read enough. How I wished two weeks would pass quickly.

# 3

It took just one week to obtain approval from both the Nurses and Midwives Counsel of Belize and the General Nursing Counsel of Belize for me to accept the travel assignment. Since the agency was internationally certified, I didn't need a work visa. They'd issue it when I arrived. Having only a few weeks of paid time off, I signed on for two weeks. Peggy had notified me that I would be working in a two-bed ICU at Belize Medical Associates Hospital in Belize City. They'd booked me a hotel five minutes away. Everything had been arranged. I locked up my apartment, hesitating before pulling the key out. I got in the car, stretched my neck in all four directions, and took a deep breath. Next stop, the airport.

After waiting for two and half hours, I boarded the plane. I took out my iPod, my books on Belize, and some gummy candy to feed my nervous sweet tooth. I hate flying, so I leaned back and tried to settle my brain by concentrating on the adventure. My stomach fluttered. I'd started rereading my brochures and itinerary when I heard my name.

"Natalie Ulster? Is that you?"

I turned around and saw a former high school classmate and groaned quietly to myself. Definitely not one of my closest friends. I would describe Erica Ehrendsen as one of those "hoity-toity" types of people that everyone else wanted to be friends with. She tried to control everything and everyone and if she didn't want you somewhere, you weren't invited.

"Natalie? Did you hear me?" She plopped herself right in front of me so I couldn't look away.

Unable to ignore her any longer, I slowly looked up. "Oh, hi, Erica. How have you been?"

"It's so good to see you," she said with such phoniness that I thought her smile would crack her face in two. "Oh, this is my new husband, Rick! We're going to Belize for our honeymoon! Isn't that fabulous?" God, she had a ton of freckles all over that makeup-free face.

I gave a small smile and nodded at Rick. He looked like a normal guy, a bit on the portly side with dirty-blond hair and nice eyes. "Nice to meet you, Rick. Congratulations. I'm going to Belize on a travel nurse assignment."

"Oh, my!" Erica exclaimed. "What does your husband think of that? You're traveling all alone?" She clasped her hands to her heart.

"I wouldn't know because I don't have one." I threw some candy in my mouth.

"Oh, I'm so sorry," Erica said, barely allowing the other passengers to squeeze by her.

"I'm not." This chick had me laughing inside.

"Well, I hope you enjoy your little nursing trip," Erica said as she gave her husband a squeeze. "Hopefully, we won't see you! I mean, hopefully, we won't be visiting any hospitals!"

"Enjoy your honeymoon." I crammed my books and candy into the seat pocket, grateful as a passenger asked to squeeze by Erica. His bald head met the overhead compartments and his voice sounded raspy. His dark sunglasses turned toward me as he grinned. Erica nudged Rick to get moving.

*Forget about her,* I told myself. *This is a chance for adventure, away from everybody. A way to see the world!*

The plane took off and I relaxed, closing my eyes to the soothing sounds of John Mayer.

Six hours later, we touched down in Belize City. Dirt and rocks formed the runway. Locals bustled throughout the airport wearing brightly colored shirts and white pants; wanting to take passengers' luggage, sell tour tickets, or lead us to the taxis. It smelled of pineapple and spice mixed with ocean air. I inhaled Belize and shifted my bag on my shoulder. One man stood out, holding a sign that read "The Travel Nurse," and I headed straight for him.

"Um, hi. I'm Natalie Ulster. I'm here with the travel nurse group."

"Right this way, pretty lady."

Erica and her new husband waited with a large group of other couples that were going to be taken to the island of San Pedro. The two of them kept kissing, hugging, and giggling. I'm sure it would be much more fun to travel with someone special than to be doing what I was doing, but hey, what was I gonna do? Never see the world because I'm waiting to share it with someone? I don't have time to wait.

I followed the driver to a black minivan with cigarette-burned seats. I briefly worried since I had heard about mites and lice in taxis, but took a deep breath and seated myself, looking out the window as the ride started. I decided to sign in to Facebook and let whoever cared know my status. *Natalie Ulster at Belize City, Belize. Here's to a new adventure!*

The landscape was flooded with jungle and flora giving way to the city as we drove on. Small houses covered with tin roofs flanked the narrow, unpaved streets and kids ran everywhere.

All shades of South American people were milling about. An unconscious man lay on the sidewalk as the locals stepped over him, unfazed. Most people in the city were barefoot, and the soles of their feet were chalky white compared to their darkened skin. I had read that Belize City was not the nicest of areas, but San Pedro and the islands really attracted tourists.

Around a corner, a woman busied herself cooking tortillas and some kind of meat on a cart covered with a tent. Tourists were taking pictures with her children. I recognized the bald dude from the plane walking up to the cart. He turned toward the van and lowered his sunglasses in my direction. I checked my watch and looked away. *Jeez.* The van crossed a little bridge over stagnant, smelly water, and I finally saw the entrance to the Hotel Radisson. It looked quaint and in pretty good shape, almost out of place compared to the buildings I had passed by. This would be home for the next two weeks. *I can't believe I'm getting paid to be here. I'm in Central America, Mom!*

The hotel itself looked as if it had been built right in the middle of the jungle. Huge palm, banana, and citrus trees surrounded the entire grounds. Exotic flowers I had never seen before hung down from lush trees and lizards scurried all over the place. It reminded me of Hawaii. I checked in and received my key. The bellhop offered to show me to my room. Walking through the grounds, I spotted a very large spiderweb between two trees. I didn't want to meet the giant spider that built the web so I quickened my pace, anxious to get inside. Insects were not my thing.

I was used to staying in luxury whenever my family traveled—my mother's version of "roughing it" had been three-star hotels. But, I liked the simplicity of the Radisson. I didn't need much more. Except for food. I needed food. My stomach grumbled and I felt grouchy. Inside my room, I grabbed my purse, tipped the bellhop after he set my luggage down, and followed him back downstairs.

I picked a table by the small pool. Pool attendants were delivering a neon-green frozen drink. It looked like the exotic drink of Belize; I wanted one and asked a passing waitress the drink's name so I wouldn't sound like such a foreigner ordering it.

"*Es una mar-ga-ri-ta.*"

My face, neck, and ears flushed. So much for exotica. I still ordered it, along with a meat pie that resembled our pot pie, but with some kind of spiced beef inside.

Eating my lunch, I pulled out my packet of information and studied the section on the hospital where I would be working. It looked like a sterile, old facility, only two or three stories high, but it seemed quaint and inviting. The idea that I would be starting there in two days excited me.

Everything I read said Belize had the best waters in the world. I had to take advantage of the world's best place to scuba dive. Tomorrow would be my one free day for a while so I called the concierge and asked him to set me up with a dive. He said he'd work on it and to come down later in the evening to purchase the tickets.

The phone in my room rang a few hours later. The concierge had arranged a dive trip for me in the morning. Belize waters appeared so clear and I couldn't wait to get in them. I decided to go down for a swim. I dove into the warm pool tasting salt water instead of chlorine. Like the heavenly water, calmness washed over me. I easily swam a mile. This was exactly what I needed.

I awoke refreshed the next morning and headed downstairs to get my dive info. A local man in a red-and-white flowered shirt gave me all my information and showed me where to go. I would be leaving in one hour on the Belize Water Taxi, a short walk down Front Street, the main road outside the hotel. At thirty feet deep, the dive would be an easy one. Locals called it Shark Ray Alley. As long as the sharks weren't descendants from *Jaws*, I'd be fine. Also, no matter where I go in this world, there better be a good coffee joint nearby. I can't live without it! I bought a cup of lifesaving coffee and a croissant from the hotel café and looked for the Water Taxi.

I turned on Park Street, passing an old schoolyard with big jungle animal sculptures that were used as climbing toys. No jungle gyms or slides. Just a few wooden swings and black stone gorillas or blue elephants the kids could play on. I turned north on Front Street and could see a sign for the taxi stop on the pier. Birds chirping interrupted the quiet scene, inhabited only by a few locals. Natives were waiting, dressed in uniforms that said they were either maids or some kind of cooks. We smiled at one another as I took a seat on the bench.

A few minutes later the taxi boat arrived and I climbed in. The ride to Ambergris Caye, an island off San Pedro, took about an hour and a half, and I used the time to admire the glass-like, turquoise waters and the clear, blue sky. The water was so clear you could see fish of all sizes and colors swimming alongside the boat. I had to get in there! If I lived here, I'd never come out of the water! The water taxi pulled up to the pier and a man helped me aboard the dive ship while another unloaded fins, dive tanks, snorkel gear, and dive weights.

In a thick Belizean accent, one asked, "Ya all alone?"

"Yup," I said, "it's just me."

The man smiled and tipped his wide-brimmed straw hat. He asked to see my diving certificate. I had a few dives logged already over the past year, placing me in the experienced group. He told me to take a seat at the edge of the boat as we waited for two more couples to board, then we motored out a short distance, anchoring at Shark Ray Alley. The man informed us that a photographer would be joining us below, and CDs would be made available once we arrived back in town. I checked my gear and received the okay to enter the water.

I sat on the side of the boat noticing several small, canoe-like crafts off the port side. Belizean men were under the water diving for conch and bringing it back to the men in boats. The men above would start cutting the conch into pieces and throwing whatever parts they didn't want back into the ocean, which caused different species of fish and sharks to surround our boat. I couldn't help but think this was largely for our benefit. Excited, I tipped backward off the side. My flippers were the last part of me to hit the warm, salty ocean. I descended slowly for about thirty feet, where I stabilized my buoyancy and began to look around. Beautiful fish were swimming all around and I could see at least one hundred feet in front of me! The dive master led us down the reef and signaled up with his hands. I tilted my head to the surface and saw an entire school of eagle rays soaring above, like ducks in V-formation flying south for the winter. Eels poked their heads out of the red and orange coral formations with mouths turned up in cute, pudgy smiles. Crabs and lobsters scurried across the smooth, sandy floor beneath me. Everything seemed so serene. The dive master again signaled, and as I turned around a four-foot-long, wide-headed thresher shark swam by. With eyes wide open, I looked at the master diver and he gave me a thumbs-up. I guess that was supposed to make me feel better. Thankfully, the shark ignored me and we swam on.

We came to a small shipwreck, about the size of a sailboat, with two portholes large enough for us to fit through. I glided through one porthole as the dive photographer met me on the other side, signaling me for a picture. Schools of fish were every-where! I tried to still myself in the water, sculling my hands in an upward motion. Not a bright move. Not only did I fail to stop moving, I stirred up tons of debris and sand. The photographer shook his head back and forth vigorously, but it was too late. The great shot disappeared. I tried to say "sorry" under thirty feet of water and swore I could see him rolling his eyes beneath his snorkel mask. Oh well. My air-tank meter pointed to 500 psi, so I let the dive master know I had to head up. Apparently he needed to surface, too, because he started following me.

At the beginning of a dive you have at least 3,500 psi in the tank, so when you reach 500 psi you need to head for the surface. During my ascension, he stopped me and showed me a giant blue grouper, which reminded me of my mom's great-aunt Molly, pudgy with big lips and gentle eyes. I smiled. Holding a spiny sea urchin, the dive master offered it to the grouper. Within two or three bites, the urchin no longer existed and the grouper swam off. I gave the dive master the okay sign and proceeded upward, out of my blue sanctum. I broke the surface, spit out the remaining salty water, and looked for the boat. The man on board reached out his hand and I climbed the ladder, amazed at what I had seen. I sat down on the bench and began to take off my gear.

"How was it down there?" the captain asked.

"Incredible! I want to go again!"

"Oh, sorry, ma'am. We're done for today. There's a storm coming in from the west and we don't want to get caught in rough waters."

"I hear you. But man, that was awesome! Thank you!"

Back at the hotel I took a shower and got into bed for a nap. After diving and breathing in such concentrated oxygen, fatigue had set in. I drifted off to sleep thinking about all the creatures I'd seen.

Three hours later I awoke and checked my phone; eight o'clock. I didn't feel that hungry, so I headed down to the bar and ordered a beer. The bartender asked what a pretty young woman like me was doing here all alone. I told him I was a travel nurse. That's it. No dramatic story. No trauma. No running away. Well, maybe a little running away. He smiled and moved on to the next customer.

"Hey, you ruined my shot," I heard next to me. I turned around and came face to face with a stranger.

"Excuse me?"

"My photograph of you in the shipwreck this morning. You killed it by stirring up all that crap!" I suddenly realized who he was.

"Oh, yeah, right. Sorry, I got kind of flustered. It's okay, though, I don't like taking pictures anyway." I started playing with my phone.

"You should like taking pictures. Those eyes are gorgeous." I furrowed my brows and shook my head. Smiling, he extended his hand. "I'm Jason, and you are?"

"Natalie. Nice to meet you." I got out my wallet to pay the tab but Jason stopped me by putting his hand over mine.

"Can I buy you a drink?"

*What?* I looked up at him, pleasantly surprised. He was thin and very tan with dark brown hair and bright white teeth. His eyes were a deep green framed by long, brown lashes. I decided to stay.

"So where are you from, Jason?" *I'm going to need another drink.*

"California. I came here after graduating high school and stayed so long, I earned myself a visa." He flipped his hair out of his eyes.

"You didn't need one coming in?" My stomach growled. Hoping he hadn't heard it, I placed my arms across my belly.

"You can stay in Belize for one month without a visa. I applied for a visa extension and before I knew it, I had been working in Belize a year and was granted permanent residency. My apartment's just down the street. So what about you?"

"What about me?" The bartender placed another beer in front of me. "Could I get a chicken tamale, please?"

"Try the conch fritters," Jason said. "They're the best!"

"I can't. I'm allergic to seafood. Sorry."

"What about when you're under the water? They don't bother you?"

I laughed. "No. Only if I eat fish. I'm fine swimming with them."

"Good. So, what's your story?" Jason turned his stool toward mine.

"Well, I'm a nurse, and I wanted to try out travel nursing. This is my first stop."

"How is it so far?" He raised his eyebrows up and down, making me laugh.

"It's fine, thank you." I took a swig of beer.

"How long are you here?"

"Two weeks. We'll see how it goes." The bartender placed my food in front of me. "Mind if I eat? I'm hungry."

"No, of course not. My parents aren't thrilled with my career choice. They wanted me to do the whole college thing but I wanted to see the world. People wait on doing this kind of stuff and then, *bam*, the chance is gone."

"Yeah, I know exactly what you mean. One day your life is normal and then, *poof*, it can be taken from you."

"Your parents approve?"

"My dad doesn't have much say in my life anymore and my mom . . . she died fifteen years ago. Breast cancer." I took a huge swig of beer.

"Oh my god. I'm . . . I'm . . . " Jason ran his fingers through his hair. Most people feel uncomfortable as soon as I bring that up. They don't quite know what to say. I'm not looking for them to say anything. It is what it is.

"Don't worry about it. You didn't know. Anyway, I'll be working at Belize Medical."

"Cool. I've been there a few times. Shark bites, jellyfish stings, you know. Occupational hazards."

Laughing, I finished my food and placed my napkin on the bar. Signaling the bartender, I asked for the check. "Very nice to meet you, Jason. I'm pretty tired and I've got a long day tomorrow."

"No, this is on me. No worries." Before I could argue, Jason threw his credit card down.

"Thank you very much. I appreciate it." I stepped off the stool and picked up my wallet.

Jason touched my arm. "Would you like me to show you around San Pedro some time?"

*Really?* I liked being all alone in a foreign country, free and able to do whatever I wanted. He seemed nice and not pushy. *Oh, what the hell.* "Um, sure. I'd like that. I have to be at the hospital tomorrow but I'm off on Thursday."

"Great!" Jason said. "Let's plan to meet here around ten o'clock in the morning? It'll be easier than me trying to call you at the hotel. We'll take the ferry to the island and have lunch."

I smiled and thanked him for the drinks. We said good night and I walked up to my room, thinking it had definitely been a good idea to come here. I'd only be here for two weeks, so there was no way things needed to go further with Jason, but it would be fun to spend my days off with him, the perfect diversion. Just what I needed.

# 4

I awoke two hours early the next morning, ready to start work. I preferred walking to places in Belize City rather than waiting for a taxi. I strolled up Marine Parade Boulevard to Gabourel Lane, then a left, two rights, and another left, which put me at the doorstep of Belize Medical Associates Hospital. Just beyond the entrance, a group of mostly women with a few men sat in the lobby under a sign that read, "Welcome Travel Nurses." I checked in with the woman manning a table there. She marked off my name and told me to have a seat. We would be greeted by the hospital CEO and the Director of Nursing, then we would receive our floor assignments and begin our orientation. I took a seat beside a woman wearing an American flag scrub top, wanting to stay in my comfort zone just a little bit longer.

"Hi." I smiled at her. "My name's Natalie. This is pretty cool, huh?"

"Good morning! I'm Ann," she said. "We shall soon see." She winked.

Trying to fill up the time while waiting for administration, we started talking.

"Where are you from?" I asked, sipping coffee that I'd gratefully retrieved from the welcome table.

"Michigan. What about you?"

"Denver. This is my virgin voyage. I'm an ICU nurse. You?"

"Welcome to the world of travel nursing. I'm an oncology nurse. I do this whenever my husband goes on one of his hunting trips." She wrinkled her petite nose.

"I'm looking for a change. Trying to figure things out, you know?"

"You're not married, are ya?"

"No. Totally free."

"Good. Let me tell you something. There ain't no magic out there. It doesn't exist."

I laughed. "What? Okay. You're the one who's married." I started rifling through the orientation packet.

"I wish someone had told me, so I'm sharing with you," Ann said matter-of-factly.

*Who does this chick think she is and why do I care? Do I have the word "lonely" tattooed across my forehead? What the hell?*

"Well, thanks for sharing." I said. *Weird chick. Don't take your marriage problems out on me, I frickin' just sat next to you!* This was why I'd chosen to be single. Love makes you nutty and then, when you lose it . . . well, you're fucked. I pretended to read through the packet. Thankfully Ann took the hint, and eventually the CEO and Director of Nursing arrived.

We were given a quick orientation on the entire hospital and shown how to document our charting. I was so glad I spoke the native tongue. I toured the twenty-four-hour emergency room, labor and delivery unit, the neurology unit, the operating rooms, and the general medical/surgical floor. The hospital looked exactly like the pictures in the brochure. The brightly colored decor, the pictures of sea creatures, and the tiny windows that were built into the cinder-block walls were so neat to see. I'd worked at only one hospital throughout my entire career and it thrilled me to be in a new environment.

This hospital had an old, used feel to it. The fluorescent white lights above flickered and the floors contained multiple gurney tracks from so many years of use.

Located on the first floor, the ICU held only two beds and I would be the only travel nurse; all the other staff nurses were permanent. The ICU was equipped with two ventilators, complete cardiac monitors, IV drip pumps, and a medicine supply room, so getting oriented wouldn't be difficult. Since there were no occupants yet, I had time to orient myself to the unit. I was exploring and familiarizing myself with the locations of the equipment when another nurse arrived and introduced herself.

"I'm Sonia. Thank you for being here." She extended her hand to me. Sonia's speech sounded like a mix of English and Creole, another language spoken in Belize.

"Hi. Natalie." Sonia wrapped both her hands around mine. "Can you show me around a little before we start getting admits, Sonia?"

"Sure. Follow me." Short in stature and very round, she had her hair pulled back in a tight bun. Strands of gray, frizzy hair framed her face and she wore an old-fashioned nurse's dress with white stockings and white orthopedic shoes.

"Our doctors deal with high acuity patients, traumas mostly, with minimal resources. It can be a real *filho de puta*."

I tilted my head to one side and furrowed my brows.

"Sorry. That means 'a real son of a bitch'!"

I laughed. "Ah yes, I'm very familiar with that phrase."

Sonia gave me a big smile and continued to tell me about the different kinds of patients who come in— "some pretty bad stuff," she warned. We sat down at the nurse's station. "So, tell me a little about ya?"

"Me? Well, I'm from Colorado and I've worked in the ICU for about seven years. I wanted to try out travel nursing, so here I am."

"You have children?" Sonia pulled out her purse and removed a stack of photographs.

"No. I'm not married." I looked down at my hands. Why did everyone ask me that?

"Oh, child, you don't have to be married to have kids! But, I am, and here they are." She showed pictures of her three children and her husband at a local carnival, smiling and acting silly.

"Beautiful. What does your husband do?"

"Oh, he works in the wood mill. Shitty job but it gives us a roof. He works the nights and I do the days. It works." Sonia shrugged.

"Looks like you have a nice family, Sonia." The phone rang, ending our conversation.

Our first admission arrived: a twenty-something male who had fallen off his horse while trying to get home to his village. He'd hit his head on the dirt road and lost consciousness. Shock from blood loss had caused low blood pressure and a fast heart rate.

"One, two, three," I called out as we moved the patient from the gurney to the bed. Hooking him up to the monitors, I noticed he looked older than the age listed on his chart. His hands were calloused and dirty, as though he had been climbing trees or digging in mud all day. His vital signs appeared stable so I covered him with a warm blanket and exited the room. While I was charting at the computer, his wife walked in, approaching her husband's side. She spoke minimal English so Sonia talked to her; my Spanish consisted primarily of bad words and slang. Sonia explained the monitors and what drugs we would be using. We reassured the woman that her husband would be okay, and that she could stay as long as she wanted. She told Sonia that her husband worked on a fishing boat and they were very poor. They had two children at home, whom she cared for while her husband brought home food and money. Putting her face in her hands she began to sob. I walked over to her and put a hand on her back to let her know we would do our best to get him well. She nodded at me as if she understood.

Throughout the day, I checked on my patient regularly, making notes in his chart and asking his wife if she needed anything. She kept repeating, "Él es mi corazón" which means *he is my heart*. I could see the love she had for him. *Screw you, Ann. Mister Rights do exist.* By the time my shift ended, my patient, Jorge, had started to move his fingers and blink his eyes. I called for Sonia and together we went to Jorge's side. "Jorge, my name is Natalie. I am your nurse today," I said as Sonia translated. "You are in the hospital. You took a bad fall off your horse but your wife is here." His wife, Maria, got up from her chair and went to the other side of the bed to hold his hand. She put her head on his chest and both of them cried. Sonia and I exchanged glances and walked out of the room, sliding the curtain closed behind us to give them some privacy. Sitting down at the nurse's station, I noticed the night nurses filing in.

"Hi, I'm Natalie," I told the night nurse. "Jorge came in with a pretty big head wound. We've got him stabilized right now. He's alert and his wife is with him."

"His wife needs to go; visiting hours are over," said the militant nurse.

"I realize that, but he's just started waking up and she's been at his side waiting to speak to him. Couldn't you just bend the rules a little and let her stay?"

"You Americans are so soft."

I gave her a blank look, too tired to get into a war of words. It appeared that I had convinced her because she went to get a cup of coffee instead of focusing on kicking Maria out. I gathered my things and Sonia asked if I needed a ride back to the hotel.

Not wanting to walk the dark streets alone, I accepted her offer and we left together.

The rain poured outside. Sonia suggested we get some dinner and wait out the storm. The restaurant we found looked like a colonial Georgia plantation—white, several stories high, with balconies and columns.

"Where about do you live?" I asked, looking over the menu.

"The city. A little house. Not the safest area, but it's where I grew up. I know how to protect what is mine." She took her hands and covered her heart. Sonia made me feel comfortable in my new surroundings. I welcomed her motherly style. It made me happy to be with her. We didn't stop chatting.

After dinner Sonia took me back to the hotel and I got into a hot shower. Then, excited about my dive the day before and my first day as a travel nurse, I grabbed my phone.

"Hi Karen, it's me," I said, glad to hear her voice.

"Natalie! How are you?"

"Fine. Just getting used to everything. I've been diving, met a great nurse I'm working with, and had a somewhat easy patient."

"You sound good."

"I am. It's nice to be away for a little while."

"Well, we miss you. Things got pretty crazy after you left."

I started drying my hair with a towel. "What do you mean?"

"They called Betty in for questioning." I stopped messing with my hair and looked in the mirror. "Judy gave her condolences and then asked her how her husband had looked when she visited; had anything been amiss, that kind of stuff."

"Why did Judy do that?" My heartbeat picked up.

"She told us you had mentioned some things weren't right in the room when you walked in, and since Betty was the last to leave, they wanted her opinion. To cover the hospital's ass, I guess."

"So, what happened?" I fiddled with my fingers and found one nail I could pick at.

"Feeling accused, Betty got upset and ran out of the unit. No one's seen or heard from her since."

"Geez. What the fuck?"

"Anyway, don't worry about it. Enjoy your time there."

*Damn.* I sighed. "Well, I'll be home in about two weeks," I told her. "Then we'll catch up."

"Can't wait. And get that whackjob out of your head. Don't worry about it. Enjoy Belize. I'm so glad you called."

"I'm glad you answered. I'll talk to you soon, okay?"

"Sounds good, Nat. Be safe!"


The next day I returned to the ICU. Jorge was sitting up in bed, eating, apparently stable. Maria helped him drink water by holding the straw in his cup steady. Sonia had already clocked in, and updated me on Jorge's status. His blood pressure had stabilized overnight and they were able to stop a few medications as he regained full consciousness. I checked his wound and it looked clean; no signs of infection. I briefly skimmed through his chart to note what else had gone on during the night. He was recuperating nicely, and it looked as if Jorge would soon be transferred out of the ICU.

I went into Jorge's room and started to explain what we were going to do. They both could understand a little English, so I kept it simple. Watching Maria caress her husband's face and squeeze his hand, I felt her devotion. They were both excited about the news and Jorge asked when he could go back to work. I told them to take things one step at a time and that he would be able to ask all those questions when the doctor came in. Placing his belongings in a bag, I heard a huge commotion down the hall. Sonia yelled to me, "Get room two ready!"

I hurriedly got the monitors and bed ready. Four policemen, a doctor, and two nurses wheeled in a bloody mess: a young man in his mid-thirties with multiple gunshot wounds to the hands, stomach, back, and head. His body looked shredded. Evidently he'd used his hands to defend himself from the gunfire, as both had almost been blown right off.

One of the policemen pulled me aside. "He's a former gang member and drug trafficker. Served ten years in prison."

"Oh wow," I said, looking over my patient. What a mess.

"Then he found God. He got out last year for good behavior." The policeman flipped through his paperwork and shoved his pen back in his pocket.

Sonia and I began to lift the covers and attend to all the gaping holes in his body. Scars all over, from gunshot and knife wounds, told the story of a violent past. Blood had soaked his cornrows and against his dark skin the blood appeared purple. Life-support machines were working overtime—ventilating, sedating, and keeping his blood pressure up. He had two bags of blood hanging and the electrode pads that had been used to resuscitate him were still attached to his chest, the hair surrounding them charred. So many injuries. Sonia and I looked at each other as we both shared the sick feeling our patient wasn't going to make it.

Nausea came over me as I changed the dressings on his hands. I put my forearm over my mouth, regaining my composure. I am usually never nauseated and always willing to treat anything that walks in the door, no matter how gory, but this poor man's body barely held together. His hands dangled by tendons and the bones were sticking out. The wound on his belly exposed ribs and vital organs, and the one on his forehead had cracked his skull wide open. I gave a look to the doctor and asked what he wanted us to do.

"Get as much as you can clean and then we're taking him to the OR."

"Why clean him? Can't you just take him now?" I asked.

Sonia glared at me, shaking her head. "We'll take care of it, Doctor," she said.

Showing my palms as if they held the answer, I whispered, "What are you doing? He's going to die. He needs to go to the OR now!"

"They can't get a surgeon. It's not like surgeons are in-house or on-call. They have to go find one from another hospital, Natalie."

"Oh," I looked down at the floor. I felt helpless.

We had to try to keep him alive until someone arrived. My patient did not have much time. Sonia went to check on Jorge and his wife as I continued to bandage the man's body back together to the best of my ability. A woman walked in, identifying herself as his sister before she sat down quietly. I introduced myself, glad to discover that she spoke English.

"Can you tell me a little about him?" I asked, soaking gauze in sterile water and wringing it out.

"His name is Norman Lornza. He was trying to do good things. He's paid for his sins," she said, rocking back and forth in the chair.

Sonia re-entered the room and unwrapped a roll of gauze. "He's been in the news lately, right?"

I gently tried scrubbing away the dried blood from his hair and skin. Sonia kept busy wrapping his hands.

"Ya. He'd become very religious and knew there were people from his past after him but he never lived in fear."

"We're going to do everything we can to save him," I said as Sonia and I looked at each other, knowing his chances were slim.

We managed to keep him alive another hour but fifteen

minutes after he was taken to surgery he died on the table. When I went to speak to his sister, she thanked me for being so compassionate and nonjudgmental. I told her that's what nurses do. I guess she had had a different experience with the medical world before this.

I decided to leave the unit for a few minutes just to get away. Jorge still waited to be transferred, and Sonia wanted to catch up on charting. I walked down to the little cafeteria and made myself some coffee. The doctor who had told us to keep Norman alive until a surgeon became available approached as I paid the cashier.

"Tough break, the gunshot wound dying."

"You mean Mr. Lornza?" I clarified. I hate when patients are addressed by their diagnoses. Doctors do it all the time.

"Yeah, whatever," he sneered. "You know what he was, don't you? A gang member and a criminal."

"I'm told he used to be. So . . . you're saying he deserved to die?" I crossed my arms, careful not to spill any coffee.

"You're not from here, miss. If you were, you'd understand. He was a bad man. The gangs run rampant around here, corrupting our children, costing this city millions."

"His sister told me he'd become religious and wanted to help. He tried to spread the word about the gangs."

"Yeah, right. A real Holy Roller."

My stomach tightened. "I don't think that's fair. His sister said he'd changed for the better." Are people not allowed a second chance? Seeing the blank look on his face, I decided this conversation was going nowhere. "I've got to get back upstairs," I said, turning to go out the door.

"Americans! Always thinking they're so perfect," I heard him mutter.

Rubbing both my temples, I made my way upstairs. I didn't

want to become jaded and angry, like a lot of medical profession-als. It's called burnout. We work long hours, sometimes holidays and weekends, and we seldom hear the word "thanks." ICU nurses often take care of the dying and it can get to you; it can make you feel like what you do is pointless. But our job is to care for the sick, no matter where they come from or who they are.

Were Sonia and I supposed to give shitty care to Mr. Lornza because of his criminal past? Did Mr. Watson deserve to die for being the asshole that he once had been? Was there some kind of justice in those two deaths? Do only good people deserve to be saved? If that were true, my mother would still be alive! I'm constantly reminding myself why I chose nursing. The nurses at Mom's bedside were the only ones who brought her comfort. They gave her the magic morphine that took her pain away and allowed her to sleep. They cleaned her and fed her while the rest of us cried over her. They made her smile while my sister and I made her cry. The nurses' power was what I had wanted to possess so badly: the power to mend the poisoned effects of a dying soul. I owned that power now and would never lose sight of where it came from.

# 5

I was looking forward to having a few days off after three days in the ICU, and the possiblility of seeing Jason excited me. I hadn't thought much about him since we met, and it would be better to keep expectations low rather than high, in case they came crashing down. Sonia and I had had a pretty stable day, with only a man who'd injured himself at a plantain mill and a woman who'd almost drowned snorkeling. Neither patient seemed critical and the day dragged.

"How about coming over to my house tonight for dinner?" Sonia asked. "I'd like you to meet my family."

"Sure! I'd love to!"

We finished up and walked to Sonia's car, an old, white Honda Civic with a dent in the back right side. My belly grumbled with hunger and excitement to meet her family. We drove the short distance down one of the few paved streets to a small section of closely packed houses. Sonia pulled up alongside the sidewalk and parked her car. The houses smelled like damp wood. Chain-link fences surrounded a few of them, and some had boarded-up windows and loose wooden slats in the siding. Sonia's house stood sandwiched between two three-story dwellings. Painted white with a red door and a red tin roof, it was the prettiest one on the block. There were loads of green plants and white flowers along her front porch and on the left side of the house stood a large, tall, shade tree with twirling vines hanging down.

We walked in the front door and two of Sonia's kids came running to her, yelling, "Mama, Mama." She bent and scooped one of them up, her nursing bag and purse still hanging on her shoulder. Jealousy poked my heart. A mother's hug offered so much comfort and a sense of home. I missed it.

"These are my babies," she said. "Say hi to Miss Natalie."

One by one Sonia's kids filed in and stood in line to shake my hand. The littlest one, named Raffy, came first, followed by her older brother Paolo and the oldest, his sister Marta.

"Your hair looks funny," Raffy said.

Her mama quickly clarified, "They're not used to curly hair. Most Americans they meet have long, straight hair."

"I think her hair is beyooootiful," said Marta. "I wish I had curls like that and not this mess." The eleven-year-old kept straightening the front of her dress and twirling from side to side, trying to make her dress flounce.

"Thank you," I told her. I noticed Sonia had finally put down her things and gone into the kitchen. She pulled out what looked like small round tortillas, some kind of meat covered in a red sauce, and cabbage. Putting the tortillas in the oven to warm, she turned on the four-burner stove to heat the meat.

"I don't keep any alcohol in the house but can I offer you some mango juice?" Sonia asked.

"I'd love some. Can I help you with anything?"

"No, bebé. We'll be ready in a minute. My man is working so you won't be able to meet him, but the kids are excited to have dinner with an American. I hope they won't drive you too crazy," she added.

"Oh, they're fine. This is so great. It's been a while since I've had a real family dinner." I glanced around Sonia's kitchen.

"What do you mean? Your parents are far from you?"

"No. Well, sort of."

Sonia froze and looked at me. "What is it?"

"My father lives near me in Colorado but we don't see each other much. My mom died when I was a teenager so . . . " I bit my lip.

Sonia came over and threw her arms around me. I laughed. "Sonia, it's okay. I'm fine."

"I had no idea. I'm so sorry." She held me at arm's length just as a mother would do to her coming-of-age daughter.

"Don't worry about it. You've made my first gig as a travel nurse a hell of a lot easier. It helps to have a friend."

"Oh, thank you, *bebé*. Now come, let us eat. You and I will talk more later."

We all sat down at her small, square, wooden table and Sonia began assembling the Belize version of tacos for her children. "Please, help yourself," she said as she moved the food closer to me. I took a tiny round tortilla and put in some meat mixture, cabbage, red beans, and a splash of lime, forming a little taco. The older kids started giggling. I stopped and looked at Sonia with the taco halfway to my mouth.

Laughing, she said, "Don't mind them. We do it different here." She then started ripping the tortilla in little pieces, using them to pick up the meat and cabbage in one scoop. Then she squirted the lime on top and popped the tasty morsel in her mouth. Using her fork, she ate some red beans.

"Sorry," I said. "I thought—"

"Eat it however you want, *bebé*."

Back at the hotel, the message light on the bedside phone blinked. Picking it up, I almost dropped it to the floor when I heard Jason's voice. "Found your room but you're not there so

I'm gonna leave a message. Just wanted to remind you about our date tomorrow. I'll meet you in the lobby around ten. Bye." I had almost forgotten. *Geez, the people here in Belize are something else. I'm not used to such reliability.* Shrugging, I took a shower and got ready for bed.

The next morning, sitting in one of the brown armchairs sipping my coffee, I caught Jason walking in, right on time. Standing up to greet him, I smiled and he came over and kissed me on my cheek. He appeared very casual, wearing white cargo shorts and an army-green tank top with sneakers. His slightly messy hair looked sexy in a surfer-boy way, and he had a bit of stubble around his face. The white shorts made his tanned skin appear two shades darker. He looked really, really good and smelled of cocoa butter. "Shall we go?" I nodded toward the exit.

"You look nice!" Jason said. "I'm ready if you are."

"Where are we going?"

"I thought I'd take you into town. We can have lunch and walk through the village. There are a lot of art galleries and trinket shops. If you like that sort of thing."

"Sounds great! No water adventures?"

"Well, I thought we'd see how the day goes. If you're not sick of me, there's a manatee boat ride through the mangroves that's awesome," Jason said, smiling.

"Oh, no. I'm glad to be doing something fun today, and not alone. Without you, I wouldn't know where to begin." That didn't come out quite the way I'd wanted it to and I looked at Jason a bit apologetically.

"No worries! I hear you. We're going to have a good time."

We started down Front Street and headed toward the water taxi depot. We climbed aboard and I settled myself into a seat at the back of the boat. The boat jutted forward and I held on to the side, becoming entranced by the clear, turquoise water and the fish, stingrays, and turtles swimming beneath me. The sun shined while the moist air caused my shirt to stick to my back and my hair to frizz around my face. Jason talked about Belize's history and pointed out landmarks he thought were interesting. Finally, we arrived at San Pedro and Jason helped me off the boat. I looked around the island. There was one narrow street, unpaved but covered with hard, packed sand and lined with little stores, one and two stories tall. Locals lined the sides of the road hocking jewelry made from seashells, ocean drawings, and woven baskets, calling out to the tourists walking by. There were a few boutique hotels and several different restaurants.

"How neat." I pulled out my cell phone and took a panoramic picture. "This is cool!"

"Yeah, this is San Pedro, the main town in Belize," Jason said.

We stopped in front of a white building with a sign that read *Gallery* decorated with colorful wooden fish. Purple, red, and orange groupers lined the stairs that led up to the front door. Each fish had a unique design along the body and the tail, with a perfectly round eye and black lips.

"Can we go in there?"

"Sure. It's your day," Jason said, extending his hand and bowing.

We walked in. Hundreds of fish hung on the walls. The artist greeted us. After spending fifteen minutes debating which fish I wanted, I decided not to purchase any. So I'm a little indecisive; what can I say? We headed down the street, slowly stopping at tables where women were selling necklaces, shark teeth, coral, and other ocean treasures. My stomach let me know it needed food.

Reading my mind, Jason said, "Let's stop in here," and directed us toward a little restaurant called Manny's. It smelled of pineapple and spices.

We sat at a little table and were given menus. I looked mine over, not having a clue what to get. Jason must've sensed my hesitation. "Don't worry; I'll order something good for you. Trust me." When the waiter came over, Jason gave him our order. Was he for real? I figured there must be something wrong with him; I just hadn't found what it was yet.

"Are you always this gentlemanly?" I asked.

"What do you mean?"

"Well, I . . . I'm just not used to this," I said, tugging my earlobe.

"Not used to someone being nice to you? I find that hard to believe."

"I'm not used to a *guy* being so nice to me. A guy who looks like you." My ears felt hot.

"A guy like me?"

"Handsome, my age, not a weirdo. I'm just not used to it." I stopped myself because I didn't want to give off a pity-party vibe. I hadn't let too many men into my life and the ones I had, I'd rather forget.

Laughing, Jason said, "Okay. Well, would you prefer I be mean?"

"No!" I said, starting to lighten up. I took a deep breath and smiled. "Sorry. Let's just forget I ever said anything. I'm good."

"So, I take it there's no guy back home?" Jason crossed his arms and leaned his elbows on the table.

"No. Actually, there hasn't been a guy for a couple of years. I like being on my own, though. Don't have to worry about anyone else."

"Aw, come on. No one likes to be alone."

"What about you? I'm sure I'm not the first chick you've brought here."

"No, you're not. I've had girlfriends. They come and go. You know how it is." The waiter brought us two ice-cold beers.

"Yeah. I guess I don't go looking for a relationship. I think it'll happen when it happens. And if it doesn't, it doesn't." I took a huge swig of the beer.

"That's not going to get you anywhere, Natalie. Sometimes, you've got to go find what you're looking for. That's why I like traveling the world."

"And have you found what you're looking for?" I raised my eyebrows.

Jason laughed. "No, but I'm not gonna stop looking!"

"I don't know," I sighed. "I kinda like how things are going right now. I can travel, I can work, I can play . . . I don't need anything else."

"Okay, Ms. Independent. Whatever you say." We both looked at each other, smiling. I glanced toward the door and saw the towering, bald man from the plane walk in and survey the room. *Is this guy following me?*

The food came and I turned my attention toward my plate. There were chicken drumsticks and thighs in a deep red sauce sitting atop a bed of rice and pineapple. It tasted spicy with a little bit of sweet: yummy. I drank bottled water and beer to cool off the heat in my mouth. We were getting ready to head out when four Rastafarians walked to the front of the restaurant and pulled out musical instruments. A fast, thumping, bass beat began and then one of the men started singing a song called "Elephant Man," a blend of reggae and Caribbean, with a jazz vibe. Customers began jumping up and down and dancing and Jason and I couldn't hear ourselves talk. The restaurant became hot and stuffy, almost claustrophobic. My mouth felt dry and I wanted to go to the bar. After asking the bartender for some water, I leaned my back against the bar, elbows propped on the countertop, and watched all the people gravitate to the center of the dance floor. They were writhing and jumping in circles.

Masses of them, like in a mosh pit. I smelled a mix of sweat and marijuana. I couldn't take my eyes off the dance floor.

"Hey! Did you just see that?" Jason asked, tugging my arm.

"What?"

"Some lady came up and stole your drink. Now she's out there dancing." Jason nodded his head in the direction of a wasted blonde having a great time on the dance floor.

I quickly turned and saw the empty glass. "Weird," I said. "Let's get out of here. It's getting too crazy!" I had to yell over the blaring music and more people were trooping in. Walking out, I glanced around for the bald man but couldn't find him any-where. Once outside, I inhaled the fresh sea air and smoothed my frizzies. I sat down on a nearby bench, fanning myself.

"Sorry about that. It gets crazy in that place. It's fun for a while, but you get tired of it quick. And things can get a bit rough."

I totally agreed with Jason. "How about that manatee ride?"

"Sure! Let's do it."

We walked until we came to another pier and Jason spoke with the local man who managed the rides. Since Jason worked for the dive company, he got a decent discount and signaled for me to come aboard. I took his hand and jumped in. We were told that we would be heading into the very calm water of the marshes, and that to really get a good look at the manatees, we needed to be very quiet. The boat traveled fifteen minutes into the mangroves before the captain turned off the engine and pulled out a long stick. He placed it in the water and began to guide the boat with it, explaining that the manatees would hide if the engine was too loud. We had to be quiet because the ani-mals wouldn't surface if they felt threatened.

Jason and I were sitting across from each other and, for a brief moment, our eyes locked. *Too bad I'm leaving next week. I'm start-ing to like this guy.* I heard a splash and looked to my right, spotting a manatee poking its head out of the water. I brought my hand to my mouth to remind myself to stay quiet, but I had a hard time containing my excitement. They were adorable—big, fat noses and tiny black eyes—and they moved so slowly in the water. I could see why they were sometimes called sea cows. We stayed still and more manatees surfaced to feed on the mangrove. After about twenty minutes, the captain turned the boat around and poled it along. When we were well out of the preserve, he turned the engine back on, and before I knew it, we were back at the pier.

"That was amazing!" I told Jason. "Thank you so much!"

"No problem. My pleasure."

We headed back to the water taxi depot that would take us back to San Pedro. The manatee trip only took about an hour and I wondered what Jason had planned for us next. Walking passed Manny's we heard a commotion in the street and sirens blaring on vehicles parked in front. "What's going on?" Jason asked a man.

"Some lady dropped dead. A tourist, I think. One minute she was dancing and drinking, the next minute, gone."

Jason and I looked at each other, horrified. We stood in the back of the huge crowd gathered around the emergency workers who were loading a woman onto a gurney. The medics raised the gurney and the edge of blanket that covered her head fell aside. Jason gasped.

"Holy shit, that's the woman who stole your drink."

"What?"

"That's her. I'm sure of it."

I stood there, frozen. "Jason, can we go back to the hotel?" My voice shook.

"Sure. You okay?"

"I'm really freaked out. One minute some lady is dancing and having a good time, then she steals my drink, and drops dead! What the hell? What if something was in the water? The water that was meant for me." I quickly surveyed the streets, not sure what to look for.

"It's probably just a coincidence, Natalie. Could've been anything. Heart attack, overdose, too much alcohol. No one's walking around putting poison in people's drinks. Come on, let's go."

I couldn't stop thinking about the blonde under the sheet. Why had she died? Her image stayed with me. I shook my head and then had a worse thought. What if the water *had* been poisoned and I'd drunk it like I'd planned? Nope, we weren't going there. *Mom's got me covered. She promised she'd watch over me. It's got to be a coincidence.* That woman had probably drunk way over her limit and died of alcohol poisoning or a drug overdose. I decided to break the silence as we came to the water taxi.

"This really has been a great day."

"I agree. Wish you hadn't seen that, though." Jason put his arm around me.

Another boat ride later, we were back on Front Street at my hotel. We stood at the front door in awkward silence.

"Thanks again, Jason. I had a great time, despite the . . ."

I wanted to go upstairs.

"Do you want me to come up with you?" Jason asked.

I tilted my head to the side and took a deep breath. I'd be leaving in a few days, I reminded myself.

"Please?" he said, looking a little like a puppy.

"Okay, come on up," I said with a smile. What the hell? If it turned out to be a one-night stand, so be it.

"I promise to be a good boy," Jason added, holding up his right hand. But for some reason, I didn't believe him.

We got in the elevator and rode up one flight. I unlocked the door. Jason followed me in and sat on the bed. I stood above him, unsure what to say.

"Look, Jason. I really like you and I'm glad—"

"Don't say anything, Natalie. I had fun today. You remind me of home." He reached for my hand.

I took it and sat down next to him. He took my hand and kissed it. Then, very slowly, he put his hand on my face and gave me a very slow, soft kiss on the lips. My heart quickened. We separated and I sighed.

"Jason. I'm not good at . . . this," I said, waving my hand between the two of us.

"I'm sure you're just fine." He lightly tugged my shirt and started kissing my neck.

I tilted my head back, raised my arms and let him lift my shirt over my head. He took my face in both hands and kissed me, our tongues dancing. All right, I'd just met the guy a few days ago, but I was going with my instincts. And my instincts were usually correct. I lay back and Jason started moving down to my bra. He kissed the lace covering both breasts and then the space between them.

"Can we leave my bra on?" I asked, breathless. I didn't want to deal with taking it off.

"Absolutely." Jason continued down to my navel. He flicked his tongue in and out. My groin tightened and I had the urge to lift my hips. *Let's do this already.*

Jason pulled my shorts down to my ankles without undoing the button. I writhed on the sheets, my hands above my head gripping the pillows. He kissed my panties and then moved them to the side. *Here we go.* He kissed the space between my thighs then tasted me with his tongue. I gripped the sheets and raised my hips to meet his mouth. He kissed my groin and went back to my sweet spot, thrusting his tongue deep inside me, his fingers following the trail of his mouth, massaging my most sensitive place. He got faster and stronger. Planting kisses all over my belly, my thighs, my . . . *Okay. Done.* I arched my back and then collapsed down. Heat rushed to my lower half and I melted into the sheets.

Jason licked his lips and slid up my body. He moved my hair out of my face and looked down at me, grinning. "I'd say you are pretty good at this." He kissed me again as his pager went off.

"I guess it's your turn?" I asked, tracing his chest with my fingers. No way I'd be able to orgasm if we had sex, but I shouldn't be greedy.

He checked his pager. "Damn it. I can't. I've got to head to the dive shop. Next time." He gave me a quick kiss and got off of me. This guy really made things easy.

"I feel bad, almost selfish." I pulled up my shorts and put my shirt back on.

"*I* loved it." He raised his brows and helped me up from the bed. We walked toward the door. Pulling a card out of his wallet, Jason winked at me and began writing his number down. "Make sure you call me before you leave."

"Um, sure. I'll do that." I looked at the card, turning it over in my hand.

"Don't sound so surprised. I'm not all about sex, you know. Just give me a call before you go. I want to go out with you again. I like you." Jason opened the door and waved before he left.

Well, this is new. *See Mom, I can meet a nice guy.* Even in another country. I stood at the window watching Jason walk down the street. It's so much easier not being attached. Relationships cloud my brain. Jason's fun and I'm glad that's all he is. I think he feels the same way. A serious relationship would mean I'd need to devote too much time thinking of ways to do everything I want to do while keeping the other person happy. I've got to keep this travel thing going, and even though I've only been doing it for a few days, I really like it. I want to live, and die, on my terms; no one else's. *Sorry, Mom. Maybe I'll see Jason again, maybe I won't.*

# 6

Unable to sleep much due to the dead blonde episode yesterday, I decided to wake up with a walk and caffeine. Savoring every sip of my vanilla coffee, I stuck to the most direct route—north on Marine Parade Boulevard—that went right along the coastline. The sounds of crashing waves and seagulls calmed me and made the mile-and–a-half walk easy. I turned onto Barrack Street noticing a group of people gathered around what looked like a car accident. A small Toyota van sat wedged under the hood of an overturned bus whose wheels were still spinning. Because I had on scrubs, a local woman grabbed me and said, "Is bahd, man. They's hurtin' and they's nee''elp." She pulled my arm and led me to the center of the scene. I hadn't seen her since the flight but there on the sidewalk, crying with her head in her hands, sat Erica.

Locals were crawling out of the bus windows and onto the ground. I walked to the van and looked in on the driver's side. Rick, Erica's husband, was pinned under the steering wheel of the Toyota, his face covered in windshield debris. She came running to me.

"What happened?" I asked.

"Oh . . . Natalie!" she cried, "Please help him! You have to!"

Somehow, even in crisis she managed to annoy me. "What happened?"

"We wanted to take a tour of this little town, and Rick drove. This bus came out of nowhere and ran into us, head on!"

"Let me see if I can help him. You okay?"

"I'm okay but please, get him out. It would be awful for me if he lost a limb or something."

I shook my head. Erica must've hit hers pretty hard to say something so stupid. Then again, she had always thought of herself first. Walking to the Toyota, I turned around when I heard Sonia yelling to me, offering help. Oh, thank God, someone I could count on.

"Our ambulances are not very fast," she said. "Let's see what we can do."

I bent in through the driver's window and looked at Rick. No response. I felt for a pulse, and positioned my cheek over his mouth. A faint breath blew against my ear. His chest was pinned under the steering wheel, his face covered with glass shards.

"He's alive! We've got to free him from the steering wheel," I told Sonia.

"I'll go in through the passenger side and try to lift up on the wheel. You pull him," Sonia said. "Try to keep his neck stabilized."

We both stuck our bodies halfway through the windows, and as Sonia pulled up on the steering wheel I pulled on Rick, with both hands tightly holding his head in place. I wasn't going to be responsible for a spinal injury. I'd never hear the end of it from Erica. He started to budge, but I knew I wouldn't be able to lift him up and out of the window. I told Sonia we needed help. She turned to a large Belizean onlooker and, in half-English, half-Creole, said, "Das goot to 'elp is git 'is mon out di cah. We nee youz stong ahms."

Sonia and I strained to support the steering wheel and Rick's neck as the man pulled him out the window. We put him on the concrete as gently as we could.

Sonia listened for a pulse with her head on his chest and she gave me a thumbs-up. We'd saved him. I started picking the little glass shards from his face, careful not to make his wounds any worse, and Erica ran to his side.

"Oh my God. His face! He's going to have so many scars!" She dropped to her knees.

Sonia's expression mirrored mine. We silently smiled at each other. I put my nurse's bag under Rick's head and started to rub his sternum to wake him up. After a few deep rubs, he slowly blinked his eyes open.

We heard the ambulance sirens approaching. Rick could move all his extremities, but he complained it hurt to breathe and blood dripped all over his face.

"Hi, Rick. Remember me from the airport? I'm Natalie. You and Erica have been in a car accident. You were unconscious and pinned under the steering wheel but we got you out, and you'll be fine. They're going to take you to the hospital." I smoothed his blood-stained hair.

"Thank you . . . for helping me," he whispered.

Erica started pushing everyone out of the way so the emergency techs could get to Rick. "Please get out of the way, Natalie, and let them take him," she said in a strident voice.

I closed my eyes and stood up, counting to ten so I wouldn't go off on her. Even now she patronized me! I started to open my mouth, but Sonia touched my arm and shook her head. "She's not worth it. Karma, my girl, karma," she murmured.

The emergency workers loaded Rick, and Sonia and I picked up our belongings. We watched as they drove him away.

"You think he'll be on our unit?" I asked Sonia.

"Nah. He's not that bad. Probably bruised his chest and has some lacerations. He's lucky we were there." She gathered her belongings from the ground.

"I really don't like that woman," I said, pressing my hands against my stomach.

"How do you know her?" Sonia asked.

"We went to high school together. They're here on their honeymoon. She's always been a bitch."

"Still is," Sonia said, making me laugh. I'm glad Sonia saw it too.

"You'd think she'd be nicer knowing we just saved her husband's life!"

"What does it matter? He's alive because of us. You know it, I know it, he knows it. Who cares what she thinks?"

"Her whole life she's had it so easy. Two parents, money, everything."

"I bet she don't have everything, child. She got her problems, too. Don't you worry, karma is always with us. You put out ugly, you get ugly. You put out good, you get good."

"Not always, Sonia." She waited for me to finish my thought, but I couldn't.

"Bad things happen to good people, too." She put her arm around my shoulder. It felt good.

"Why are people so ugly? Life's too short to treat each other so shitty. Erica's mean-spirited."

"She will learn from her mistakes and karma will show her. Now come on, Natalie, you're better than to let someone like that ruin your day. Think of her no more!" Sonia pretended she had a magic wand and waved it over my head, making me laugh. Her kids were lucky to have her as a mom. Always knowing what to say and how to make them feel better. We arrived at the hospital a few minutes later and, as we walked by the emergency room, doctors and nurses were attending to Rick. I overheard Erica asking how long it would take for the gashes on his face to heal. I sighed, and we headed upstairs to the ICU, apologizing for being a bit late.

My new patient was a sixteen-year-old girl, Nicolina Arroyo, who had been thrown thirty feet after being hit by a car as she was walking home to her village. She'd been selling trinkets on the beach, counting her money as she walked along the narrow path leading from the beach to the jungle. A pickup truck full of workers from one of the resorts struck her when she came to the sandy road. She had brain swelling with a fractured skull, broken ribs, a broken pelvis, and her right leg and arm were fractured. Her parents were at her bedside, crying.

I walked into the room and introduced myself. The parents didn't say much. They held her hands, one of them on either side of her, stroking her. I decided not to ask them to leave during my assessment. I opened my patient's eyes and shined a light at each pupil. No response. I went over to her ear and said, "Nicolina, my name is Natalie. I'm your nurse today. Can you move your toes?" Nothing. "How about squeezing your mom's hand?" Nothing. I put my stethoscope on her chest and listened to her heart beating: normal rhythm. She required a respirator and her lungs were expanding and deflating in sync with the breathing machine at her bedside. Her vital signs were stable and I began checking her IVs. There was saline to keep her hydrated, a powerful steroid to reduce the swelling of her brain, and sedatives to keep her asleep and calm.

"Is she going to be okay?" her mother whispered.

"It's hard to say," I answered. "She's not responding to anything. Her vital signs are good, but we won't know how her brain is for another twenty-four hours or so. We'll do the best we can, though."

Her parents kept crying. I stepped out to go chart. Sonia waited for me at the nurse's station.

"How she doing?" she asked.

"Doesn't look good. She's not responding and completely dependent on the ventilator to breathe for her. It's so sad."

"I know her parents. She's their only child. A quiet girl, hard worker, not a lot of friends."

"Sad," I continued, diligently charting.

"Her parents are older, in their early fifties, I think. They had her very late in life after trying for years. The dad works with my husband. The mom and Nicolina walk the beaches all day selling whatever they can . . . hats, beads, artwork. They don't bring home a large amount."

"Why doesn't she have any friends?" I asked.

"You can't tell now, but she's awkward looking. Real thick glasses make her look like she has bug eyes. A lot of the kids here play soccer in the streets; they grow up with it. Boys, girls, all of them. Nicolina can't play. Can't kick a ball if you held it for her. Not coordinated, I guess. Keeps to herself a lot. Always with her parents."

"Where was her mom when she walked home yesterday? She was alone, wasn't she?"

"Not sure. Ana's usually with her," Sonia said.

I let out a long breath and moved my chair away from the desk. I kept watching Ana and her husband cry, their foreheads pressed against each of Nicolina's hands. Something in my gut— "the nursing gut," as we call it—told me the next few days were not going to be good. I had a strong feeling that Nicolina wouldn't make it.

Later, back at the hotel, I went to the bar for a stiff drink. Watching Nicolina's parents had bothered me. No matter what we did, she would die. I had been there before. I finished my drink and went up to my room to shower. My eyes burned and I could barely keep them open. Here was a young girl, dying in the ICU while her parents cried over her, and then there was Erica, crying over some facial scars! Her husband lived, but Oh Lord, he'd be damaged! Where were her priorities? Why couldn't she see what she had? If you took things for granted in life, it might be too late before you realized they were gone. And then you'd be left feeling . . . empty. I resolved not to give Erica any more thought; she didn't deserve to be in my head, nor did she deserve any more of my time. To hell with her. Man, had it been a long, depressing day.

The phone rang and I didn't feel like answering it, but the continued ringing eventually started driving me nuts.

"Hello?"

"Natalie, it's Jason."

"Oh, Jason, hi. It's good to hear your voice." I looked at myself in the mirror and fixed my curls.

"Can I see you before you leave?"

"I don't think so. I'm working the next two days and I leave Tuesday morning."

"Damn. Okay. So I guess this is good-bye."

I twirled the phone cord between my fingers. "I had a lot of fun with you. A lot. I wish I had more time, I really do."

"Hey, things happen for a reason, you know. It's been cool. This doesn't have to be good-bye forever. I'll get back to the States at some point."

"Will you look me up when you do? We can also e-mail. Do you have that here?"

Laughing, he said, "Of course we do! What's your e-mail address?"

We exchanged addresses and I didn't want to hang up, but sleep called the shots. "I have to go, I'm really tired and it's been a bad day."

"Well, good luck, Natalie, wherever life takes you."

"Thank you, Jason. So much. I owe you," I told him in a sultry voice.

"And I will definitely take you up on that. Until then." We hung up.

I gently put the phone back in its cradle and collapsed to the bed.

Over the next two days, I took care of Nicolina but saw little improvement. Doctors did all the tests to determine if she was brain dead, and if her remaining organs were healthy. Once they determined that her heart, lungs, and liver were good, they put Nicolina into "harvest mode." The medical team would try to keep those organs alive so others in need could benefit. This was the hardest part of being a nurse. How could I comfort her parents? They'd lost their daughter. What remained now was only a shell.

*"Natalie, would you like to see her before she goes?"*

*Sitting next to my mother on the bed, it felt as if her body had become a cocoon, only no butterfly lay inside waiting to emerge. It was empty. Her face felt cold as I kissed her cheek; her arms were nothing but bones.*

*The nurse asked my dad if he'd like to be alone with her. No, he told her, and walked out of the room. My sister kissed Mom on the forehead and followed my father out. I was alone. Again.*

*One nurse turned off the oxygen while another nurse pulled the blanket up to Mom's chest and fluffed her pillow, then smoothed Mom's hair. A third nurse recited the Kaddish, the Jewish prayer for the dead. Finally, in death, Mom looked peaceful. Instead of gaping open, her lips now formed a smooth line, slightly upturned at the corners. She looked as if she was smiling . . .*

The night nurse finally convinced Mr. and Mrs. Arroyo to go home, change clothes, and get something to eat. Reluctantly, they left Nicolina's bedside. I went to her and once again forced her eyes open, shining a bright light at her pupils. No response. I spoke loudly in her ear. Nothing. Her vitals were stable and her heartbeat regular. I walked to the head of her bed and put my hand on her cheek. Both eyes were swollen and bruised. Her lips were swollen from the tape around the tube that kept her breathing, and her arm and leg were in casts. Her face appeared four times the size of a normal sixteen-year-old's, while her hair, matted from blood and bodily fluids, lay mashed against the pillow. I took one of her toes between my index finger and thumb and applied hard pressure to the toenail. This would make a normal person hit the roof in pain. Nothing. If there was any brain activity, that pain would have caused a twitch or something. I checked the IV bags to make sure they were still running, emptied her urinary catheter bag, and went out to the nurse's station to chart the morning's assessment.

The rest of the day, Nicolina remained unchanged. A neurologist, surgeon, hospitalist (a doctor who manages the hospital patients only), and a pulmonologist all made their rounds and assessed Nicolina. Each one came to the same conclusion. By late afternoon, talk of donor transplantation started to replace prognosis. Her parents kept crying. When a trauma surgeon came in to discuss a patient in need of Nicolina's heart, Ana's legs gave out. Her husband caught her before she hit the ground. I went in and asked to speak to the surgeon outside Nicolina's room.

"Excuse me, Doctor, but I'm not sure they're ready to hear this," I said, crossing my arms.

"Well, excuse me, Nurse, but if we're going to have a successful transplant, we need to do it soon. Get the consent. The girl's gone."

*Fucker.* The surgeon walked away briskly and I was left with the awful task of asking these parents to let their daughter die, and to donate her organs so someone else could live. Impossible. *Everywhere I go it's the same b.s.*, I thought angrily. Doctors were all the same. Stoic and unmoving, only thriving on those they could save.

Dragging myself into Nicolina's room, I saw her parents at her bedside. I took a washcloth to her face and cleaned some of the tape residue and dried saliva off her lips. I attempted to wash some of the debris off her hair, face, and hands. I put a large emesis basin on the ground and a towel under her head. With a pitcher, I wet her hair and lathered it with shampoo. Running my fingers through her soapy hair, I watched her mother stand up and join me. She took the pitcher and poured it slowly, washing away the dirt and blood. We finished cleaning Nicolina's hair together in silence. I found a dry towel and placed it over her wet head, gently massaging the moisture out of it. Even when there was nothing a nurse could do or say to make a situation better, simple things, like giving a bath or making the patient look nice, soothed a heavy heart, including my own. I felt useful. Ana took a brush out of her bag and took over for me, wanting to brush out the tangles herself. I went to sit in the chair to speak to Ana's husband Reynaldo.

"Do you understand what they're asking of you, Mr. Arroyo?" I put my hand on his shoulder.

In broken English, he said, "Yes'm. We don't want to let her go. She our *bebé*."

"I understand," I said. "They don't think she is going to wake up, Mr. Arroyo."

"And you?" He looked up at me, pleading. His eyes were red and brimming with tears.

I drew in a breath, then released it. "No. I don't think she will wake up."

Ana stopped brushing Nicolina's hair for a brief second, gave us a vacant stare, and then started again. Just then, a professional, businesslike woman walked into the room. She clutched a clipboard to her chest and wore a badge around her neck that read Donor Team.

"Hello, Mr. and Mrs. Arroyo. My name is Shanesha and I'm a caseworker here at the hospital. I work with donor patients and their families."

Ana stopped brushing Nicolina's hair and gave her a lingering kiss on the forehead. She walked around the bed, stood up straight, and faced the intruder.

"What we need to do?" asked Ana. Her husband rose to his feet.

I went to Ana and put my arm around her. She looked at her husband.

"My *bebé* is gone, Reynaldo. There's nothing more to do. If her heart can live on, then she can, too. We must do what they ask."

Mr. Arroyo began to sob. In a matter-of-fact way, Shanesha pulled out the paperwork and handed Ana a pen.

I sat with Sonia near the end of my shift, my chest hollow. The transplant team had come from Karl Heusner Memorial Hospital, the largest hospital in Belize City, to take Nicolina. Her parents walked silently behind the stretcher. I got up and Ana stopped. I hugged her tight and told her, "I'm sorry I didn't know Nicolina, but I know she was wonderful."

Ana's dry eyes met mine. She had no tears left. "Thank you."

I walked back to Sonia, who reached her arms out. We hugged each other tight. I had seen many sad things in my life and as a nurse, but this girl had struck my heart. I wanted to do all the living I could while I still had time. And I wanted my life to be meaningful, never taken for granted. Death doesn't care if you're good or bad. It just takes you. I'm a good nurse and a good person. I thought of what Sonia had told me: "You put out bad, you get bad. You put out good, you'll receive good." I wished I believed that. Had any good come of my mother's death or Nicolina's?

I told Sonia that although I was happy to be going home, she would be the one thing I would miss the most about Belize. "You've been so great, making me feel comfortable here and showing me around. We met for a reason and I'm so glad we did!"

"It's been great meeting you. I've never met an American like you! You are a wonderful person," Sonia told me.

We exchanged addresses and I told her that if she ever came to America, I would love to see her. This wasn't good-bye forever for us; it was only good-bye for now.

Our shift over, Sonia and I gathered our belongings and walked out of Belize Medical Associates. I took one last look at the hospital. Back at the hotel, packing up my luggage, my thoughts were not of how I would make things better for myself in Denver. Nope. I didn't want to go back there. I wanted to keep doing this. To travel around and meet new people, experience new hospitals. Experience anything and everything I could. I needed to chase life. I had to figure out how to do that. Leaving Porter would have to be the first step.

# 7

I decided I liked traveling and staying a short time in different places. A month after I returned home from Belize, I informed Peggy that I would sign on full-time and I was ready for another travel assignment. I still had to put in my two weeks' notice at Porter and let everyone know my plans.

I went back to work on a Monday, letter of resignation in hand. Judy and Karen were the most upset.

"After one assignment, you're ready to do this full-time?" Judy asked.

"Yeah. It feels right. I need a change."

"I don't want to lose you, but if this is what you want, I wish you the best!"

"Thanks, Judy. I really appreciate everything you've done for me. Hey, I meant to ask you: Have you heard anything about Betty Watson?" I chewed my nails.

"You haven't heard? Are you kidding? Natalie, she's wanted by the police. She hasn't been seen or heard from since I questioned her after her husband died."

"What? Wanted? For what?"

"We thought you knew. After you left my office, I called risk management, and they advised me to call the cops. Just to cover our ass. Well, apparently Betty cashed in her husband's life insurance and skipped town. Police are looking for her."

"Holy shit. Was I right? Did she kill him?" I took in a sharp breath.

"I don't know about that, but something happened."

"I can't believe she worked with us! What the hell, Judy?"

"I know. It's kinda scary. She's the police's problem now and can't come back here. Don't worry about her; you're off to bigger and better things." She wrapped her arm around my shoulders.

"I hope I never see her again," I sighed, shaking my head. "What if they never find her?"

"Natalie, the police will take care of it. Now let's stop talking about Betty and more about you."

"Jesus, you think you know someone . . ." I'd have to do an Internet search for Betty later, just out of curiosity.

"I know. Makes you wonder about some of the other nurses we work with, huh?" Judy nudged my elbow and I nervously laughed.

I put thoughts of Betty aside and focused on my new decision. Judy and I hugged and talked about some memories of me as a new nurse, she as my preceptor. I would miss her! We came up with a definitive end date and I finished the day easily. Karen and I walked to our cars together after our shift ended. There wasn't much to say because I knew I'd always keep in touch with her.

"I hope you find what you're looking for, Nat," Karen said solemnly. "You know what they say: if you love someone, let them go, so I'm letting you go." Her smile warmed my heart.

I stopped in the middle of the parking lot and touched her arm. We embraced and I said, "I love you too!" Like Sonia, this wasn't good-bye for us; it was more like . . . "see ya later."

Peggy called me a few days later and told me there was nothing available internationally. However, she had a six-week spot open near Phoenix, Arizona. I had been to Arizona several times as a kid. My parents took us there every spring break and I remembered the clear, blue skies and the smell of orange blossom and lavender in the air. The pools were sparkling clear and the temperature range hovered between seventy and ninety degrees. In the spring! You could swim year round there!

"Sounds good!" I told her.

"Great. I'll put you down for the second week of April. In the meantime, I'll keep my eyes open for a global assignment. Does that sound peachy?" Peggy asked.

"Yes! I think I'll drive myself to Phoenix if that's okay. I'd like to have my own car there. It's not too bad of a drive."

"No problem. Just keep track of your gas receipts and we'll reimburse you. Let me know if you need anything else and I'll get the paperwork going. Jane will call you with the info next week."

"Thanks, Peggy. I look forward to it!"

"Welcome aboard, Natalie! We're glad to have you!"

It's very difficult to pack for a six-week trip, but I managed to squeeze everything in two pieces of luggage. For work, I only needed scrubs; easy. For the rest, jeans, T-shirts, sundresses, and bathing suits. I figured if I forgot or needed anything else, I would just get it when I got there.

On the night of my last shift, the girls at the hospital threw me a good-bye party. We all went to Pott's Bar on Sixteenth Street, the most popular nurses' hangout. If you worked at Porter, you hung out at Pott's. We had a great time drinking and talking about memorable patients we'd had together—some good, some bad, and some very, very bad. Laughter and camaraderie filled the bar. I felt lonely all of a sudden.

"What's wrong?" Elizabeth asked.

"Just starting to get a little nervous about Thursday. I'm leaving the day after tomorrow. Possibly for good. I never thought

I'd leave Denver. So much of who I am is here. Do you think it's bad that I want to leave it all behind?"

"No, I don't. In fact, I admire you. You recognized you needed a change and you went out and found options. That takes balls, Natalie. It's okay if you want something different. People do it all the time. You're going to be fine."

"Thank you," I told her as we hugged. I'd never thought of myself as having "balls" other than on the nursing unit. It felt good to hear her say that and I started to believe that everything would be okay.

Back in my apartment I put on some Norah Jones and sat on my balcony, taking it all in. I never thought I'd like moving around so much. I used to love being in the ICU at Porter. I knew the ins and outs of the hospital, could do my charting in a quick ten minutes, and knew who everyone and where everything was. It was my comfort zone. Going somewhere new required getting oriented to the unit, having to learn the hospital's way of charting, and making new friends. Not an easy task, even in your late twenties. Frankly, change had scared me up until Belize. Caring for those patients in Belize had made me see life in a different way. I realized that I needed to be grateful for what I had and not worry so much about the little stuff. Life is too short; you've got to take it by the horns and ride.

I leafed through the packet Peggy had sent about the hospital and the city I would work in. The hospital, called Marisdale North, was set in an upper-class town with the same name about twenty miles east of Phoenix. The ICU had twenty beds, all fully equipped with ventilators, computer charting, and other high-tech medical machinery. This should be easy. If I could survive Belize with its third-world conditions, then I could definitely survive this. Now if I could just survive a phone call to my father . . .

"Hello? Dad?" I started playing with my hair.

"Natalie? What time is it?"

"It's ten o'clock. Why do you sound so shitty? I can barely hear you."

My father cleared his throat. "Um, oh . . . Natalie."

"Yes, Dad, it's Natalie, your daughter. What's wrong with you? Are you drunk?" I cursed under my breath.

"No! I mean . . . yeah. I went to a cocktail party and had too many . . . I must've passed out on the couch."

"Great. I'll be quick. I wanted you to know I'm heading to Arizona. I left Porter. I'm going into travel nursing."

"You what? How could you do that? Why?"

"Why not? There's nothing keeping me here anymore." Nothing but silence. "I want something different."

"Nothing keeping you?"

"No. Nothing." Cricket silence.

"Well. Be safe."

*Be safe?* That's all he could say? "I will. I always am." I swallowed the huge knot that had consumed my throat. My eyes were stinging. I wished Mom were with him right now. "Bye."

"Natalie. Wait . . ."

"What, Dad?" I held my breath.

"Nothing. Take care. Please."

I laughed bitterly, shaking my head. He sucked at this. "Good-bye, Dad." I hung up the phone and threw the heart-shaped stress ball I found on my counter at the nearest wall, knocking down my shelf of swimming trophies.

After a thirteen-hour car ride, tons of coffee, three stops at disgusting public bathrooms, and a slew of shitty comfort food to keep me happy and awake, I arrived in Marisdale. The temperature outside read eighty-two degrees and the heat penetrated my face. I guess I was used to springtime in Denver, a cool fifty or sixty with a lot of snow. I followed the directions to my furnished apartment and pulled into the assigned carport. Absolutely gorgeous! Throughout the complex, little streams wove in and around cascading waterfalls while large queen palms and ficus trees surrounded the grounds. I walked up one flight of stairs to my door.

The entryways were arched and a large bay window completed the quaint kitchen area. The balcony off the bedroom and living room overlooked a three-tiered waterfall that made the most relaxing sound. A beautiful, high-backed, old-fashioned couch made of mahogany with flowered upholstery sat along the east wall and an entertainment unit with a few lamps and a coffee table furnished the family room. The bedroom had a metal sleigh bed and matching dresser and nightstand, and the bathroom reminded me of the Southwest, decorated in reds, greens, and oranges. The soffits contained fake greenery in baskets, and the kitchen, although tiny, looked functional. A wooden table sat under a glass chandelier by another bay window in the dining room, complete with a blue-tiled top with room for four. "I'll probably never use that," I said out loud. I pictured myself eating dinner on the couch in front of the thirty-two-inch TV. Table for one.

I reported to the hospital bright and early and received directions to the conference center. A wing of its own, the conference center seemed more like a convention center! I quickly took out my phone, took a picture of the entry and posted it to my Facebook wall: *Natalie Ulster at Marisdale North Hospital, Marisdale, Arizona. Here's to a new chapter!* Hospital staff were busy running around the halls, transporters pushed patients to different departments, and the overhead speaker paged doctors, reminding me of a scene out of the TV show *ER*. My nursing juices flowed and I bit down on a smile.

But the excitement waned abruptly after an hour of orientation, when I realized that if I weren't getting paid for today, I'd be gone. Policies, procedures, and pathways were boring the hell out of me. The "Three Ps", they called them. More like the "Three Bs": bland, boring, and blah.

Finally, I received my name badge and headed to the second-floor ICU. An older nurse named Deb met me outside and showed me around the unit. Her badge kept bouncing up and down against large breasts, causing jingling sounds to resonate off her bejeweled lanyard. She looked like a seasoned nurse, walking around the unit with a great deal of confidence. Deb brought me to the nurses' station, located right in the center of the unit. No matter where you were at the station, you could see all the rooms. Love it! At Porter's, the nurses' station sat at the end of a long hallway . . . stupid. That always led to a lot of patients who couldn't find their call bells yelling "Nurse!" After seven years, the shouted word had grated on my eardrums. Deb showed me the touch screen monitors and the supply room, with scanners and bar codes for anything needed.

"Wow, very high tech," I told her. "Fancy schmancy."

"Only the best here in Marisdale!" Deb said.

"Hey, where I'm from, we were still paper charting and going down to the basement to get supplies. Right by the morgue! *This* is nice."

"Well, with all this fancy stuff comes demanding, elitist-type patients. Not all of them, but most of them. The other populations here are either poor or uninsured. We've got quite the variety."

We continued to tour the unit. I stayed with Deb for the day but would get my own assignment tomorrow. We had two patients: one elderly woman on a ventilator, suffering from valley fever, and a construction worker who'd developed seizures after being stung by a scorpion. Not at all in my comfort zone.

"Should I be worried about scorpions here?" I asked Deb.

She laughed. "Not unless you live or work in the desert. You don't see them around grass or developed neighborhoods much."

"Although you do have to watch out for the one that sneaks into your bed at night," said a deep voice from behind us.

I turned around, startled, but the fear of scorpions quickly disappeared as I looked up and saw the most striking man I'd ever seen. He was over six feet tall, with tanned, olive skin and jet-black hair, and biceps sticking out of his short-sleeved polo shirt. *No way this guy's a doctor.*

"Hi, Dr. Lansfield," Deb said. "This is Natalie. She's a travel nurse here with us for what—a month?"

"Six weeks," I said. "Nice to meet you." Distracting myself, I sat down at the computer screen and started reviewing my patients.

"Glad to have you here, Natalie. It's nice to see a new face. And I'm just kidding about the scorpions," he said, winking at me. "Let 208's nurse know I left some orders on the chart. I'll be by early tomorrow morning to discharge him," he told Deb as he strode out of the unit.

Deb looked at me and smiled. "A word of advice. Don't join the bandwagon of Lansfield groupies. He's a great doc and good to the nurses, but he never goes out with any of them. Guess he doesn't want all the drama or gossip that goes on."

"I don't blame him. It's a bitch. Hospitals can get pretty sleazy." I continued perusing the chart.

"Right? He's the most eligible bachelor in the hospital, been here almost five years, but you'll never hear a rumor about him, good or bad. He stays out of it all and likes it that way. Leads to many a sad nurse."

I agreed with Deb. He was good-looking, but so what? I didn't have time for that crap.

Deb introduced me to the rest of the nurses and most seemed very nice and appeared to know what they were doing. Of course, every unit has a token bitch. This one's name was Emma.

"Great! Just what we need, another travel nurse. Can they not find permanent people anymore? Is the pay that good? You just stay a few weeks and then go somewhere else and earn twice what we earn?" Emma candidly asked, throwing her hands in the air.

"Is she always this pleasant?" I asked Deb as Emma walked away.

"Don't worry about her. She's a little prima donna. She went into nursing to find a doctor husband but she hasn't been too lucky in that area. Funny, though, she's actually a good nurse, and good to her patients. She's not so bad once she gets to know you."

I blew off Emma's comments and figured that if she was the worst of them, I could definitely handle it. It had been a long day and relief came as our shift ended. I thanked Deb and headed to the parking lot to make my ten-minute drive home.

I was searching in my purse for my apartment key when I looked down to find a little furry friend at the bottom of my staircase. He was the cutest dog I had ever seen. Laying flat against his back, a very tightly curled tail wagged like crazy. He had a black face that looked like he'd flattened it running into a wall, and a short, tan body. Deep wrinkles across his face made him appear chronically worried.

"Well, hello, little fella," I said, petting him. "Where did you come from?"

"So sorry. He's mine. Ozzie, come!" said an elderly lady who came out of the door directly under my apartment.

"It's totally okay; he's adorable. Ozzie, is it? My name's Natalie. I've moved in, temporarily, one flight up."

"Oh yes, I saw you come in yesterday. Nice to meet you. I'm Mary, Mary Nelson."

"Nice to meet you, Mary. And you too, Ozzie," I said, holding Ozzie's smushed face in both my hands. "Well, I've got to get upstairs. I guess I'll be seeing you around."

"Oh, yes. I'm glad to have a young medical person living right above me. I'm assuming that's what you do, wearing that uniform. I'll try not to bother you much," Mary said. She appeared to be in her early seventies and I had a feeling Ozzie was her only companion. She used a cane and her hunched back reminded me of Quasimodo.

"No worries! You can bother me. Especially if you bring Ozzie. He's too cute!" I kissed the air toward Ozzie's direction.

"He's a great dog, and a great friend. We won't keep you. Have a good evening," Mary said as she scooted Ozzie back inside.

Smiling, I walked up the stairs and into the apartment. I opened the balcony door so I could hear the fountain while I changed out of my scrubs, then sat down in the Adirondack chair and looked up. *It's nice here, Mom. The weather, my apartment. This is going to be good. I can feel it.* I clutched a picture of my mom and I, taken right before the cancer diagnosis, firmly to my heart.

# 8

His hands were all over me, starting at my lower back. He moved them down and caressed each butt cheek, gently squeezing and kneading. I threw my head back, wrapping my legs tighter around his waist. Wanting . . . more. I moved my head so I could look him in the eyes as our lips smashed together, our tongues searching the insides of each other's mouths. Little moans escaped my throat and then our pelvises met, moving rhythmically up and down. Again, I leaned my head back and tried to control my breath. I was panting. Wanting . . . more. Finally, both of his hands gripped my waist and he positioned me perfectly, gently sliding into me. I let out a groan and . . .

I shot straight up in bed and felt the cool sweat on the back of my neck. I moved my hand down between my thighs and felt . . . wet? Oh God, did I just orgasm? What the hell? What kind of dream was that? And, *who* . . . Oh, shit! Catching my breath, I saw him clearly in my mind's eye: the doctor I'd met on the unit. Damn! What was his name? Dr. Longfield? It didn't matter. Why did I dream about him? And why did it have to be *that* kind of a dream? Dr. Lansfield! That's it. I guess my libido hadn't received the memo about him not wanting to date nurses. I grabbed my head with both hands and shook it side to side, forcing him out of my brain. How could this not be awkward, the next time I saw him? *It'll be written all over my bright red face because that . . . was . . . so . . . good!* I lay back down and looked at the clock: 2:45 a.m. I had to get up in three hours. I put one hand over my heart, took a deep breath, and fell back asleep. Strangely satisfied.

I arrived at the hospital ten minutes early and got a cup of coffee in the lounge. They'd given me a little cubby where I could leave my purse, and I sat down to wait for the nursing assignments to be printed. Emma came in next. She walked right by me, put her stuff away, and walked back out, her upturned nose in the air and her strawberry-blond hair flipping behind her. I just kept sipping on my brew.

A tall, beautiful woman strode in. "Good morning! I'm Yvette. And who are you?"

"Natalie." I took another sip. "I need at least one cup of this before I can really talk to you." I told her, lifting up my coffee and smiling.

"Oh, no worries," said Yvette. "Take all the time you need. Nice to meet you." She sat down across from me and started pulling out vitamin packs, a powdered something which she put into a large bottle of water, and her stethoscope from her nurse's bag.

"That accent? Where are you from?" I asked.

"South Africa, poppet. And you?"

"Denver, born and raised. What is all that?" I pointed to her powder and vitamins.

"Oh, this? It's how I get through the day at my age."

"Your age? How old are you?" I said, really wanting to know.

"Fifty-two."

"What? You look fantastic!" Yvette's perfectly smooth skin glowed. She had flawless makeup and bright white teeth. Her shiny black hair rested tightly in a French twist and her petite frame couldn't have been more than a size four.

"Thank you, poppet," Yvette said. Other nurses started filing in and the assignments were brought to the table.

I looked for my name and saw my patients. The first one read "Begay, 28-year-old male, septic infection, 800 lbs." The next one, "Meyers, 34, gastric bypass surgery, 650 lbs." Great. Every nurse dreaded any patient over 500 pounds. They were impossible to move, caused major back pain, and often their personalities were just as difficult. It was a known fact that travel nurses were given the shittiest assignments. No one knew exactly how good a travel nurse was when he or she arrived at a hospital, so they would always get the short end of the stick. This is true at any hospital; I'd just never thought I'd be the nurse holding that stick.

"Good luck with those," said Emma. I happened to glance at her assignment: a 1:1. One nurse to one patient. These patients were very critical, very near death, and intense as far as lots of medications and machines . . . majorly hands-on. Only the most experienced nurses got those. Most ICU nurses loved these patients. You relentlessly did things to keep the patient alive, making the day go by very quickly. Although very stressful, you couldn't beat the adrenaline rush. Whenever I would get a 1:1 at Porter, I'd always say, "You're not going to die today. Not on my watch." It's what ICU nurses spend all those years training for. But I guess I'd have to wait a little while before I could get one of those again. For now, I'd have to settle for the two biggies.

I received a brief report and walked into the first room. I had never seen a larger man. The Native American lay in a specially made bed that almost filled the entire room. The night nurse explained that no one would come visit him because the family was afraid to come in. Usually, when a Native American was in the hospital, it seemed like the entire tribe would be at the bedside. Why wasn't anybody visiting? Begay's kin had spent the last few nights in the family waiting room, just outside of the unit.

Yesterday, the nurse had tried to get one of them to come in, but none would. There wasn't much room for visitors anyway. The only way I could get by the bed to the monitors was by turning my belly toward the rails and sidestepping alongside the bed. I pulled the V-neck of my scrub top up over my nose. The room stunk like moldy feet and infection. I almost gagged. *That's why his family won't come in! Their noses can't take it.*

The extra-large gowns weren't big enough for him so two flat sheets and a cover were spread across his body. The respirator helped him breathe and he had a huge catheter called a Swan-Ganz coming out above his left clavicle. A Swan is placed in the heart of very sick patients to monitor the heart's function and blood flow. I checked the monitor and jotted down the numbers. I had to pull from my brain what everything meant because it had been a while since I'd worked with a Swan, and by my calculations, Mr. Begay's heart appeared to be failing. None of the numbers looked good. Two medications were running by IV to keep his blood pressure up and a sedative kept him asleep—although, with all the infection, his brain wasn't very active anyway.

The smell in the room started to drive me crazy. Where did it come from? I checked his urine catheter, his breathing tube, and his rectal tube, all of which were intact. Then, I saw his feet. There must have been about fifty layers of dead, white-and-green skin on the bottoms of both feet. Disgusting. I don't think this man had ever owned a pair of shoes! I knew I wouldn't be able to get through the day with those pudgy feet peeking out from the sheets, mocking me with their stench. This had to be why the family stayed away. Before I moved on to my other patient, I brought in the charge nurse to get her opinion.

"Can we do anything about this?" I asked her, showing her his feet.

"We don't have the tools to do anything ourselves. And that's the least of his problems." She pulled her glasses down and looked at me over the rims.

"It's not a big deal, I know," I told her, "but it's real bad and it can't be good for anybody's health. What about a foot doctor? Can't they scrape it or buff it or something?"

The charge nurse laughed. "A podiatrist? Natalie, where are your priorities? The man's dying!" I stared at her blankly. "I'll tell you what. If he is completely stable, you can see if one of our local podiatrists will come in. I'm warning you, though, it's a very unusual request. You may piss off a few people. He's not expected to be around much longer."

"I hear you; it's just so *bad*. None of his family members want to come in here. He's going to die alone while his family waits outside. I'd like to try and get someone to look at him later, if I can. As long as you're okay with it."

"I'm fine with it. Good luck with that." She walked off, shaking her head and smiling.

I knew it sounded crazy but I didn't care. I didn't want him dying alone. No one should. Ever. I wrote down "podiatrist" on my nurse's sheet and planned to call someone later. I wanted to get the other patient moving so I could start charting. I entered the room and saw my second rather large man of the day, sitting in a very large bed positioned like a recliner, watching TV and sucking on a wet washcloth. Yes, sucking. I introduced myself to him and asked him why he had half a washcloth in his mouth.

"I'm not allowed to eat anything for another twenty-four hours, right? Well, I'm hungry and thirsty NOW!"

"Mr. Meyers, you can't have anything except a few ice chips. You're sucking all the water out of this thing! It's too much. Your stomach can't take it," I said, taking the washcloth from him. "Anyway, it's time for your walk."

"What? I can't walk right now. I just had surgery."

"Mr. Meyer, they explained to you that we'd walk you around the unit every two hours, didn't they? It's all in the packet you received before the surgery. The surgeons are very strict about that. Every two hours." I pushed a humongous wheelchair closer for him to use as a walker and positioned myself in front of him.

Just then Yvette walked by the door. "Yoo-hoo! Natalie, what are you doing?" she said, running into the room.

"I've got to walk him. Every two hours. It's the same with all gastric bypass patients. You guys do that here, don't you?"

"Yes, but we have a lift team to help you. You don't have to lift him on your own. What are you, crazy? Wait, I'll go call them." She flew out of the room and placed an overhead page.

*Lift team?* Damn. Where were they my last seven years? About twelve of my lower vertebrae could've used that. I'd always lifted my own patients. One thing swimming has given me is strong muscles. My legs can lift anything. Well, not really, but I am strong. A lift team? Arizona was looking better and better every day! A few minutes later four hefty guys arrived, and it still took all of us to get Mr. Meyers moving. I walked next to him, holding the IV pole, and encouraged him to keep going. Each slow, tiny step forward took years off my life. We were supposed to make it once around the unit, but we barely made it around the corner.

"I can't . . . I'm dying," my patient said, gasping like a fish out of water.

Signaling the lift team with my hand, as if I were chopping my head off my neck, we turned him around and headed back to the room. I wasn't going to kill myself this early in the morning. We had all day to play.

"Rest and I'll be back in two hours to do it again," I told him. "And no washcloths!"

I left the room, ignoring the whining and whimpering. I sat at the nurse's station and logged on to the computer. Looked easy enough. I began diligently entering all my vital signs and documented my exam.

"Who has room 213?" said that sexy, low voice. *Oh, shit.*

I hunched further behind the computer screen. I knew if I looked at Dr. Lansfield, all those sensual feelings I'd had this morning would show in my face. Luckily, one of the other nurses spoke up and he followed her to his patient's room. Phew. Once the coast was clear, I asked the nurse charting next to me which podiatrist who came to the hospital seemed the nicest. She gave me a name, and I called Mr. Begay's attending physician for the order. Sounding young on the phone, I assumed he was a resident. Good! I could usually get the baby docs to write whatever I needed. And I needed a consulting podiatrist.

"You want me to come check out a dying guy's feet?"

"No, no. It's just that his family members won't come in the room or visit because the smell is so bad. And it looks really gross! I don't want him dying alone while his family sits outside because of some ugly feet."

"So cover them up!" the podiatrist said.

"Believe me, it's more than that. It's the smell. Please, doctor. If you have time?"

Sighing, he said, "Since you're being so nice about it, I'll try." He hung up the phone.

Well, it was a start. At least I knew I'd tried to do something. I finished up charting and got up to walk my patient again. Had it been two hours already?

Right after lunch the podiatrist showed up with what looked like an old medical bag. "Who's got room 210?" he asked. He was short and balding with soft, blue eyes.

"That would be me," I said. "Thank you so much, Doctor Baker."

We walked into Mr. Begay's room together and I quickly pulled the sheets off his feet. I didn't have to show him anything because the stench had already reached his nostrils. The doctor just stood there, mouth open, his shirt collar over his nose. He looked at me and I gave him a crooked smile. "See? It's bad."

"All right. You probably won't want to be in here when I'm doing this. It's not going to be good for the lungs. If you're going to stay, you'd better get a mask on." He began to pull things out of his bag: a full face mask, similar to a welder's shield, some sort of saw with a round blade, and several rolls of gauze. He started to drape the room.

"I'm out. I'll be at the nurse's station if you need me."

Minutes later, it sounded as if *The Texas Chain Saw Massacre* had come to Marisdale. I looked at the monitor that showed a live feed of the patient's room. Clouds of debris flew all over the place, like a Denver snowfall. I checked the vitals monitor and everything looked stable for the moment. The whole process took about an hour and finally, Dr. Baker came out of the room and asked me to call housekeeping.

"How'd it go?" I asked him.

"It's days like today I ask myself why I take care of feet. I buffed most of it down and the smell should subside over time. It's probably not a good idea to go in there for a while. If possible."

"Okay. Anything you need from me? I really appreciate what you did."

"No. I think you've done enough. Call me if you need anything else. Better yet, don't." He walked out, bag in hand, white dust clinging to the back of his head.

Half an hour later I decided to check on Mr. Begay. Housekeeping had cleaned up the room and the only odor that remained smelled a bit of lemony bleach. I happily breathed it in. Checking his vitals again, I went to the foot of the bed and lifted the covers. His soles were pink and his heels were slightly white with a thin layer of rough skin. They almost looked normal. Now, that's what I'm talking about! I called to the ward clerk to see if she could locate the family in the waiting room and let them know it was safe to come in. Seconds later, a group of seven or so people came to the door.

"Hi, I'm Natalie, Mr. Begay's nurse. Come in. It's tight, but you all can gather around this side." I pointed to the end of the bed.

They hesitated at the door, then willingly went in. They were quiet, making very little eye contact. An older woman saw his feet poking out and she placed her hand on top of the sheets, softly chanting something. Another man took out some kind of herbal plant and brushed it along Mr. Begay's forehead, again chanting. Lastly, a young woman placed a feather on his pillow, right by his head.

"Thank you, miss. Now he can go with the spirits." I gave a respectful nod and smiled as they all walked out together.

I was glad he got his own send-off and hoped he knew his family had been with him.

"Glad you're here. You're a good nurse. Tomorrow I'll give you a better assignment, I promise."

"Oh, don't worry about it. Every patient needs a nurse, even less appealing ones."

"Fair enough. You did well, though. I've got to go help Emma out; she's having a horrible day." She patted me on the back and walked away.

Snickering at Emma's misfortune, I reminded myself of Sonia and her words about karma: you put out ugly, you get ugly. Maybe if Emma had been a little nicer the nursing gods would be smiling down upon her right now. *But she isn't, so now she gets to have a shitty day.* I smirked.

It's nice to get recognized once in a while for the work we do. It rarely happens. I went back to the nurses' station to chart and finish up the day. *Travel nursing is the best thing I've done for myself. Today has turned out to be a good day.*

I got home and, again, couldn't find my apartment key, muttering to myself to put it on my keychain tonight. This was ridiculous! Once I found the keys at the bottom of my purse, I looked up and saw Ozzie waiting for me at the stairs, his tail wagging and his tongue hanging out. He appeared to be smiling. Mary slowly came out of her door.

"He's been waiting by the window all day hoping to see you."

"Awww. What a great thing to come home to!" I knelt down and started to pet him. He put his front paws on my thighs and licked my face.

"I think he gets tired of being cooped up all day in the apartment." Mary said. "It's just too hard for me to walk him anymore."

"I'd be happy to walk him, Mary. I can take him when I get home from work, and I can help you out on my days off."

"Oh, no. That's too much to ask, dear."

"It's okay, trust me. The dog makes me happy."

"If you're sure, dear. I know Ozzie would love it," Mary said.

"Of course! I'll even take him for a walk now. Just let me go change and I'll be down in a few." I took the stairs two at a time.

"Oh, you're an angel! I'll go get his leash and a bag. Thank you, Natalie." Mary shuffled into her house with Ozzie scampering behind.

I've always been a dog person but never had one growing up. I couldn't get one myself as a nurse because of the long hours.

How perfect would this be? Keeping the benefits of having a dog, yet not having to worry about what to do with it while I went to work? This worked for all of us! Then it dawned on me ... *I'm only here a short time. What will Mary do when I leave? What will Ozzie do?*

# 9

Today was my last day of working three twelve-hour shifts in a row. Most nurses like to work two twelves and then have a day off before working another. I preferred to get them all over with at once. I was beginning to feel comfortable with my new surroundings and people's faces were getting more and more familiar. I knew my way around the unit and was developing some friendships. I decided to keep my same two patients instead of getting new ones. I knew them well. I thought it'd be best to keep things simple during my first week in Marisdale and it was working.

I had begun listening to the report on my patient's status from the night nurse when a loud, rather obnoxious woman in scrubs came barreling onto the unit.

"Why isn't my patient up and walking? Two hours! I ask you guys to walk them every two hours!"

We all stopped listening to each other and looked toward the double doors leading into the unit. A roly-poly of a woman, with messy brown hair shoved under a scrub cap, walked onto the unit.

"That's Dr. Goldenauer," the night nurse said. "She does the gastric-bypass patients. She's a real bitch on wheels."

"I *have* been walking him every two hours," I whispered. "You've been walking him, haven't you?" I asked her.

"I try. But last night I got stuck with three patients and things got busy. For the most part he's walked. He's a real pain in the ass, though. He doesn't want to move."

"Who are you?" the doctor asked, looking in my direction and startling the night nurse and me.

"I'm Natalie. I'm a travel nurse. I have Mr. Meyer." My knuckles turned white as I gripped my clipboard.

"What? I don't want *any* travel nurses taking care of my patients. It's a rule I have. The charge nurses know my rules!"

*Jesus.* The charge nurse came running up. "Good morning, Dr. Goldenauer. Natalie has been taking great care of Mr. Meyer. She walks him all the time. But Mr. Meyer doesn't want to get up."

"It says here you guys haven't even made it around the unit and he's been here three days now! You want me to transfer him or you want him to stay here? I'm not moving him until he's walking around the unit!" She slammed her fist on the counter.

Margo, the charge nurse, explained that we'd all been walking Mr. Meyer as much as possible, but if the patient refused, we can't force him out of bed. "We're doing all we can with him. He acts the same way with the regular nurses, too. It has nothing to do with Natalie being a travel nurse," she argued.

"No travel nurses on my patients, period. Change it," said the surgeon as she stormed into her patient's room.

"I'm so sorry, Natalie," Margo said. "It's not you. We all know that."

"Well, after that, I don't want him as a patient anyway. Who wants to deal with her again? What do you want me to do?"

"I'll give you Yvette's patient in room 206 and the empty bed. If we get another patient, you're first in line. Let's go before she gets too in-depth with report."

We walked over to where Yvette was receiving report, and happily, she switched with me. I would get a little old lady with blood loss from a stomach ulcer and very low blood pressure. Sadly, she was a Jehovah's Witness and it's against their religion to receive a blood transfusion. We could easily have saved her with a few pints, but she had refused. She would most likely die soon.

Scanning through my notes and getting ready to head into the room, I felt someone touch me on the shoulder. I turned around and looked up to see Dr. Joel Lansfield. *Fuck!*

"Hi," I said, swallowing some saliva to wet my dry throat. I felt my face burning a deep red.

"Hey. Just wanted to let you know that Dr. Goldenauer is nutty. The only reason people kiss her ass here is because she brings in a lot of money with those gastric-bypass patients. Don't let her get to you."

*I wonder how he got that little scar along the left side of his chin? I want to touch it.*

Smiling, I squeaked out a "Thanks, I appreciate that," and hurried into my patient's room. Grateful for the reassurance, I straightened my scrubs and introduced myself to Mrs. Robinson. Lifting her shoulders and neck, she struggled to breathe. I explained that her anemia had worsened and that she didn't have enough red blood cells to carry the oxygen her body so desperately needed.

"Any chance I can change your mind about the transfusions?" I asked her, raising my eyebrows.

"No, sweetie, I can't. It violates God's laws," she answered, smoothing out her blanket and resting her hands, fingers intertwined, on her lap. "You believe in God, don't you?"

I hate these kinds of discussions. "I'm Jewish but I don't practice. I consider myself more spiritual than religious."

"Why don't you practice your religion, dear?" Mrs. Robinson reached for my hand.

"I don't know. It doesn't give me much comfort. When my mom died, I didn't think there was any point to her death. What did God mean by taking her from her family?"

"There's always a point, child. God has a plan for us all. Mine is to be with him soon. I know that."

I cocked my head and smiled at her. Such a sweet lady. *A lady I could save with one order for a transfusion!* I let go of her hand and checked her IVs and heart monitor. She got the hint that I didn't want to talk about religion anymore and picked up some kind of prayer book from her night table. It's nice that some people find comfort in their faith and believe everything has a purpose. I don't. I believe our souls continue on once we're gone, but is there a holy being associated with that? I don't know. It's all up in the air for me.

Knowing Mrs. Robinson wouldn't change her mind, I had to admit to myself that I would soon lose her. She looked terrible with her ghostly white skin and purple lips. She just needed a few units! She'd pink right up! I asked my patient if she needed anything at the moment, and of course she said no. Sighing, I walked out of the room and sat down at the computer.

For the remainder of the morning, my stomach churned in knots due to my internal struggle. I felt so frustrated knowing that I had to respect Mrs. Robinson's wishes, whatever they were, even if I thought they were wrong. How could someone's religious beliefs cause them to choose death? Why did they admit her to the unit if her religion prevented us from doing anything? I wanted to march into her room, grab her by her bony shoulders, and shake some sense into her. But I couldn't. I couldn't do anything. I felt helpless. Nursing gave me a sense of accomplishment, a sense of purpose, but the only purpose I had with her now involved charting Mrs. Robinson's vitals and watching her die. I would almost rather have taken care of two Goldenauer patients.

The charge nurse relieved me for lunch and I still had yet to receive another patient. The day dragged. Yvette and I went down to the cafeteria and ordered some food.

Yvette gestured to the guy behind the grill. "Hi. I haven't seen you before. You new?" She asked him.

"Uh, yeah." The toothpick in his mouth shifted from one side to the other. His face reflected the fluorescent lights of the cafeteria and he had a douche-bag goatee: not well-groomed, but with scraggly hairs and no order to it. I thought about changing my mind about ordering from the grill but I really wanted a burrito. He quickly turned his back to us and busied himself with toasting bread. We found a table and sat down while I waited for my food. Yvette started sprinkling her magic powder over her salad. How long did it take to make a burrito? Yvette had already finished eating when finally, my number got called.

"That took a long time," Yvette said. "Usually they're very quick here."

"You'd think they went and killed the chicken themselves," I told her, my mouth salivating.

I took a bite and started chewing rather fast, swallowing some huge pieces, because our lunch break only lasted thirty minutes. Something didn't taste right. All of a sudden, my eyes grew big and I spit out what remained in my mouth. I grabbed a fork and started frantically tearing the burrito apart.

"What's the matter?" Yvette asked. "Are you okay?"

Then I saw it. Shrimp! All over the place! There were some pieces of chicken, but mostly shrimp!

"I'm highly allergic to shrimp, Yvette! I ate some of that!" I yelled, my face draining of blood.

"Oh my gosh! How did that happen? They don't even make shrimp burritos here! Okay, let me look at you." She came over and knelt down in front of my chair, reaching for my face.

I started to feel my throat close and it became difficult to breathe. I had to pull in every breath of air with my neck and chest muscles. I could feel my tongue and lips growing tight and painful and the inside of my skull started itching so much I wanted to rip my eyes out. I gripped Yvette's hands and squeezed, forcing out the words, "Epi . . . Pen . . . purse . . ." as I frantically pointed toward the floor. Yvette understood me and started flinging things out of my purse until she had the EpiPen in her hand. With one swift movement she took the cap off and jabbed the syringe into my thigh. I guess if you ever come close to dying and happen to have a choice of locations, you'll want to choose around lunchtime in a hospital cafeteria. About ten people, all in scrubs, were at my side within seconds. Then, darkness came over me.

When I awoke, I could feel tubing up my nose and my mouth felt parched. I looked around the room and saw the monitors. A curtain had been pulled around my gurney. My lips burned and it hurt to swallow. I felt like a truck had hit me. On the TV monitor above the bed I read a message that said, "Welcome to Marisdale ER where we care about you." Seeing me struggle to boost myself up, Margo came to my side.

"Hi, Natalie. That was fun. If you wanted a longer lunch hour, all you had to do was ask."

I forced a smile, pulling the oxygen tubing out of my nostrils. I struggled to keep my eyes open. "What happened?"

"You went into anaphylactic shock right before Yvette gave you your EpiPen. Good thing you had that with you. Things could've been a lot worse. We tried to question the grill chef but Yvette said they must've changed shift because the guy that served you disappeared."

*Sonofabitch!* "I asked for a chicken burrito. It was filled with shrimp. I would never order shrimp. I know what happens if I eat it, hence, the EpiPen." My breaths quickened and my head pounded.

"Relax, Natalie. I'm trying to figure out what happened. Try not to worry about all that right now; just let the medicine kick in. They've given you IV steroids and an antihistamine. You should start to feel better soon."

"Thanks," I told her. "What about my patients upstairs?"

"You don't have any for now. Mrs. Robinson went into cardiac arrest from her blood loss and died. We haven't gotten any new admissions. I'm sending you home. You need rest and you can't work with all those drugs in you."

"Okay," I told her, not registering what she'd said about Mrs. Robinson. The ER doc walked in and Margo excused herself. He checked me over and filled me in again on what had been given to me. My body felt tense and I caught myself grinding my teeth. The whole chef thing didn't make any sense. Did this kind of thing happen often? How new was this guy? I guess the salad bar would be the only thing on the menu for me from now on. Who makes a chicken and shrimp burrito anyway? It's either chicken *or* shrimp, not both!

Another hour in the ER and they finally released me. I went to the unit to see Yvette and thank her before heading out. I would be off for the next three days and wanted to make sure she knew how grateful I was.

"You'd better get another EpiPen. Don't want that happening again," Yvette said.

"I'll call in a refill as soon as I get home," I told her. "Thanks. If you hadn't been there . . ." I looked at my feet, shaking my head.

She hugged me tight. "Nonsense, poppet! You would've done it yourself. I know you would've."

"I'm not so sure about that, but thank you anyway." We hugged again and I waved good-bye.

Driving home with antihistamines in my system probably wasn't the most brilliant thing to do. I slowly made my way out of the car after parking it safely in my carport. I couldn't wait to get into bed and forget this whole day. Approaching the stairs, I heard Mary and Ozzie come out of their apartment. I stopped, one hand on the rail, one foot on the second step. Energy drained out of me, mentally and physically. I felt too tired to take Ozzie on a walk tonight. Somehow, Mary saw that.

"You all right, dear?" she asked. Ozzie stood next to her, wagging his tail, tongue hanging out.

"It's been a real crappy day. Do you mind if I walk him tomorrow? I'm off for the next few days. I can spend a lot of time with him then."

"Oh, don't worry about Ozzie; he'll be fine. Just let us know if you need anything." Mary turned and called for Ozzie to come with her. He didn't budge. He came to my step and sat right on my foot, looking up at me. I sighed and knelt down to give him some attention. He made the whole day's events disappear.

"Mary? Would you mind if I took Ozzie inside for a little? I could use a friend right now and I get the feeling that he wants to come with me. I'll bring him down later," I pleaded.

"What a wonderful idea! You take him, sweetie. He's good for the soul! Just bring him back to me," she said, winking.

"Thank you. I'll take good care of him. I'll bring him back, I promise." Scooping Ozzie up under one arm like a football, I showed him my apartment. While he sniffed around, I changed into pj's and opened a bottle of pinot grigio. Collapsing on the couch, I flipped on the TV and opened my laptop. Ozzie jumped up on the couch, did a few circles, then plopped down along my thigh. Within seconds, he fell asleep, snoring like a kid who desperately needed their tonsils and adenoids out. I rubbed his belly and started to wind down. Even though I'd chosen to leave

Denver and travel, lonliness visited me at night. I was with people all day but at night, in my little apartment, the silence always reminded me that it was just me. And now Ozzie. Tonight, he would keep me from feeling lonesome.

The *bing* from my e-mail alert made me look at my laptop. A message popped up:

> *To: natalieicurn@cable.com*
> *From: jasoncam1@godiving.com*
> *Subject: Hey*
> *Hey Natalie! What's up? I wish you were still here! Hope all is well and wanted to let you know that I may be in California next month. Not sure where you are, but just checking. Would love to see you! We need to pick up where we left off*
> *Cheers, Jason*

The e-mail stimulated me and I smiled, remembering that day in Belize. I could always visit Jason somewhere, but I couldn't see myself being with him for long periods of time. I preferred it this way. He was there, and I was . . . well, everywhere. Who knew where I'd be in the next month, or even in the next year? I thought for a minute about what I wanted to say and picked my words carefully:

> *To: jasoncam1@godiving.com*
> *From: natalieicurn@cable.com*
> *Subject: Re: Hey*
> *Jason, hi! I do miss seeing you and the dives and Belize! I'm not sure where I'll be in the next month but if I get to California, I will definitely let you know. All the best! Natalie*

It sounds cold, but I didn't want to think about the what-ifs or how we could see each other. There was no point. We were both doing our thing in different places. I closed the laptop and searched for a good movie on TV.

Ozzie rolled to his side and put his head in my lap. *This is good, I'm happy.* His unconditional love lifted me. I didn't have room in my head for more. Betty still hung out in my thoughts, gnawing away at me. Where was she? Had she killed her husband? Weird things had happened. Like seeing that woman take my drink and then . . . I leaned back into the couch and closed my eyes. It hit me: the shrimp! Could someone have known about my shrimp allergy and snuck it in my food? Just like with the water? Impossible. Who would want me dead? All the nurses I'd worked with back home knew of my allergy, and of course my family did, too. I hadn't done anything to anybody, had I? Except . . . Betty. The cold image of her taking jewelry from her dead husband penetrated my bones. Betty knew I had a shrimp allergy. Could she have somehow . . . no! How could she even know where I was? And how would she get into a hospital kitchen? And how would she know I was going to order food? Impossible. It had to have just been an accident. *Or a series of accidents.* Another coincidence. But, two close calls, in two different places, both putting my life in danger? No. It couldn't be her. Could it?

# 10

One week down in Arizona, five more to go. I hadn't gone for a good swim workout since leaving Denver and I missed it. I found a club with a pool right across the street from my apartment. There were people all over the place: working out in the weight room, shooting baskets out front, diving off the high dive in the deep pool, or just swimming leisurely. A separate lap pool for serious swimmers looked awesome; it was super clean, with real lane lines made out of plastic, not cheap rope, and a stainless steel gutter system to reduce any waves caused by swimmer's wake. The pool looked crowded. I found one open lane and placed my goggles, cap, and kickboard on the edge of the diving block to reserve my spot. I shed my clothes and jumped into the eighty-degree water.

The water felt so good I didn't want to get out. After an hour, the lifeguard informed me that the swim team needed all the lanes and I needed to exit. I did, and had started drying off and gathering my things when a familiar voice said, "Hi! Natalie, right?"

Could I not escape him? Dr. Lansfield stood above me and I had no place to run. "Hi. Funny meeting you here. You swim?" I asked, shaking the water out of my ears.

"I did in college. Now I do it to stay in such great shape." He winked. "You look like you know what you're doing out there," he said, gesturing to my equipment bag.

"Yeah, I've been swimming my whole life. Almost made it to Junior Nationals when I was thirteen. Then . . . well, I wasn't into it as much anymore. Now it seems like it's the only thing that keeps me sane these days."

"Clears my head too," he said, taking his goggles out of his bag. Then he took off his shirt. *Damn.*

"Um, okay. So . . . this place is pretty busy. Is it always like this?" I asked him, wrapping my towel around my waist and putting on my shirt.

"It's the nicest pool in the area and it's close to the hospital. All staff get a discount. The pool's heated year round and you can get access to the weight room, too."

"Well, I'm glad I found it. It's great to swim in. Feels fast. I'll look into that discount. Thanks. See you around!" I slung my bag on my shoulder and slid into my flip-flops, ready to head out.

"Take it easy," Dr. Lansfield called after me.

*I'm trying to.* Okay, so the whole wet dream thing was over. Done. I could talk to him without feeling a warming sensation creep up my body. That would have made work really tough for me over the next few weeks. Feeling good about how casually I'd handled the situation, I headed home looking forward to walking Ozzie. Just the thought of him with his curly tail and flat nose made me giddy.

The next day, Kate, one of the other nurses, asked if I wanted to have lunch with her, and I agreed. Nurses usually decide who goes to lunch with whom so there are enough nurses on the floor to cover. I started reviewing the chart and realized that I had a sad patient assignment: Lisa Duvane, twenty-four years old, had gone through a very difficult labor. A globule of amniotic fluid broke off and traveled to her lungs, causing respiratory arrest. Lisa went into cardiac arrest in the OR and now needed life support. To make things worse, because she'd been on the table for so long, compartment syndrome had consumed her left arm. When pressure is applied for prolonged periods of time on a limb, high pressures in the muscle tissue cut off circulation. The only treatment is surgery, where they slice open the arm lengthwise from wrist to shoulder to release the pressure and recirculate the blood, similar to fileting a fish. I had seen compartment syndrome only one other time, when I worked in Denver. A young woman had been jogging at night and a car struck her, pinning her against a tree. She lost her leg after the swelling cut off all circulation. Things didn't look good for Lisa, who had undergone an emergency C-section and gave birth to a healthy baby girl—whom she still had yet to hold.

I entered her room and saw her left arm wrapped in so much gauze she looked like the Michelin Man. It hung from a trapeze bar at a ninety-degree angle. Sedatives kept her from fighting the breathing tube. She had one IV running to keep her blood pressure up and another to keep her hydrated. She would remain unconscious until tomorrow when we would attempt to wake her up. Once sedation is removed the patients realize they're breathing through a tube, and lying in a hospital bed, totally helpless like that, can be very disorienting. Some patients panic and cause further injury to themselves, which means they have to be sedated again and remain on the ventilator. Right now, she needed rest. In a few days, they would try to bring in the baby and see if the two could bond.

Lisa's case confirmed my reservations about having children. Who knew if I'd even make it to forty? Breast cancer is usually hereditary. I wouldn't want to have a baby then be diagnosed a few years later, never to see it grow up. Or God forbid, pass the gene on. My mom had a great thirteen years with me but it wasn't enough. We were both cheated. It would be easier for me not to go down that road. Who needs it? No way!

By mid-afternoon, Lisa had started to wake up. Her ventilator alarms kept going off because she resisted the tube. I tried reassuring her, but she continued to pull the airway out with her good arm. I tried to calm her down but she kept on fighting. Her traction arm had to remain absolutely still, otherwise she would tear the incisions even farther apart and could possibly bleed out. Her right arm, crazily flailing about, had caused the IV tubing to pull and stretch beyond its capability, sending the IV pole flying. Lurching over her kicking feet, trying to catch the pole before it ripped the whole thing from her arm, I yelled "Help!" to anyone who would hear me. The weight of my body across hers immobilized her enough while the charge nurse began applying the restraints. Another nurse ran in and started adjusting the alarms and straightening out Lisa's respiratory tube.

Dr. Lansfied poked his head in. "May I suggest some Vitamin H?" Vitamin H is our term for the drug Haldol, an anti-psychotic used in the ICU to sedate agitated patients.

"I know, I know. I'm trying to get her restrained first so she doesn't cause any more destruction. That's next, trust me," I said as I finished tying off her arm restraint. I quickly checked the standing orders and whispered "Thank you" under my breath that the hospitalist had placed an *x* in the Haldol box. I ran to the med room and drew up 10mg to push into her IV.

Once Lisa fell asleep from the sedation, I breathed a sigh of relief and went out to the nurses' station to chart. Staring at the computer screen, I leaned back in my chair to catch my breath. I could've used some of that Haldol, too. I didn't want another surgeon bitching at me for allowing Lisa to get so out of control and causing further injury to her left arm.

"Having a rough day?" Dr. Lansfield asked, writing in one of his patients' charts.

"What are you, following me? You're everywhere I turn," I said to him, grinning.

"Guess you're just that lucky."

Shaking my head and rolling my eyes, I began to document the incident with Lisa in the computer.

"I'm going to make your day. Are you ready?" Dr. Lansfield began. "A buddy of mine is having a party tonight and if you want to come, I've got a map with directions here." He patted his pocket.

I looked up and tilted my head. "Are you asking me out?" *I thought he stayed out of the hospital dating scene. I doubt I'm the one that's changed his mind.*

He took a step back. "Who said anything about a date? It's a party and I'm trying to get more people to come so my buddy has a good time. You've got really pretty eyes; you know that?"

Completely ignoring the compliment, I said, "Oh, so I'm like a seat filler at the Academy Awards. There to fill space." I raised my eyebrows, my tone flat.

"You're welcome, by the way. You should learn how to accept a compliment." I continued to stare at him. "Look, I thought you could use a good time. You're new in town, he's having a party, why not invite you? If you don't want to come, don't." He put his pen in his pocket and turned to leave.

Realizing I'd sounded like a total bitch, I apologized. "Sorry. I'm not trying to give you a hard time. You caught me off guard. A party sounds fun. I'll take the map and we'll see what happens. Okay?"

He handed me a folded square piece of paper and said, "Should be a good time." *Maybe I should go.* If I could get some other nurses to come with me, even better.

Lunchtime came and Kate and I headed to the cafeteria. She loved her job and seemed fun to work with. Married with no children and in her late thirties, she usually arranged all the social events for the unit and had no problem going out for a drink after working twelve hours. Kate took a bite of her sandwich as I started telling her about Dr. Lansfield's party. She almost choked on her bite of tuna salad. "What? He asked you to go? What did you say?"

"You don't want to know. But it's not like he asked me to go *with* him. He's looking for more people to invite."

"He's close friends with another doctor here named Winger. They've been friends forever and that doc *loves* to date nurses. I bet it's his party. He always has parties. Maybe he's trying to set you two up."

"No, I don't think so. We ran into each other yesterday at the pool. He's probably looking for a big turnout, that's all. I don't think it has anything to do with me. But I'm thinking about going and would love for you to come with. What do you say?"

"Sure. I think it's so funny. There are nurses who've been here for years who would die to be asked to a party by Dr. Lansfield and here you are, here three weeks, and you don't seem to think this is a big deal. Hysterical!"

"It's not a big deal, trust me. And he's asking everybody to go. I've heard he doesn't want to . . . what's the term . . . dip his pen in the company ink. I totally agree with that. I'm the same way. Not interested," I explained to Kate.

"I like how cool you are. Other nurses would be all giddy and stuff. Tells me a lot about you. You're very down to earth. I like that," Kate said, smiling. "I'll come over to your place after work. I've got a change of clothes in the car. Jerry, my husband, is out of town so I was planning on doing something anyway."

As the day went on, my shift got easier. Lisa remained comfortably sedated and her vital signs remained stable. I drove home figuring out what outfit I would wear to the party and hoping that the directions led to a real house. I've looked stupid before and didn't want to look stupid again. I didn't think Dr. Lansfield would be cruel enough to give me a fake map and decided to trust that his invitation was good.

After a quick walk with Ozzie, I let him come upstairs with me while I got ready for the party. He followed me around everywhere. When I stood at the mirror fixing my makeup, he sat right on my feet. I wondered if I could adopt him from Mary and make him mine. But what would I do when I traveled? I would miss him. I really loved the little guy. The doorbell rang and Ozzie burst out of the bathroom, barking. I let Kate in and finished putting on my party face.

"Ready to go?" I asked, standing there in a knee-length black sundress with silver sandals.

"Yup! You look good," Kate said. She wore short black shorts and a pink halter top.

"So do you. Let's get out of here. I just need to drop Ozzie off downstairs."

"He's so cute! He's not yours?" Kate asked.

"I wish. He's my neighbor's dog. He and I have a thing going on and she lets me take him whenever I want. He always waits for me when I come home."

"Sounds almost better than having a man. So cute," Kate said as we bustled down the stairs, Ozzie in tow.

Dr. Winger's house was located ten minutes from my apartment. The map proved correct! Cars were packed in the driveway and lining the streets. A sign on the door read, Come On In! The Party's Here. Kate and I walked into the foyer and discovered people everywhere. She recognized a bunch of hospital employees and took my hand, guiding us in their direction. Walking past the kitchen I saw Dr. Lansfield standing at the counter with some cougar chick draped over him, while a pack of what I assumed to be nurses were laughing and hanging on his every word in a little crowd around him. Mama Cougar looked to be a size one, with the tightest, shortest strapless sundress and white high heels. Very tacky. She had a blond pixie haircut with frosted tips, and was probably in her early forties, way too old for the outfit she wore. Dr. Lansfield's body language showed he couldn't care less about her. I chuckled and kept walking.

We got some beers and sat down on one of the brown leather couches in the living room. Kate introduced me to a female kidney doctor, another hospitalist like Dr. Lansfield, and then she pointed out Dr. Winger. A few nurses from the medical/surgical floor joined us. I must have been really thirsty because I think I chugged my Corona Light within five minutes. Excusing myself, I went outside to the patio for another beer. Once outside, I reached into the cooler and took out a cold one, surveying the host's perfectly manicured lawn and sparkling Pebble Tec pool.

"Having a good time?" Dr. Lansfield said behind me.

"Yeah, nice place. Thanks for inviting me," I said, taking another sip of beer. "You have quite the fan club."

"Those girls? They're just having a good time."

"I've heard about you. You don't date nurses. Every place I've worked, there's always doctors sleeping with nurses. Hospital culture, I guess. I stay away from that stuff, too. Although, those girls seem *very* nice. Must have been hard swinging around the dance pole, working to pay off their nursing school loans."

Lansfield laughed. "Be nice. Not everyone can be as smart as you."

"What makes you think I'm smart?" I asked. Nobody had ever said that to my face before, other than my parents.

"I don't know. You seem to know what you're doing out there. Patients are lucky to have you."

I jerked my head back, not sure what to say. I remembered how I'd ignored his last compliment so I decided to throw him a bone. "Thanks. That's a nice thing to say." I took another sip of beer. After a brief silence, I added, "So if you don't go out with anyone at the hospital, who do you go out with?" I suddenly became curious.

"I'm still recovering from a pretty shitty relationship. Messed me up. I'm not looking right now. What about you? How are you going to hook up with someone, being a travel nurse?"

"I don't 'hook up', thank you very much. Well, sometimes I hook up. I'm trying to see the world and get shit done. That's it. I don't have time for a relationship," I told him, shrugging my shoulders.

"Sounds kind of lonely."

"I think I'm doing okay," I smirked, taking another swig.

His mouth formed a sly smile that rose up higher on the right side. "I think you are, too."

"Can we change the subject, please?"

"Sure. What about your family? Do you see them much?"

"No. My dad abandoned his fatherly duties when my mother died and my sister's a physician in Denver who works her ass off so she doesn't have to think or care about anyone else." Lansfield's eyebrows furrowed. *Next subject.*

"I'm so sorry. How did she die?" He touched my shoulder.

*Wait, what?* "Who?" I asked.

"Your mom. What happened?"

I stared at him blankly. Most people never knew what to say so they never asked questions. "Oh! Um, she, uh . . . breast cancer." I chugged the rest of the beer, hoping for some liquid courage.

"How old was she?"

"Forty. I was fourteen. Her nurses are the reason I went into nursing. They were amazing."

"Is that why you stopped swimming? Competitively?" *Wow, this guy really pays attention.*

"Yeah. I stopped training so I could be with her. After she died, I lost my edge. I guess I didn't care about winning so much. Not after losing ..." I stared at my feet.

"The cancer spread?"

"Yeah. It spread to her lungs and then her brain. She was in so much pain. It was almost a ..." The lump of guilt in my throat made it difficult to speak and my eyes felt wet.

"A relief?" This guy understood.

"Feels shitty to say, but, yes. When she died I knew she was at peace. She looked happy." I pinched my eyelashes to rid myself of the tears that were forming on my mascara.

"Same with my dad. I didn't make it in time, when he died. He lived two hours away and I almost got there, but by the time I did, they had already taken him to the morgue. He had a smile on his face, though, like he could finally relax." The good doctor smiled and opened two more beers, handing one to me.

"What happened to your dad?" I searched his eyes, looking for more comfort.

"Pneumonia. He also suffered from dementia and became paranoid at the end. It was hard to watch."

"Death sucks. And yet, we see it all the time." We both stared out into the backyard, sharing the silence. "Do you have any other family?"

"I'm from a huge family. Everyone always is in everyone else's business. I even had to share a room with my little sister."

"That's not so bad. Lots of kids have to share rooms."

"Even when they're teenagers? One day, I placed a strip of

masking tape down the center of the room because she was such a slob and I couldn't take it anymore."

I laughed. "What are you, some kind of clean freak? Why'd you do that?"

"If I'm trying to work or relax in my house or at my desk and it's a mess, I can't concentrate. I get depressed. If you have a clean place, you have a clean mind and you can focus. Get shit done."

"Never thought about it that way, but makes sense. I'll be sure to clean up my place if you ever happen to come by." I beamed, taking another sip of beer. *Good one, Natalie. Smooth.*

"Make sure that you do." Our gazes danced with each other. "Are you going to swim tomorrow? I'm planning on going after work."

"I can try. What time would you go?"

"Between five thirty and six. Whenever I get done at the hospital," he said.

"Well then, I'll see you when I see you. Thanks for the chat, and for the beers. I don't get to talk about my mother too much."

"You should. She's part of you."

*Is this guy for real?* "I'll try to be there tomorrow." My heart skipped a beat but ignoring it, I headed back inside. Kate was probably wondering what had happened to me. I turned around to catch a glimpse of him one more time. Watching me leave, Lansfield waved.

Talking to him felt like talking to . . . a friend. Someone who understood. Someone who let me share. The best part was, neither of us were interested in each other so I didn't feel any pressure. *Although, he is very easy on the eyes and that smile, and the biceps, and his dark skin . . . . Stop, Natalie. Just stop.*

Kate and I stayed another hour before leaving. We were both tired and had to be back at work the next morning. We said our good-byes and as I got into the car, Kate started in on me.

"I saw you and Dr. Lansfield talking outside alone for quite a while. What did you guys talk about?" Kate asked as she fiddled with the radio.

"Nothing really. I just made a comment about the bimbos hanging all over him when we walked in and then we talked about our families. I asked him why he doesn't date, strictly out of curiosity," I told Kate, adjusting my rearview mirror.

"Why? Are you attracted?" Kate asked, batting her eyelashes.

"No! I'm surprised he's not snatched up already. I wanted to know why."

"You like him!" She nudged my elbow that rested on the white leather console.

"No, I don't! I wanted to know his story for some weird reason . . ." My turn to fiddle with the radio.

"Did he tell you?" Kate prodded.

"No. Only that he's still getting over someone. Anyway, who cares, right?" I turned to look at her.

"Apparently you do," she said as she grinned and turned to look out the window.

I looked at her and opened my mouth, ready to respond, but for once in my life, nothing came out. Turning my eyes back to the road, I drove the rest of the way home in silence.

Good thing I hadn't had much to drink at the party because the next day sucked. We were going to remove Lisa's breathing tube, hoping she could breathe on her own. If she could, then I would try to have her sit on the side of the bed and bring her family to interact with her for a while, which seemed easier said than done. First, I turned off her sedation so she could wake up. The tricky part was keeping Lisa calm. Having to breathe through a tube, I've been told, is like breathing through a straw. Patients tend to panic when they're awake.

I began talking very gently to Lisa, explaining that soon she'd be awake and we'd try to get her tube out. I held her hand as she started to open her eyes. Her initial response was to thrash around but I kept smoothing her hair and reassuring her. Her pupils expanded. She looked right at me and I explained that I wanted her to follow the respiratory therapist's instructions so we could get the tube out. Lisa had to pass a few breathing tests before we could call the pulmonologist and get the order to pull the tube. She did very well and I stayed right with her during the whole process.

Thirty minutes after we shut off her sedation, we were ready. The respiratory therapist and I positioned ourselves on either side of her and I explained what was going to happen next.

"Lisa, on the count of three I want you to take a deep breath and then blow out as hard as you can. Dana here will pull out your tube at the same time. Okay?"

Lisa nodded at me and squeezed my hand tight.

"Here we go. One, two, three! Blow, blow, blow," I coached her as Dana pulled her tube out and suctioned the secretions pouring from her mouth.

Lisa started to cough and gag, kicking her legs. She flailed her arms anxiously, wincing, and sorely reminding herself about her tightly wrapped arm in traction.

"Don't move your arm, Lisa. You've had major surgery and your arm has to stay still. Just try to relax. Are you hurting?" I asked her, still holding onto her good hand.

"My arm and my throat hurt," Lisa said, whispering as her vocal cords recovered from the trauma.

"I'm going to get you some pain medication. Do you remember anything that happened?"

Lisa shook her head. "I remember my water breaking in bed

but that's it." Then, all of a sudden, Lisa's eyes opened wide and she sat straight up in the bed. "The baby? What happened to my baby?"

"Your baby is fine. A baby girl. Your husband has been with her. Do you want to try to see her today?"

She lay back, hard, against the pillows. "No. Not today."

"Are you sure? She's beautiful and I'm sure she'd love to meet her mommy."

Lisa turned her head away from me, and with her good arm, started to run her fingers along the gauze and padding that held her left arm together. I briefly summed up what had happened with the amniotic bubble and how her arm had ended up being operated on. She sobbed.

"Lisa, I know this is a lot to take in, but you've got a beautiful baby girl now. She needs to be with you. Your husband's doing all he can, but there's nothing like the bond between mother and baby."

"How am I supposed to hold her? What am I supposed to do with her? Can I even breast feed her with all the drugs I've had? What's the point?"

"Lisa, come on. I understand this isn't what you had in mind for childbirth, but we're here now. It won't be easy, but you have a baby. And she needs you."

"No. Not today. I'd like to rest now." Lisa rolled over on her side, her back toward me. I clenched my teeth. *Please don't let that little girl grow up without a mother. It's not fair.*

I made sure she didn't need anything and then walked out of the room. Her husband stood waiting outside the door, stooped, with dark circles under his eyes. I explained to him that we would keep trying and maybe tomorrow he could bring the baby in himself and all three of them could be together.

"What if she doesn't ever want to see her?" he asked me. The bags under his eyes made the dark circles above them look even darker.

"Not going to happen. Don't worry, we'll keep trying. She'll come around. Right now I think she is associating all her trauma with the baby. She may be having some resentment toward her without meaning to. I've seen it before. We'll call one of the post-partum nurses to help Lisa and the baby bond. Give her some time. She'll realize that what she went through was worth it once she sees her newborn."

He went into the room to see his wife. I only hoped that she would soon want to see her child. My energy drained, I finished charting and got ready to give report. I filled the night nurse in on what had happened and told her I'd be back in the morning. I needed a hot shower, a glass of wine, and a long walk with Ozzie, not necessarily in that order.

I parked the car outside my apartment and grabbed my bag, looking forward to being greeted at the stairs by my furry friend. When I got to the stairs, he wasn't there. Where was Ozzie? I suddenly thought about Mary and worried that something might have happened to her. I knocked on the door, shouting, "Mary? Are you in there?" After several seconds, the door finally opened.

"Oh, Natalie. It's you," Mary said, dressed in a housedress and slippers.

"Are you all right?" I asked, anxiously looking around the apartment. "I got concerned when I didn't see the little guy at my stairs."

"Oh yes, I'm fine. Ozzie seems to have a little infection in his rear end and doesn't feel well. I took him to the vet and he's on antibiotics. He should be fine in a few days, dear. Not to worry."

"Okay, I got scared. For you and him. Can I see him real quick?"

"Sure, he's in the bedroom. Go ahead."

I walked down the hall into Mary's bedroom and saw Ozzie on his blue-and-green plaid pillow, asleep. I knelt down on the floor next to him. My nursing gut told me something was wrong. I've always been able to treat sick, dying, or hurt people no problem. But a dog—can't do it. They're so dependent on humans and so loyal. I'd thrived on the unquestionable love Ozzie had given me. He hardly knew me, yet he always wagged that curly tail, happy to see me when I got home, every day. That was more than I can say for some of the humans I've known.

There appeared to be blood right below Ozzie's tail. I said hi to him and sat there, petting him. He slowly lifted his head, slightly opened his eyes, and placed his head onto my lap. I leaned down to kiss him and told him he'd be feeling better soon and we would go on all the walks he wanted to. He took a deep breath, which sounded like a snort, and went back to sleep. I gingerly repositioned him back on his pillow and told Mary I'd check on him tomorrow.

Back in my apartment, I showered, got a glass of wine, and plopped down on the couch. Strangely, my thoughts were far from the frustrating day I'd had with Lisa. Ozzie worried me. He fulfilled my temporary need for companionship and he made me happy. Looking up toward the ceiling, I took a long sip, swallowed, and said out loud, "Oh, please let him be okay."

# 11

isa, you've got to try!" I said, fighting with my patient to get her to dangle her legs off the side of the bed. Now that Lisa no longer needed the ventilator, she could start moving around. The ICU team—doctors, nurses, and social workers—had decided that Lisa's baby would be brought into her room today. And I assured her family Lisa would be ready to meet baby Ava. She showed no interest. I understood her pain and the trauma she had suffered while giving birth, but now it was time to buck up and meet her daughter.

"It's no use! I can't even hold her! What's the point?" she said, her voice shaking.

"Okay, you know what? This is what's going to happen. You *are* going to see your baby today. Period. You're stable enough and it's time. I'm sorry, Lisa, but you're doing it." I began straightening out her remaining IV. I untangled her monitor wires to make room for her to hang her feet off the side of the bed. Leaning directly in front of her, my arms hooked under her armpits, I said, "On the count of three, I'm going to help you sit up. Understand?"

Lisa looked at me, her face softening.

"One, two, three!" I pulled Lisa to a sitting position. "Now, I'm going to swing your legs to the left. Don't worry about your left arm, the traction will go with us."

In two swift movements, Lisa dangled off the side of the bed, steady enough to receive her newborn. After a few words of encouragement, I left the room and notified the nursery it was a go. Several minutes later, Lisa's husband Dean arrived, pushing an incubator. I followed him into the room. He sat on the bed next to Lisa and put his arm around her. She laid her head on his shoulder and started to cry. I walked over to the incubator and lifted little Ava out of her synthetic womb. Swaddled in a pink-and-white blanket and wearing a little pink beanie, she slowly opened her eyes. They were round pools of sparkling blue and her cheeks glowed rosy pink. "Hi, Ava," I said and she gave me the tiniest toothless grin I've ever seen. Babies usually had no effect on me but as I held her, I felt . . . warmth. Lisa going through so much, enduring so much pain, and having this beautiful being as a result gave her whole ordeal meaning, or, a purpose. I couldn't get over the baby's pure innocence. It made me smile . . . Ava made me smile.

"Can Lisa see her?" Dean asked.

"Oh my gosh! I'm so sorry. I got carried away. She's absolutely beautiful." I brought the baby over to Lisa.

Lisa looked at me, eyes wide, in fight-or-flight mode. I explained to her that I would stay right there and put the baby in her right arm, her husband at her left. I nodded to Lisa, letting her know everything would be fine, and gently placed the baby in her arm. I took a step back. Both mother and father were weeping. Lisa kept looking up at me and I kept reassuring her by nodding and smiling. After fifteen minutes, Lisa began taking deep breaths and leaning back against the bed. Reading her fatigue, I helped her lie down and gave the okay for her husband to take Ava back to the nursery. It was a start—a small one—but at least a start.

I helped Lisa lie back down, placing one pillow under her

knees and another under her left arm, and securing her IV back in place. "You did great," I told her. "We'll try for more tomorrow."

"It's so hard to see the baby. I'm so frustrated about what happened to me. I know it's not the baby's fault, but I'm a complete mess! I don't know if I'll be able to use my arm again or not! This is so not what giving birth should be about!" She sobbed.

"Lisa, I know this is hard for you but you need to remember one thing. Your husband told me how happy you guys were when you found out you were pregnant. Sure, things are hard now, but that child is here. And she's yours. You're going to have to accept that. It's not about you anymore. Things don't always go as planned. Today was tough, but it was only your first day. It'll get easier. Don't take your frustration out on the baby; she didn't ask for this either."

Lisa turned her face away from me and silently cried. I decided I would leave her alone for a while and let her rest. She'd endured enough of my nagging. I left the room and pulled the curtain behind me, leaving the sliding glass doors open so I could hear her. I recalled holding little Ava and feeling my heart melt. How hard it must've been for my mother to know she'd never hold us again. Now I understood why she cried every time I sat with her. *I can't do that to myself. I won't fall in love, have kids, and then leave them. Cancer doesn't give a shit who you are or what you do. One day you're taking your kids to the park, laughing and soaking in the sunshine, then the phone rings and boom, your life's over.*

Now that Lisa had set foot on the road to recovery, I knew with time she would come to love little Ava. Why couldn't she see how lucky she was?

Back at home, I practically ran to my stairwell, hoping to see Ozzie. Having finished the last of three twelve-hour shifts, I couldn't wait to have the next two days off. I came to my staircase and saw Mary sitting on a folding chair outside her door, Ozzie in her lap. I moved toward him, ears twitching as he lifted his little head.

"How is he?" I asked.

"He's real tired. I think it's the medication. I wanted to bring him outside to see you. Thought it would boost his spirits."

"Can I hold him?" I asked, not really waiting for her to answer as I scooped him out of her arms. He felt lighter to me. How much weight had he lost? My nursing instincts gnawed at my gut. Something just didn't feel right.

"He had a seizure today, Natalie. He was walking around one minute and the next he fell over, all four feet in the air. Peed everywhere and then it was over. He got up and went to his bed," Mary told me, wringing her hands.

"What did the vet say?" I asked.

"They told me to stop one of the antibiotics and gave me another one. I just want him to feel better." She petted Ozzie, who lay in my arms.

"I'm off for the next two days. I'll help you with him. Together, we'll get him well, I promise you. He's going to be just fine." I kissed Ozzie's head and handed him back to his owner. I figured he needed rest rather than to keep me company tonight. I'd check on him first thing in the morning.

Mary took Ozzie back inside and I waited for her to close the door before going upstairs. Depressed and worried, I started a bath. I threw my clothes on the bed and heard the computer ping, signaling an e-mail.

*To: natalieicurn@cable.com*
*From: jasoncam1@godiving.com*
*Subject: It's me*
*Hey Natalie! Still thinking about you. Wanted to let you*

*know that I'm going on assignment with my dive company to Australia! California fell through. I figured you came all the way to Belize for nursing, maybe you'll end up in Australia? Anyway, I'll be there through the month of July. The waters will be cold, but hey—it's Australia! Let me know . . . Cheers, Jason*

Wow. Australia. He was still thinking about me? I hadn't heard where I'd be going next, but I should find out soon. I only had a few more weeks. Maybe I could suggest Australia? No. I was just going to let things unfold, although it would be nice to see him. Australia has the Great Barrier Reef and who wouldn't want to dive that? I decided to answer him before jumping in the tub.

> *To: jasoncam1@godiving.com*
> *From: natalieicurn@cable.com*
> *Subject: Re: It's me*
> *Hi Jason! Australia sounds great! I don't know where I'm going yet, but if the option is available, I'd love to join you. Not sure about diving in cold water, though :) Will let you know ASAP—It was good to hear from you. Talk soon, Natalie*

Smiling, I stepped into the tub and tried to relax. Seeing him would be fun and I needed it. Things were great here, but I could use the excitement, the distraction, and the fun. A fellow traveler, no baggage, no commitments. Just . . . fun. I'd see what I could do when Peggy called me. Leaning my head back against the cold tile, I closed my eyes and took a deep breath. My thoughts quickly turned to Ozzie. He'd just have to get better; he had to.

The next morning I got up, made some coffee, and headed downstairs. Mary answered the door in her robe and slippers, her hair rolled tightly into pink foam rollers. Ozzie came to the door slowly, still not himself. His tail wagged and his wrinkly face smiled. I knelt down to give him some love.

"How did he do?"

"Good. He slept without a peep other than his usual snore. I'm taking him back to the vet today," Mary said, walking to the kitchen.

"I can go with you. Would you mind?"

"Not at all, dear. You're sure this is how you want to spend your day off?"

"Of course. I want to help. I . . . I love him." I held Ozzie's face in both hands and kissed him on his flattened, wet nose.

A few hours later we arrived at the vet clinic and Ozzie rested in my lap. The vet tech called Ozzie's name and brought us back to an exam room. She told us that Doctor Gutterson, a vet Mary wasn't familiar with, would be in to see us. Apparently, the vet who normally saw Ozzie had been out ill for the last few weeks. Mary whispered to me that this was the third doctor she'd seen in the office.

"How's Ozzie doing this morning?" asked the doctor.

"Not great," said Mary. "No more seizures, though."

"Good!" said Dr. Gutterson, a woman in her mid-forties with long, gray-brown hair and Birkenstocks peeking out from a long broom skirt.

During her examination of Ozzie, I asked her what she thought about his weight loss. "I know Mary's been trying to get him to lose weight, but this seems like an awful lot over such a short period of time. Are you concerned about that?" My arms were crossed firmly against my chest.

"And you are?" the vet asked me.

Taking my hand, Mary interjected, "She's my neighbor and very close to Ozzie. I want her here."

"I think his weight loss is good considering how overweight he was, but I can draw some blood and make sure everything's okay."

I didn't like the woman. It worried me that Ozzie had lost weight so quickly and I didn't believe the infection had caused it. My medical background gave me ideas about what could cause such an abrupt loss in weight, including . . . cancer. *Figure it out, Dr. Gutterson!* She finished examining him and told Mary to continue the antibiotics for the next two weeks, claiming he still had signs of an anal gland infection. When I asked her about the seizure, she quickly responded that it could be a side effect of one of the medications. A vet tech came in to take Ozzie for some blood tests.

"Mary, he'll be okay. Don't you worry." I squeezed her hands, wishing I could believe my own words.

When they brought Ozzie back to the room, the tech placed him on the table and I stood up to get him. Just then he let out the most horrible cry, like a bleating sheep in pain, toppled over to one side, and seized . . . again. I clapped my hands over my ears because I couldn't bear to hear his yell. Mary had her hand over her mouth and tears spilled onto her cheeks. Dr. Gutterson heard the commotion, came running into the room, and suggested they watch Ozzie for the day. I rolled my eyes. Didn't she just say he had a simple infection? We'd almost taken him home! After Ozzie settled down and started to come around, Mary and I kissed him good-bye and I put my arm around her as we walked out of the clinic, feeling terrible about leaving him behind. I told Mary we'd come back this evening and get him. We hugged each other in the car and I quickly wiped away the tears filling my eyes to hide them from Mary. I didn't want to upset her any further.

I returned to the vet alone later that night around six thirty. Mary asked if I could pick Ozzie up. She didn't have the strength to return to the vet. How had I gotten so involved in this? I loved Ozzie and so far, he'd been very easy to take care of. Mary'd had him for a little over five years and she had been doing just fine. She took great care of him. Anger brewed in me. I had become so close with Ozzie and now, once again, I would be deprived of love. I've been here before. Goddamn it! I'd come here to get away from pain but it seemed to follow me everywhere.

Sitting in the exam room I anxiously waited for the vet, chewing and biting my nails. Finally, a young girl brought in Ozzie and placed him in my arms. He barely moved but did not appear to be in pain. His left front paw was wrapped with gauze where they'd taken blood from him and inserted the IV. Another doctor finally walked in—*not* Dr. Gutterson.

"I'm afraid I don't have great news. Ozzie has no ability to clot his blood and is bleeding out from somewhere—we don't know where. It appears to be hemolytic anemia. That's when—"

"I know what that is, doctor, I'm an ICU nurse. The body eats up its own red blood cells. His body can't stop bleeding." My heart dropped.

"That's correct. Most dogs in this situation have a fifty-fifty chance of survival."

"How did this happen?"

"We can't be sure. Could be from the antibiotics, could be hereditary, or . . ."

"Or what?" I held my breath.

"Poison." The doctor peered at me over his glasses.

My mouth fell open. "Excuse me?"

"Just a possibility. I doubt it, but it can cause this type of reaction."

I felt nauseous. "No. Why would anyone poison Ozzie?"

"Mary didn't have any enemies, did she? Someone who wanted to hurt her?" He led me to a row of chairs.

I sat down and put my head in my hands. "Not that I know of." My voice broke. *Please don't let this be because of me.*

"I didn't think so. Probably a medication reaction. He's also purebred and sometimes those bloodlines run thin. Lots of inbreeding. He may have been born with a blood disorder." He put a hand on my back.

I looked up at him, my body numb. "What are the options?"

"It depends on how much you want to put into this. I've known Mary for years and I'm not sure she can afford a lot right now, both financially and emotionally speaking. You can take him downtown to the specialty hospital and look into a blood transfusion. There are also immunosuppressant infusions but those are very expensive and sometimes have worse side effects. Or, we can try some steroids and see if he turns around," the doctor explained, clutching his clipboard to his chest and pushing up his glasses with his middle finger.

"I need to talk to Mary. Can I bring him home on the steroids and let you know? I'd love to tell you to do everything you can to save him, but it's not my decision." I stroked Ozzie's back. He let out a big sigh and nuzzled his head deeper into my arms.

"Sure. We can do that. Let me get the medication for you and my card."

Over the next few days Ozzie got worse. Each day I'd come home from work and hope to see him waiting for me at the bottom of the stairs wagging his tail, but it never happened. I checked on him frequently and for the most part, he'd lie on his pillow in Mary's bedroom, acknowledging me each time

I visited by putting his head in my lap. Mary kept hoping he would improve with the steroids. I couldn't tell her what the vet had said about poison being a possible cause. Why instill fear in such a vulnerable woman? And what if I was to blame? She'd never forgive me. Mary had decided that the steroids were all she could do. She couldn't afford hospitalizations, transfusions, or anything else at this point.

A week and a half after Ozzie's diagnosis, Mary called me around eight o'clock at night. Ozzie was having a very bad seizure. By the time I ran downstairs, the seizure had ended and he lay still, gently breathing in his bed. I started petting and soothing him. Thinking some fresh air would be nice, I carried him outside and placed him on the grass to see if he would walk around a bit or even pee. He sniffed the area directly in front of him and then squatted. I thought maybe that would make him feel better but within seconds, out came a huge amount of dark red, almost black stool. Blood, and tons of it. He was hemorrhaging! Ozzie's legs started to shake, and I quickly picked him up, clutching him tightly under my arms. I kissed his head. *He's dying; I know it. Right in front of me.*

Back inside Mary's apartment, I decided we needed to talk. "Mary," I said gently, "this doesn't look good. He's pooping blood and he's so weak. It's not good." I reached over to take both her hands.

"I know, dear, but what can I do?" She started to tremble.

"I think we need to let him go. He's suffering." My heart broke, again.

"Oh honey, I can't. I can't put him down. I can't." Mary began to sob.

"You understand that we can't let him go on like this?"

"I do. But *I* can't." She looked at me, her shoulders quaking. After a very long silence, I said, "Will you let me?" I couldn't watch this anymore. My heart ripped further apart. The easy thing to do would be to let Mary deal with this. Ozzie was her dog, after all. But the truth was, I thought of him as mine and I loved him. We couldn't let him suffer just so we wouldn't have to feel the pain of losing him. That's the worst thing a person could do. Completely selfish. Love means putting someone else's needs above your own.

Without a word, Mary nodded yes and got up from her chair, one hand over her mouth. She went to the refrigerator and brought me a plastic magnet with an emergency number for a veterinary hospital down the street. I gathered Ozzie in my arms, like a newborn baby, and clutched him against my chest. He started panting and not because of the heat. He couldn't get enough oxygen without an adequate number of red blood cells. *If I find out that someone poisoned Ozzie, whoever it is better watch the hell out.* Mary placed one of his blankets over his back. She kissed her hand and placed it on his head. She held it there for a long time. Then she turned away, walking toward her bedroom and shutting the door. Her one companion, taken from her. I could hear her sobbing as I left her apartment with Ozzie, for the last time in my arms but forever in my heart.

I had two more weeks in Arizona and after what I'd been through, I welcomed the thought of a new place. Every time I passed the stairs, I felt the ache of Ozzie's absence. Hell, he hadn't even been mine! I'd known him for just a few weeks, but he'd brought me more happiness than some people had given me in years. How much pain can one heart take? I think I hold the record.

Peggy called with three options: extend my stay in Arizona—apparently the ICU liked me and wanted to keep me another three months; go to Kansas to one of their smaller, rural hospitals; or go global to Australia. I couldn't believe that option existed! Australia! Another sign I needed to follow. I jumped at the chance to meet Jason in Australia. I had two more weeks here and then sayonara AZ!

# 12

I decided that I needed to find out all I could about Betty Watson. Ever since I had begun traveling, strange things had happened to me that almost cost me my life. And now Ozzie was gone. In two weeks I'd be leaving for Australia and I wanted to make sure Betty stayed as far away from me as possible.

Searching Google, I found three websites with stories about her. Shortly after Mr. Watson's death, the *Denver Post* reported she'd finally been arrested in Denver, but then Betty jumped bail. A story from the *Las Vegas Tribune* reported a sighting of her at a casino, but when security approached her, she fled. The last entry, from the FBI website, scared me the most. Betty had actually made the FBI's most wanted list. Apparently, Joseph Watson had been tied up with some pretty scummy crimes—embezzlement, employing hit men, and tax evasion. Not only was Betty wanted for his murder, she was also wanted for participating in his white-collar crimes as well. In addition, I read that she'd once had ties to the most notorious Russian mobster of all time, Sergeiv Lovevich. He had been on the FBI's ten most wanted list for years and his torture chambers and brutality had made him notorious. The hairs on my arms were at full attention.

According to what I could find in the FBI material, Betty had been one of Lovevich's mistresses in the early 1990s and had helped to lure young Eastern European women into working at strip clubs. There she would promise them money and arrange fake marriages to "nationalize" them. However, the women were eventually sold as sex slaves.

*Oh my God. How did she ever get by the U.S. authorities and obtain a nursing license? Shit!* Her name back then had been Dominika Montov and the article claimed she'd been presumed dead.

But where was she now? Everything I read said she'd "once again evaded police." How could one woman be that good? We'd all worked with her for years and never suspected anything like this! I knew she was out there somewhere. And what if she'd been running from Russian mobsters this whole time? Or worse, what if she still had ties with them? What if they were helping her? *Fuck! I can't dwell on this crap.* All I knew was that I didn't want to read another word about Betty or Dominika or whatever the hell she called herself. The police were looking for her and I prayed they'd find her soon. Thoughts moved too quickly in my head to process.

I shut the computer down and decided I needed to feel good again. I'd been moping around since Ozzie's death and now I'd been letting myself become consumed by thoughts of Betty Watson. I needed to work out.

I had one more week at the hospital and surprisingly, I felt a bit sad about leaving. I liked it in Marisdale. I liked the people, the patients I took care of, and the environment. I could see myself living and working here. But if I stopped traveling, I'd get complacent and then . . . maybe I'd get that life-ending news. Cancer. Fuck that. I grabbed my swim bag and headed to the pool.

A few minutes later I walked out to the swim deck. Sadly, all the lanes were full. The lifeguard saw me and said, "Give it a few minutes; some of these guys are close to being done." I sat on one of the bleachers, propping my feet on the next lowest step. Elbows on my knees, I placed my chin between my hands and waited.

"Having a bad day?" Dr. Lansfield stepped up to where I sat.

"Hey. Had a few bad days lately. Trying to cheer up, if I could just get in the water."

"What's going on?"

"It's a long story," I said, not sure whether he really wanted to hear about Ozzie.

"Well, we can't get in the water yet, so . . . tell me." He sat down next to me.

I closed my eyes and tilted my head back. Taking a deep breath, I filled him in on the last few days with Ozzie, trying very hard not to cry.

"That's a tough gig. Going through something like that. I've done it a few times myself. Hurts."

I sniffed away the tears as I pictured Ozzie lying across my lap. "Why does the topic of death always come up when we're together?"

"It doesn't. We've talked about other stuff." He put his arm around my shoulders.

I looked up and inhaled, then let out a huge sigh. "I don't know how much more of this kind of shit I can handle, you know?"

"You know what? Screw this. Let's go get a beer. It'll take your mind off things. Come on," Dr. Lansfield said, taking his bag and offering his hand to help me up.

"What? No. Swimming always helps my mood. Where would we go?" I asked, looking up at him.

"Oh, shut up. Come on." He pulled me to my feet and I reached for my bag, slinging it over my shoulder. "I'll drive. I know a cool place."

"I bet this is unusual for you. Taking a nurse out for a drink. You sure you want to back out of your little rule?" I nudged his elbow with mine.

"First of all, I'm taking *you* for a drink. You're more than just a nurse. And second, anything for a beer in the middle of the afternoon." He winked.

What the hell. I needed to feel better and the thought of having someone to talk to didn't sound like a bad idea. We drove about twenty minutes, mostly talking about mutual patients and medical stuff. I liked speaking medical lingo with someone who completely understood.

We arrived at a place called Kiki's, a restaurant in the shape of a big beach hut with a thatched roof and Tiki torches lighting the entrance. Live music blared from within. We sat down at a table and ordered beer. I found it funny to be here with him after all I had heard. He wasn't this great big untouchable being. Like a lot of people, he'd had his heart broken, that's all. He happened to be an extremely good-looking guy I found very easy to be with. I looked at him, half-smiling, half-smirking. He appeared vulnerable.

"So where were you before you came here?" he asked.

"Actually, I went to Belize. Have you ever been there?"

"Yeah, I did go there once. Great diving."

"You dive? So do I!" I said. "It's scary sometimes, but so awesome."

"I think it would be much more fun to dive with someone. I'm always the guy who buddies up with the dive master." He pushed out his bottom lip in a pout.

Laughing, it dawned on me that I, too, usually partnered up with the dive master. I remembered the picture Jason tried to take of me in the shipwreck, the last time I dove. Guilt poked my conscience, sitting here with the good doctor and thinking of Jason. It's not like I'd committed myself to either one . . . so where did all this guilt come from?

"Well . . . maybe you and I should go on a dive trip." *Yeah right, Natalie.* I took another sip of beer.

"Hmmm. That would be fun." Dr. Lansfield raised one eyebrow.

I began to feel flushed. "I'm hungry. Should we order?"

"Sure, get whatever you want. It's on me," he said, perusing the menu.

"Nope. That would be a date and we are *not* on a date. We go fifty-fifty or I'm out," I looked up at him with my hands on the table, pretending to be ready to push my chair out and stand up. Of course, I wasn't going to do that, but he needed to know where I stood.

"Why do you keep bringing that up? We're two people having lunch and hanging out. If I want to pay, it's because I can. Can't you just enjoy being here and relax?"

"Sorry. I'll try. For you." I leaned back in my chair.

While we were waiting for our beers, we both began talking about the hospital. "Wanna hear something cool?" the doctor said.

"Sure."

"Ever hear of belladonna syndrome?"

"It's from a plant, right? Where your eyes get really big?"

"Sort of. Back in the day, Italian women would put it on their eyelids and chew on the leaves, causing their pupils to become dilated. They thought this made them more beautiful. Anyone can grow it if they have the seed."

"Ooo, a history lesson," I said, rubbing my hands together and smiling. "Go on."

"Anyway, we had this seventeen-year-old girl come into the ER yesterday. Her parents brought her in because her behavior was off. Agitated, yelling, couldn't sit still."

The waitress brought our drinks. "What else can I get ya?" she asked. We ordered some food and dessert to share.

"Yeah, keep going," I urged him once the waitress left. This sounded intriguing.

"We did a urine drug test, labs, and scanned her head. Nothing. Everything normal. The girl spoke in tongues! Crazy shit."

"So how did you figure out belladonna was the culprit?"

"Patience, my padawan. I'm getting there. Well, I started thinking about anything else it could be and then I remembered how huge her eyes looked. The pupils."

"You're using Star Wars lingo on me? Padawan, really? I'm beyond apprenticeship, Jedi Master." Lansfield let out a laugh, then I added, "But the drug screen came back negative."

"Belladonna doesn't show in a tox screen. So I showed the parents a picture of the belladonna plant and told them to go home and check the backyard."

"Let me guess. A huge grove of it."

"Yup. The mom came back with a bag full of branches. I told them they had a lot of talking to do with their daughter."

"What about treatment? What did you do with her?"

"Nothing. The effects wear off after a while. She's fine now."

"Damn. I would never have figured that out. I didn't even know people could grow it."

"High school kids do it. One kid gets a seed and then anybody who wants it can get it."

"Wow. Nice work, Doctor. I don't think very many physicians would've picked that up. You're very good." For a moment, I had forgotten all my stress.

"I'm a badass," he said, showing off his biceps and then kissing each one.

"Oh my God," I said, rolling my eyes and laughing. "You are too much." After we finished amusing each other, I realized that

I respected his intellect. And his handsome looks. And his . . .

"So, I'm curious. What's your background? Lansfield sounds so American, or Jewish, or something, but you look Spanish? Or Greek? What the hell are you?"

"My mom is Spanish, my dad's from Arizona. He was twenty-five years older than my mom. He worked as part of the Civilian Conservation Corps. The government would recruit unemployed men to work in camps planting trees in national forests or working on roadways."

"Wow. Sounds gutsy." I leaned in closer.

"Yeah. He was also a Marine. He met my mom while living in Phoenix."

"Your dad sounds like a hard worker, dedicated."

"Yeah. He built our first house from the ground up. The plumbing, the roof, everything. Made me help him, too."

"You must be an awesome handyman." I smiled.

"I can hold my own, thank you." He looked down at the table. "I learned a lot from my dad."

Our eyes met and he held my gaze. Usually I'm uncomfortable with eye contact but not with Dr. Lansfield. It came easy and I felt safe and reassured. "It's so easy to talk to you. I'm usually a different person when it comes to men."

"What do you mean?"

"I don't know. I get weird. Self-conscious. I tend to talk about things they want to talk about. And then if they find out my mother died, they never know what to say. The conversation goes back to them. I guess I kind of 'conform' to what they want to talk about," I said, using my fingers as quotation marks.

Dr. Lansfield leaned across the table. "Don't conform. Just be you. I like you."

This guy killed me. My mind raced. Being with him felt right. Very comfortable, almost meant to be. We left Kiki's two hours later and Dr. Lansfield had succeeded in taking my mind off of Ozzie. I loved listening to him talk and was getting medically smarter by the minute. I could get used to this. To him. But now I wanted go home, relax, and watch TV. Swimming would have to wait until tomorrow. After he dropped me off at my car, we said our good-byes and made plans to work out together in a few days. I gave him my cell number without thinking twice.

My last week at Marisdale challenged me. Apparently, a few nurses had seen Dr. Lansfield and me at Kiki's and I made it to the top of the gossip list. Listening to shift report, I could hear whispers and feel the stares of my coworkers. Unfortunately, Emma loved every minute of it.

"So . . . what does Dr. Lansfield see in you that the rest of us don't have, huh?" she bitchily asked, her chin held high.

"What are you talking about?" I sighed and put my pen down. *You want to go, bitch? Let's go.* I guess blabbermouthing first thing in the morning was more important to her than taking notes on her patient.

"Your little date with Dr. L. What do you do . . . love 'em then leave 'em?"

"Not that it's any of your business, but we both happen to like beer and food, which is available at these places called rest-aur-ants." I pronounced each syllable so she could understand. Yvette giggled behind me.

"Way to make a name for yourself, Natalie. I'm sure you'll be getting all sorts of offers now," Emma snarked as she walked away.

Shaking my head, I apologized to the night nurse for the rude interruption and focused back on receiving report. Yvette came up behind me and put a hand on my back.

"Don't listen to her. She's been after him for years, like most nurses here. They're just jealous. Don't let those buggers get to you."

"Thanks. Nothing happened. Two people going to lunch. That's it. I'm not looking for anything else . . . I'm only here one more week!"

"You don't have to justify it to me. Toughen up your skin, poppet. Gossip is everywhere, no matter what hospital you're in."

"I know. I don't like being at the center of it, though. So glad I'm leaving for another assignment."

"I thought you liked it here, my love."

"I do . . . I did. But now this shit. That's why I want to keep moving around. So I don't have to deal with any of it." And I didn't mean gossip; I meant everything. My dad, my forever grief, my wondering if cancer would catch up with me. The list went on.

"Well, poppet, at some point you will need to decide what's most important. Do you keep running from place to place to avoid difficulty, or do you go after what you want and ignore the shit? It's up to you."

"I think I'd prefer avoiding difficulty," I told her with a soft voice.

"Oh, I think you're much stronger than that, my Natalie." I stared after her as Yvette walked off into her patient's room. Deep down, I knew she was right, but I ignored the feeling. I managed to finish my shift despite all the whispering and bitchy looks. After shift change, I quickly grabbed my bag and headed down the back stairwell, not wanting to hear more nurse bullshit on the way to my car.

"Whoa, slow down, speedy," Dr. Lansfield said as we almost collided.

"Oh, sorry." I kept going without even looking up at him.

"Hey. What's your problem?"

Stopping below him, I turned around. "My problem? Apparently, several nurses saw us out the other day and now I'm the talk of the ICU. This is why I don't do relationships! I don't need this crap!"

"Oh, please. I thought you were tougher than that." He rolled his eyes.

"Well, you were wrong! I'll see you later," I said, pushing open the door.

"Sorry to have caused you so much trouble. I'll think twice next time! And there is no relationship. It's called friendship. Do you know what that is?" he yelled after me.

I got in the car and wiped my nose. I felt bad for what had happened between us in the stairway. He hadn't done anything wrong. I've always cared too much about what people think of me. Maybe I don't think enough of myself so I let others' opinions of me define who I am. But they don't know me. *Now everyone thinks of me as just another nurse looking for her doctor husband so she can stop working and flash a big ring, instead of the infamous surgeon's daughter who wanted to be like Daddy but settled for nursing. I chose nursing school because of what those nurses did for my mother. No other reason. I like being a travel nurse and I'm not going to stop. I can't let a bunch of catty dumbshits ruin this for me. They aren't worth it.*

Thankfully, my last day at Marisdale proved better than the day before. Lisa had been discharged days earlier so both my patients were new to me. The hospital had very few beds filled so the ICU received any patient, regardless of how sick they were. My two patients were GOMERs, Get Out of My ER patients— both over eighty years old, demented, and needing total care. GOMERS usually were admitted for bladder infections or falls, nothing major. Normally, I would bitch about getting two patients like this, but today I didn't mind. I could be a babysitter. I didn't need to think much. I just had to get through my last twelve hours.

I'd begun charting at the nurses' station when my nurse manager told me I had a visitor. Surprised, I walked toward the main doors and in walked Lisa Duvane holding little baby Ava, with her husband behind them. Lisa had cut her hair because it had become so matted with all the tape and "bed shampoos" during her long ICU stay. Her left arm remained wrapped, although with much less gauze than before, and was now immobilized by a sling. She had makeup on and wore a beautiful yellow sundress.

"Wow, you look great! How are you?" I gently hugged her and focused my attention on the baby.

"Hi! I wanted to come by and say thank you. There were three of you who really stood out to me and I wanted to bring y'all something." She handed me a tiny white box.

"Oh my gosh. You don't owe me anything. It's my job." With her yellow sundress, she reminded me of a beautiful, blooming flower, shining in the sun. "I can't believe how great you look!"

"Please, open it." She directed her gaze at the box.

I unwrapped the ribbon and lifted the lid. On top of a soft pillow of cotton lay a pink metal heart pin. On a little piece of white paper were the words written in calligraphy, *Thank You for Your Strength*.

"It's a locket," Lisa said, shushing the baby and putting Ava against her left shoulder. "Each of you got a different one. I chose *strength* for you."

Touching my fingertips to my lips, I opened the heart and inside posed Lisa's and Ava's pictures, one on each side. "It's so beautiful. Thank you."

"I want you to know that because of you, Ava and I are

bonded together, forever. A lot of nurses would've been focused on getting me well and out of the ICU, but you took care of all of us," she said, gesturing to all three of them. "It means the world to me. I can honestly say that when all this happened, I doubted I would be able to take care of Ava. Thanks to you guys, I believe I will completely recover and I couldn't be more happy to be a mom to this beautiful girl." She kissed the top of Ava's head.

I hugged Lisa tight and rubbed Ava's back. I shook her husband's hand and wished them all the best. "I will cherish this," I said, clutching the box to my chest. It's very rare that patients come back to the ICU to thank their nurses. Patients like Lisa make all the days of changing bedpans, fetching water, and cleaning up vomit totally worth it. I realized that I, too, had come to possess that nursing power I'd so wanted since I was fourteen years old.

After Lisa thanked the other two nurses, the happy family of three left the ICU. My nurse manager came out to acknowledge each of us. She asked me to come to her office. I quickly let a nearby nurse know I'd be off the floor for a few minutes and told her to come get me if my patients needed anything.

"Natalie, I want you to know, if you decide you want to work here permanently, I will be happy to make a position available. We really have enjoyed having you." She smiled.

"Oh, wow. Thank you. I'm going to Australia, but then I'm not sure where else. Can I keep the option open for a while? I promise if I choose to come back, you'll be the first person I'll call."

"Please don't lose my number. I'd love to have you. Call me anytime."

"I will, I promise you. Thank you." I shook her hand. I felt closure leaving Marisdale ICU, knowing that I had given the best nursing care I could and that my manager and patients recognized me for it. And soon I'd be gone and there would be another nurse to gossip about. I would be old news.

Driving home I allowed the guilt over how I'd ended things with Lansfield consume me. He didn't deserve being treated like that and the truth was I really enjoyed being with him. Why should I let other people dictate who I could and couldn't be with? No ... I needed to fix this. I decided to swing by the pool and see if I could find his car. Luckily, I spotted it under a tree. Parking my own vehicle next to his, I sat back and waited.

Thirty minutes later, Dr. Lansfield walked out. I stepped out of my car and walked over to him.

"What's up?" he said, his tone flat.

"I ... I'm sorry for the other day. I was upset and took it out on you." I looked up at him.

"Okay. Why do you care so much about what people say? It's hospital life; you should know that."

"I know. I've always cared ... too much. I'm working on it." I tilted my head up and smiled. I didn't want to let him go yet. Something pulled me toward him. "Hey, would you want to follow me back to my apartment? I've got beer and wine. We could talk some more."

He looked quizzically at me. "Hmmm ... sure. Why not?"

Lansfield followed me to my apartment. I unlocked the door, setting my keys on the counter, and told him to make himself comfortable. He picked up the picture of my mother.

"You look like her. Beautiful."

"Thanks." I opened two beers and sat down on the couch. He came over and sat next to me.

"Nice place. The hospital put you up here?"

"No, the nursing agency. It's not bad. I like it. And look how clean it is," I said, waving my hand around to show off the place.

He laughed. "Yeah, so anyway, who gives a shit what those nurses think? We had a good time, right? It's not like we were doing anything wrong. Just hanging out." He shrugged.

"I guess so. They're not used to anybody going out with you. Much less the new chick. I can see why you don't want to socialize with nurses. We're a bunch of pains in the ass."

"It's not that. Well, it's a little bit of that, but like I told you, I had a really shitty breakup and I'm trying to lay low."

"Will you tell me what happened?"

"It's a long story."

"I'd like to hear it."

It took him a while to answer while I sat patiently, waiting. He took a deep breath, leaned back against the sofa and folded his arms across his chest. After a brief moment, he finally began. "Okay, here it is. I was engaged once, in residency, and she had recently graduated from college."

I looked at him, my mouth open. Engaged? Damn. "So . . . what happened?"

He took a gulp of his beer. "She got pregnant."

"Okay . . . that happens," I said, tilting my head to the side. "And . . . ?"

"She didn't want it. Neither of us were expecting it. We had had a plan. I wanted to finish residency and then when I had a good job in a hospital somewhere, or even in a practice, we would try for a family. But that's not how it happened."

"She didn't want it? You guys were in love, right?" Why did it bother me to say *in love*?

"Now that I think about it, no. Where I grew up it was the thing to do. Meet someone and get married. Or get pregnant. We were young."

"So not a fairy-tale romance."

"Not really. I didn't know what I wanted back then. We

talked about the pregnancy—well, more like argued about it—
for several days. I had to go in for a thirty-six-hour shift at the
hospital and things still weren't resolved. I told her we'd talk
about it more when I got home and we'd figure something out."

"Okay. What did she say?"

"Nothing. We didn't talk much during my shift. I tried to
call once or twice, but she didn't answer. I got home two days
later and found her sitting on our couch, twirling her hair. When
I walked in, I just knew."

"Knew what?" I leaned toward him.

"She'd had an abortion."

I fell back onto my side of the couch, stunned. I gasped.
How could a woman do that to someone she supposedly loved?
A woman has a right to choose what happens to her body, but
when you're involved with someone they have a right to be part
of the decision. Or, to at least be told of the decision. Strange for
me, I didn't know what to say, so I said the only thing I could
think of. "I'm so sorry. I would never do that to a guy. How
cruel." I felt honored, though, that he'd chosen to tell his story
to me. He respected me as a friend, not someone who would use
him for his money or his position. He trusted me with his story
and it meant the world to me.

"Yeah, it sucked. I mean, I was willing to sacrifice a lot of
nights and weekends to make ends meet. It would've been
rough, but we could've managed. We were getting married, for
God's sake! Granted, we didn't have the greatest relationship,
but I didn't deserve that."

"I don't know what to say. I'm all for abortion, under certain
circumstances, but you two were . . ." I had to swallow down the
word— "together. What a bitch."

"I was thinking more of the 'c' word, but that would probably offend you. The rumor that I'm . . . what do they say . . .

untouchable . . . is not true. It's the fact that I can't get over what she did to me, without me being there, and without my consent. I might have even agreed to it if she'd been honest with me."

"Where is she now?" I really wanted to know. Maybe I could beat the shit out of her. Maybe I should send Betty after her. *Not funny, Natalie. Not funny.* How could she have done such a thing to him?

"Don't know and don't care. She left a few days later and I couldn't care less. I'm not against abortion either, but what she did was wrong. I had a right to know her plans!"

"I hear you. I really am sorry," I said, putting my hand over his. "You didn't deserve that. Nobody does. Just know that not all women are like that."

"And not all guys are bad, either."

"I never said they were. Why do you say that?"

"You're running from something, Natalie. I haven't figured out what, but I know you're running."

"I'm not running. I like this travel gig. It suits me," I told him, pressing my hand against my sternum.

"But for how long? Don't you want to settle down some-where eventually? The travel thing seems impermanent. Always moving around, forming friendships and then leaving . . ."

"It's safe for me this way, trust me." Lansfield stared blankly at me. "Look, I know it's hard to understand, but . . . I'm afraid if I don't keep moving . . ."

"What?"

"Do you know how genetic my mom's breast cancer is? It usually hits the grandmother, the mother, and then the poor daughter even quicker. My mother was forty when she died, my grandmother a few years older than that. I may not have that long."

"That's bullshit, Natalie." His voice sharpened. "I'm sorry

your mom is not with you anymore. But, Jesus, that doesn't mean you're dying!"

"You don't know that. None of us know when or where. It'll just happen. And I want it to happen on my terms. Wherever I'm at."

"Don't let your mother's death define you." He reached over and lifted my chin with his hand. My heart pounded. *This guy has so much empathy; no wonder he went into medicine.*

We put the heavy talk on hold and moved on. For the next few hours we talked about the hospital and gossiped about the staff. I didn't want this day to end. Then, thoughts of Australia reminded me that I would be leaving soon. I didn't know if I'd be back. I felt . . . sad, and he needed to know that. I took a deep breath.

"Doctor . . ."

"When we're away from the hospital, it's Joel."

"Sorry. Joel, there's something I need to tell you. I'm leaving for Australia in two days. I don't know whether I'm coming back. I'm telling you this now because I want you to know these last few weeks have been really cool. Swimming with you, joking around with you at the hospital, Kiki's . . . tonight." I looked at him, waiting for his response. I suddenly felt like I didn't want to go. I didn't want to let him go. I felt a connection with him. A level of security that I had never experienced with another guy, not even Jason.

"What? After I just poured my heart out to you? Why didn't you say something earlier?"

"I didn't think about it . . . sorry. I . . . I'm glad you told me." I moved closer to him.

"Damn, Natalie! I wish you had told me sooner." He wore a pained expression.

"What would it have mattered? You told me. It's okay."

He got up from the couch and headed to the door. I followed him, putting my hand on his back. Sighing, he turned to look at me.

"I don't know what it is about you. You're frustrating as hell but . . . I'm drawn to you."

My heart leaped. *Oh God.* "Joel . . . I . . ."

I didn't know what to say. Leaving now didn't feel so great. I couldn't change my mind; I had already received my next assignment. "You have my cell, here's my e-mail," I took a sticky note off the ledge by the phone and jotted down my electronic address. "Just in case. My timing sucks, but it's not like I'm disappearing off the face of the Earth. I wouldn't mind if you kept in touch with me. In fact, I really want you to."

"How bold of you." Joel's eyes sparkled as he raised one eyebrow and smiled. I could just kiss him right now.

"Well, Doctor Joel, let's just say I've become a little more open-minded over these last few hours." Then, my heart took over and I leaned up to kiss him gently on the lips. I didn't stay there long, just enough to let him know I cared. He stood there, looking down at me, grinning. Without a word, he unlocked my door and walked out. *No! Please turn around and look at me,* I said under my breath. Midway down the stairs, Joel turned around and waved. *Thank you!* Beaming, I waved back. *I will see Dr. Joel Lansfield again,* I promised myself. *I will.*

# 13

I couldn't sleep on the plane. There were very few people on the fourteen-hour flight to Sydney from Phoenix and I had an entire row to myself, but I kept playing my last conversation with Joel over and over in my head. *Don't let your mother's death define you* set up camp in the crevices of my brain. What did that mean? I chose my profession because of what had happened to her, but I didn't think I let myself be defined by it. I know for a fact that the risk of getting breast cancer more than doubles if a first-degree relative is diagnosed. It was bound to happen.

Mastectomies and lumpectomies could take care of it temporarily, but in my experience, when someone gets cancer, it usually comes back in other places in their body, eventually ending their life. So what was I supposed to do? Ignore the facts? Bullshit. I've got to do everything I can to keep cancer from catching me. Australia seemed like as great a place as any. *And if I see Joel again, fine, if not . . . Who am I kidding?* I want to see him again. Joel is a friend, a confidant, a man who allows me to be me, and who likes me anyway. Jason is equated with fun and noncommitment. It's what I'm used to. I don't have to dig too deep with Jason.

I had been traveling twenty-four hours by the time I reached Sydney. A cab took me to the Sydney City Lodge, located one mile from the central business district. Known as "The City," the central business district held the famous Sydney Harbor Bridge and Opera House. St. Vincent's Hospital was located half a mile from the hotel, which would make it an easy ten-minute walk to work.

The cab took off and I stood outside my new temporary home, looking around. *Oh, thank God!* A Starbucks sat right around the corner! *Now I'm good to go.* Small pine trees graced the entryway of the hotel, lining a black iron fence decorated with a fleur-de-lis on each pike. *Here's to another adventure,* I said to myself as I entered the lobby. A woman in a gray dress with a yellow scarf smiled as I checked in. Listening to her Australian accent, I wanted to say "crikey" like Crocodile Dundee but decided to keep my mouth shut. What a great accent the Australians have! She escorted me down a narrow corridor to a set of red stairs that led up to the rooms. I glanced at myself in the big, gold, gaudy mirror on the wall. *Man, I look like crap.* I couldn't wait to shower. She opened the door to my room and it took me no more than ten seconds to see all of it. It was a tiny studio apartment—one double bed, a kitchenette, and a tiny bathroom, all right there in front of me. She gave me a short speech about using the shared kitchen and laundry facilities and handed me a map before walking out.

I dropped my luggage on the floor and flopped down on the bed. I wanted to clean up and get some food, maybe explore the city a little bit before crashing. Even at four o'clock in the afternoon I needed sleep. Jason would have to wait; I didn't want to call him yet. Work at the hospital wouldn't start for a few more days so tomorrow I'd be totally free.

I stepped into the stark white, sterile bathroom with its stall shower and square sink. The fixtures were stainless steel while the accessories were modern clear Lucite. After turning on the water and undressing, I stepped into the shower and began to relax as the water spilled onto my head and down my body.

I headed outside to the center of Sydney and an area called Circular Quay. Several restaurants and little clothing and jewelry shops surrounded Sydney Harbor. People were milling around everywhere! It reminded me of being back in the States, like you see in the movies, where people are walking in huge masses down Times Square. It was such a metropolis. I stopped at a place that served food outdoors with a perfect view of the water, and ordered a barbeque snag, the Australian staple similar to our sausage sandwich. Tiny bats flew over my head and, judging by the way people ignored them, they were probably pretty common down under. While I ate, I could hear the sound of a didgeridoo played by an Aborigine sitting cross-legged on the pavement in front of the restaurant. Passersby threw money into his glass jug as payment for the entertainment. I felt a floating sensation, like all my burdens had been lifted . . . for now.

The next morning I called Jason. We decided to meet at his dive shop in Kogarah, a suburb about eight miles from Sydney. I would have to take a train to a town called Rocksdale, then catch a bus. I entered King's Cross Train Station and waited along the tracks amid other travelers. Within minutes, I heard the *ding-ding-ding* of the train approaching and boarded. Outside, the city changed to countryside as we zoomed past lakes and meadows. Quaint bridges connected roads and neighborhoods lined with narrow streets. The train passed some poorer areas where trash collected in alleys and people were sleeping in ditches or under overhangs. A few miles later, the announcer came on the loudspeaker, notifying travelers we were at Rocksdale. I needed to find the bus stop for Kogarah and I had several maps and directions from the hotel and from Jason. Trying to keep my eyes on the street and not on the map, I walked through the center of town, noticing fruit stands on almost every corner. I stopped at one to buy a huge, fresh peach that called my name, and finally made my way to the bus. It would be a short ride to the Abyss Dive Shop.

"Natalie!" Jason stood waving to me from across the street. He looked so good standing there—casual and still tan with hair that looked like he'd just come out of the water.

"Hi! Oh my God! This is so awesome!" I ran across as soon as the cars cleared. We hugged and, taking my backpack, Jason led me to the shop.

"How was the ride? You do okay? Sometimes the trains can get a bit scary. Especially in Rocksdale." Jason asked as we went inside.

"I'm good. Everything was fine. What's the plan for today?"

"Well, I thought we could go for a dive if you want, then maybe dinner? It's up to you. I'm just so glad you're here." He looked into my eyes and we were almost close enough to kiss, but I quickly stepped back and looked around the shop at the scuba gear.

With warm, sweaty hands, I began rooting in my purse and applied more lip gloss than I needed. The sexual tension had gotten to me. At our last meeting things had gotten a bit hot and heavy, but in a way I was relieved we didn't go further. Now, I felt sex looming over my head, like it had to be the next step. Sex was always a "next step" for me, something I felt obligated to do. Never something I really *wanted* to do. *Let's just see where this goes, Natalie.*

I turned back to Jason. "I'm ready to go when you are." He already had our gear, including a wetsuit for me, ready to go by the door. I hoped he'd gotten the size right.

"Let's go, then." He smiled as he handed me my stuff. I glanced at the tag of my suit. Perfect.

We drove to a place called Bare Island that Jason told me used to be a hotspot for movie locations. Unfortunately none were filming then. Because I had traveled in late May, the water temperature seemed chilly, around seventy degrees according to my internal thermometer. Luckily, Jason had chosen full-body wetsuits. We walked down to the entry point and dove in. The visibility sucked. I swam out a few yards and Jason signaled me underwater to look down. Right at my feet swam a wobbegong shark. It lay on the ledge of a rock, completely camouflaged, almost like a spotted rug. If stepped on, they attack. I quickly darted away from it and looked back at Jason, my eyes wide. He nodded and came to swim beside me, taking my hand. The rest of the dive was uneventful. We spotted a few schools of colorful fish, a huge blue grouper, and some small barracuda.

We surfaced and headed to a grassy hill to dispense with our heavy gear. Sitting on the grass, I stretched my legs and watched the waves roll in, then the tide pulled them back out. It calmed me. Jason opened a cooler and retrieved a thermos, some rolls, and a few gummy worms.

"Interesting snack you have there," I said, raising my eyebrows.

"Tomato soup, white rolls, and gummies. The soup and bread help fill the gap in your belly after diving and the gummies take the taste of salt water out of your mouth. It's good. Try it."

He poured me a cup of soup as I took a bite of the soft roll. "So, what do you do when you're not diving?"

"Nothing much. I hang out. Organize my photos, make CDs for tourists to buy, and wait for the next dive, I guess. What about you? What have you been up to since Belize?"

"Same old, same old. After Belize I went to Arizona, which

was pretty nice. I could see myself going back there. The weather, like here, is almost always gorgeous and I love the palm trees and flowers that are all over the place." I sipped the warm soup.

"After you left, I missed you. I wished we had more time together."

"What do you mean? Seeing a person die in front of you, knowing it could've been me, wasn't enough for ya?" I said, winking at him.

"Not that, silly. I just . . . wanted you."

"Oh, that. Well, here I am." I gave him my best seductive glance. Jason leaned in and planted a soft kiss on my lips. He pulled away slightly, as if unsure of my response. When I wrapped both my arms around his neck and pulled him in, he responded. Open-mouthed, tongues finding each other . . . a hot, heavy breath escaped me, yet the thrill no longer existed. *It's easier this way; why fight it?* It wasn't earth-shattering, but for some reason, I wanted it to be. I could let Jason in without *really* letting him in. *He's sweet, he's fun . . . he's a snorkeler cruising superficially, looking down at me from the surface.* I liked it that way.

"Follow me." He stood up and pulled me to my feet.

"Where are we going?"

"You'll see." He led me down the hill to a cave at the far end of the beach. I didn't see anyone else around.

We walked into the cave and I could hear the roaring waves crashing above us. Little droplets of water fell onto our heads every few seconds. Looking around, I said, "You bring all your diving chicks here?"

"Only the worthy ones," Jason said with a smirk. We stood there facing each other, in a cave in the middle of Australia, and kissed. And kissed. And kissed.

Jason's skilled hands found the zipper to my wet suit and

pulled it down the length of my back. I took in a sharp breath. He stopped there, not peeling the suit off me. Yet.

"Sshh," he said. "Relax, I've got you."

I hugged him harder and turned my head up to meet his lips. Jason pulled the zipper behind his neck and peeled down his wetsuit to his waist. I studied his tan body. I felt his flat chest and the lean muscles of his arms with both my hands. Then I looked up into his eyes. He took my face in both his hands and once again, our lips met.

My brain kicked in midway through our makeout session. *I don't want to have sex here, in this cave, as romantic as that sounds.* It didn't feel right. "Jason," I said, breathlessly. "Not here."

"Really?" His hands froze on my lower back.

I put my hands on his chest, separating us. "It just . . . not here."

"Okay. No problem," he said, pulling back and turning me around to zip me up.

We walked back up the hillside, gathering up the food we had left out. I had to make sure Jason wasn't upset. I'd been called a tease all throughout college and didn't want him to think I meant to lead him on, especially after the last time we met. I had also been called a cold fish. Fuck 'em. I liked Jason physically, but something felt different. Not as fun as before. My hormones and body were certainly good to go, but my heart and brain needed to catch up.

"I'm sorry, Jason. I just . . . I need a little time. Are you mad?" *Why am I having such a problem here?* I touched his arm.

"Me? No worries. I'll get you soon enough. You won't be able to resist me much longer." He beamed.

"You think so, huh?" I placed both hands on his chest and gave him a playful push. All seemed good.

We finished lunch and went back in the water for one last

quick dive. The water became so cloudy that Jason thought we should surface before the sharks came out. Sharks prefer cold, murky water and neither of us wanted to be on their menu. After we packed up the car, we headed back to the dive shop. Jason suggested I return to the city before dark and he'd meet me there for dinner. I agreed, not wanting to risk the train alone, when night fell. I caught the bus back to the train station and boarded the one heading back "home" to Sydney.

Two dives and the passionate cave rendezvous were about all I could handle for the day. I needed sleep. I had time for a little nap, which I welcomed. I climbed into bed with my laptop and signed in for my e-mails. Junk, junk, and some more junk. Wait! Joel? I had an e-mail from Joel? I opened it, my heart skipping beats. Damn my emotions!

> *To: naticurn@cable.com*
> *From: jlansy@yahoo.com*
> *Subject: What's up*
> *Hey, Natalie. How's it going there, halfway across the world? Just want to know that you're safe and things are good. Nothing going on here. One of the nursing directors told me they're looking for some permanent ICU nurses, even a charge position is available, so they tell me. I thought of you. If you're ever interested in coming back . . .*
> *Later, Joel*

Holy shit. *He's thinking about me. Does he want me to come back to Arizona? I can't deal with this right now. What about Jason? I'm here now, without Joel. I need to stay focused.* My mind raced and my chest tightened. Was I doing the travel thing so I didn't have to face my real issues? The hole that had been left by my mother's death, my absent father, Betty Watson, a permanent job? A chance for a real relationship? Had I become a Hollywood movie—a motherless child traveling the world to find inner peace? It had seemed like the right thing to do at the beginning, but how many more travel assignments would be available? I could hide from everything here. *And I think Joel knows it. He knows . . . me.*

I didn't want to e-mail Joel back right away; I didn't know what to say to him. That I missed him? No, I didn't want to miss him. I was in Australia now with Jason. That was it. I'd think beyond that later . . . maybe after my nap.

I had fun at dinner: good food, good company. Jason took me to a steak-and-seafood restaurant right off the harbor. We talked about his travels, the best dive sites, the most interesting things he'd photographed underwater, and the strange people he'd encountered. I listened, laughed when I was supposed to, asked a few questions. He loved talking about his job. It wasn't until he asked me what I had been up to since we left each other months ago that I told him about some of my patients, including the reformed gang member in Belize and Lisa and baby Ava. Jason didn't ask me much about them. He told me that the sight of blood made him sick so no details or gory stuff were necessary. I'm not used to that. I usually surrounded myself with medical people who liked to share stories with one another. Nurses don't hold anything back, either. I don't usually think twice about describing how someone's wound had opened up and pus drained out all over the bed. Nursing is such a huge part of who I am and I like talking about it, I love doing it. Nevertheless, I cleaned up my conversation and talked about more normal stuff, like Arizona weather and traveling on planes.

After dinner Jason walked me back to the hotel. I had three more free days before reporting to the hospital for work.

"I had fun today, Jason. Thank you," I said, linking my arms around his neck.

"I can't come up?" Jason tightened his grip on my waist.

I leaned up to kiss him. "Not tonight. It's . . . not you. Sorry, I just . . ." I smiled and released him.

"You're very difficult, you know that?" Jason said, slapping me on my ass. "I don't know how much longer I can be a gentleman."

"Shouldn't be too much longer," I said with a wink. I turned up the stairs. A neighbor had just come out of the front door and held the door open for me. Mouthing the words *thank you*, I turned to look back at Jason. He stood at the bottom of the stairs, hands in his pockets.

"Wanna go to the zoo tomorrow?"

"Yes, I do." I stood there with the door open.

"Pick you up around ten." Jason looked adorable standing at the bottom of the stairs, hands in both pockets, looking up at me.

"Ten it is. I can't wait." I gave a wave and headed inside, the door shutting behind me, a confident smile on my face.

# 14

I got out of bed early to check my e-mails before getting ready for my date with Jason. I hadn't replied to Joel's e-mail yet; maybe I would later. I wanted to keep him at a distance.

Jason met me outside my apartment and took me to the ferry for a quick ten-minute ride to an island off of Circular Quay dedicated entirely to Toranga Zoo. My mom used to take us to the zoo all the time. We'd pack a picnic and spend hours strolling around the animals, holding hands and laughing at how the warthog looked like my uncle and the gorilla reminded her of her father. My heart wrenched.

"Hey. Why so quiet?" Jason placed his arm around my shoulders.

"Oh, I'm sorry. Zoos remind me of my mom. She used to take me to the zoo all the time."

"Yeah . . . that's hard."

"Yeah." *Hard? Okay.* I continued to stare out into the ocean.

"Come on," Jason said, nudging my ribs. Speaking in a Jamaican accent, he said, "Don't worry . . . be happy. I've got an awesome day planned here!"

I couldn't be angry with Jason. No one wants to hear a sob story, but I missed my mother so much. Not everyone can handle that. Resolving to put thoughts of her away and start enjoying the day, I said, "You're right. It's all good. Onward!" I stood on my tippy toes and pointed toward the island.

"That's more like it!"

The only way to the zoo's main entrance was to ride the Sky Safari, a cable car several hundred feet in the air that offered an aerial view of the Sydney waterfront. We traveled from the lower wharf entrance to the main plaza, soaring over lush trees and man-made jungle habitats. I could see the Opera House and the harbor disappear behind me.

"Wow, this is beautiful," I told Jason.

"One of the best zoos I've been to. Come on, I'll take you to the koalas."

We got off the car and walked to the koala habitat, where patrons are allowed to come face to face with them in their own environment. The koalas were in an enclosure surrounded by a short chain-link fence. A large, iron gate marked the entrance to the habitat and once we stepped inside, a jungle of eucalyptus trees surrounded us. Koalas climbed all over the trees, right in front of us. I felt as if I had just walked into the Australian outback.

"Go up there," Jason urged, pointing in the direction of a tree hosting four koalas.

"Right up there?"

A female zookeeper dressed head to toe in khaki took my hand and placed me beside a giant eucalyptus tree. She started kissing the air and within seconds, two koalas came down the tree. One of their fuzzy ears tickled my cheek and I could even hear the other munching on the eucalyptus leaves. A photo snapped, and two more people stepped forward.

"I've never been so close to koalas before! That was so awesome! They're so cute," I said to Jason as he took my hand.

"So glad you're having a good time. There's lots more so let's go!"

We found great seats in the seal show auditorium. It reminded me a lot of Sea World in San Diego where we used to go as kids all the time. As a kid, I dreamed of becoming a dolphin trainer, but my parents had explained that my seafood allergy wouldn't do well with that profession. After the show, we moved on to the kangaroos resting in their open enclosure with only a long piece of wood separating us. I stood on it and snapped a picture of one relaxing on his side and licking his paws, right in front of me. I could almost touch him. Next door dwelled the ugliest bird I have ever seen, the emu. Nothing between us but the same kind of block wood on the ground. No cages at this zoo! I stood right next to the emu after handing Jason my camera. There were going to be some great shots from this trip. My stomach started rumbling so loud, Jason took the hint and we stopped for lunch at a little café.

"Jason, do you ever think you'll go back to the States?"

"Not sure what I'd do there. I've thought about it, but I kinda like what I'm doing right now. What about you? How long you gonna do this traveling thing?"

I shrugged. "I don't know."

"Well, I don't plan on settling down any time soon. I'm too young. It's too fun out here, diving all day, taking pictures of fish, meeting people from all over the world. It's a great life."

I nodded slowly, not sure that I agreed, but wasn't I doing the same thing? After all, it's called *travel* nursing. "It's nice out here. Thank you for another great day. It's all been so amazing."

"I've got more amazing things in store for you," Jason said, raising and lowering his eyebrows several times. I laughed and then he took my face in both his hands and pulled me in for a kiss. My body completely relaxed and I opened my mouth for his tongue.

Pulling the tiniest bit away from me, lips almost touching, Jason whispered, "Natalie, I don't want to wait any longer. Please, don't make me."

*Oh fuck it. Give it to him already.* Maybe I'll feel different after we have sex.

Sighing, I replied, "You don't have to wait. I'm here." I wrapped my hand tightly around the back of his neck and kissed him, hard.

"We're out!" Jason grabbed me and started walking quickly to catch the cable car back down to the wharf.

Jason's apartment seemed . . . homey. Because it was a small studio, everything lay right in front of me as I walked in the front door. Futon, tiny kitchenette, and bathroom, much like at my hotel. I excused myself and went to freshen up. Looking in the mirror, I didn't want to analyze the situation. It was pretty simple. *I know we want different things for our futures, but I don't care. It may be my loneliness, hormones, or the need to feel close to someone, but either way, sex is going to happen.* Anyway, what would it hurt to sleep with him?

When I came out of the bathroom, the futon had been turned into a bed and Jason, with his shirt off, lay on his side facing me. He did look sexy. He had one eyebrow raised, an elbow propping him up with his head resting on his hand. He was thin with no major muscles bulging out; you could barely see the outline of his pecs and his skin shimmered with a golden tan. I couldn't see any hair on his body, anywhere. His stomach looked concave. I hoped I wouldn't crush him with my weight.

"Mind if I lie next to you?" I asked him, well aware of what his answer would be.

"Please do."

I crawled along the bed like a cat and hovered over Jason. He pulled me down on top of him and began kissing my ears, neck, and throat all while his hands were working their way under my shirt. I backed away from him and got up on my knees, straddling him. I held both arms above my head and Jason lifted my shirt off. He started working on my bra. I felt the latch open, and quickly moved my hands to my breasts, holding the bra in place.

"Let it go," he told me. "It's okay."

Still on my knees, I looked at him for what seemed like a long time. I can't stand being naked. Some women can strip in front of their lovers or stand in front of them stark naked while they get admired. Not me. I can't do it.

I got off the bed, still holding on to my bra. Jason stared at me in confusion.

"What are you doing?" he asked.

"Getting more comfortable." I walked around the futon and turned down the sheets. I climbed in next to Jason and pulled the flat sheet up to my breasts, shimmying out of my thong and shorts, and letting go of my bra. I pulled it from under the covers and threw it on the floor.

"Oh, got it." Jason got under the covers too, pulled off his pants and underwear. Only when both of us were completely naked beneath the sheets did I move in for another kiss.

"Hi." I breathed heavily, face to face with Jason.

He maneuvered one foot between my feet and pushed my legs apart. He rolled on top of me and reached over me to the nightstand drawer. Pulling out a condom, he opened it with his teeth and, resting on one elbow, used the other hand to put it on. All underneath the covers, the way I liked it.

With one smooth motion, Jason entered me and I inhaled sharply. So much for foreplay. I liked foreplay. It seemed less intimate, easier. I brought my hips up to meet his thrusts and together we moved in synchronous rhythm. My hands traced the contours of his back as he rocked back and forth inside of me.

I never make sounds during sex. I'm always quiet. Not Jason. He started groaning and saying things like, "Oh yeah, that's it, that's good. Come on." I didn't care for the dirty talk but felt bad stopping him. Guys don't like it when you correct them. I kept telling myself, *Come on, Natalie, enjoy this. Feel it, come on. You're almost there.* Why did I feel the need to coach myself? Shouldn't it come naturally?

Jason thrust harder and harder into me. I couldn't relax. I just moved with him until he gave one last push.

"Oh shit!" he yelled out, collapsing on top of me.

*Well, I guess it's good as long as one of us finishes.* Jason rolled off me and got out of bed. Typical male thing to do. Real life is not like the movies. You don't lie next to each other and snuggle, talk about the future, or whisper wonderful things to each other after sex. At least, I never had. This experience with Jason was pretty typical of all my other sexual encounters, which I could count on one hand. *I've got to stop watching romance movies.* Jason went into the bathroom and I heard the toilet flush.

"You okay?" he asked me, climbing back into bed.

"Yeah, I'm good," I said, smiling politely. I hadn't hit the big O, but who cared? In fact, I hadn't begun to climax at all. Was I being self-centered? Disappointed that I didn't get off? Only thinking of myself? I'd been told that younger guys forget that there's a woman there, too, wanting to be thought of a little bit. To be pleasured in her own way. To this day, I hadn't met one guy I'd slept with that took care of me first. Jason pleasured me the first time we were together, but when it came to sex, it was all about the man. It seemed to me like they were all out to pleasure themselves, forgetting that a woman lay beneath them. *Oh well, what's the big deal? Sex is overrated.* Don't get me wrong; it feels good, but sex, to me, had always just been . . . okay. I guess I had been hoping that Jason might be the one to change that. Guess not.

"What are you thinking about?" Jason asked, bringing me out of my thoughts.

Lying, I said, "About what a great day this has been. Thank you."

"When do you start work?"

"The day after tomorrow. Which reminds me, I should really get back. I've got to get some stuff ready before I start and I need to wind down a little. It's always stressful going somewhere new for the first time." I reached for my clothes.

"Yeah, I'm with ya. I'll take you back whenever you're ready."

It would've been nice to have him argue with me for a little bit. Another wham, bam, thank you, ma'am. Maybe I should lower my expectations a little bit, then I wouldn't feel disappointed every time. Jason hadn't done anything wrong. I had just hoped this time would be different.

Jason took me back to my apartment and we kissed goodnight. The song "I Still Haven't Found What I'm Looking For" by U2 popped in my head, making me laugh at myself. "Thanks again, Jason. I'm off next week for three days if you want to get together then."

"Absolutely. I'll call you in a few days. Give you time to get settled at the hospital, okay?"

"Okay. Talk to you soon." I headed up the steps and unlocked the safety door at the lodge, waving to Jason as the door closed behind me.

"A non-fat skinny vanilla latte, please?" I asked the Starbucks guy, stopping in on my way to the hospital. It felt good knowing I wouldn't have to do without my daily staple!

"Sorry, love," he said with that Hugh Jackman accent. "We don't have skinny here; that's an American thing. Only the real stuff."

"Okay, that's good, too." Grateful to be sipping any hot brew, I walked the rest of the way to St. Vincent's.

The hospital looked like a modernized Buckingham Palace. There were several adjoining buildings, each advertising a specialty: Gastrointestinal, Oncology, Women's Center, etc. The grounds were beautifully kept, with grassy hills and brightly colored flowers. In the center of the courtyard stood a statue with a plaque reading, St. Vincent. I stopped at the welcome desk and asked for directions to the ICU. Passing by several units on my way to the second floor, I saw a fifteen-bed ICU, and noted that the hospital had all the latest computers, machines, and plenty of people bustling around. It had all the technology I had seen before and patients occupied almost every room. The ICU, as well as the rest of St. Vincent's, had sterile white walls and grey linoleum floors. The only splashes of color were a brown wooden rail along the middle of the walls and some small pieces of art. Pictures of birds, leaves, and nature scenes were framed in little, black shadow boxes. The entire unit and monitors were visible from every angle thanks to the centrally located nursing station. Each patient had his or her own room with large sliding glass doors. I found my way to the staffing office and met the nurse manager.

"Natalie, so good to have you. Welcome," said the older woman. She had short gray hair and wore pink scrubs. "I'm Martha. Let me show you around. You can put your stuff in here." She pointed to a small room with lockers.

Martha introduced me to the nurses and I found the unit to be very easy to orient myself to. Shaped as one big circle, I quickly found my way around. Martha explained the charting system and gave me my assignment. An open bed for an admission and a forty-six-year-old gentleman with a unique problem.

"What is that?" I asked the night nurse as I examined the pelvic x-ray hanging on the viewing lamp outside my patient's door. *No . . . that can't be what I think it is.* Sitting perfectly upright between the rib cage and the pelvis appeared to be some sort of cereal bowl.

"That, my friend, is a pottery bowl. Right there in the pelvis. A pottery bowl," the nurse said with wide eyes. "Ready to hear report?"

"Can't wait."

"So this man, Mr. Biemers, is in his forties and is also a minister. He started having abdominal pain a few days ago and went to the ER. They did an x-ray. A bowl rested perfectly in his pelvic cavity, the only way in being . . . his anus," the nurse said, stopping to see my reaction.

I couldn't think of anything to say except, "Okay. How does that happen? And how do we know that it's pottery and not plastic or something?" I put my pen down. I didn't want to be distracted with writing.

"Great question, American. The clay lights up differently on x-ray than plastic. It's enhanced, like metal. They're going to have to surgically break up the pieces and take each one out through the abdomen. It's going to be a huge surgery. As far as how he got it up there? No clue. Maybe you can ask him? Welcome to St. Vincent's, Yankee."

"Gee, thanks," I called after the night nurse as she walked out, giggling softly to herself.

People are fucking crazy everywhere you go! How the hell does a bowl end up in a guy's pelvis? And a minister? Jesus! This story's one for the books. *Thanks, Martha, for the great assignment. Once again, the travel nurse gets the shit.* I reviewed Mr. Biemers' labs and vitals from throughout the night along with the pre-op history and physical. Other than a kinky fetish for dishware, he appeared to be very healthy. I couldn't put it off any longer. I had to start my morning assessment. Now if I could just keep my smile from creeping up, I'd be good. I couldn't help it; I'd never seen this before. Ever.

"Good morning, Mr. Biemers. I'm Natalie, your nurse for today. How are you?" I asked, looking down at a slender, tan man with teeth so bright I didn't have to open the drapes.

"Well, thank you." He wouldn't look at me.

"Are you in pain anywhere?"

"Not too bad. When is my surgery?" He grimaced as he tried to sit up.

"I think around two thirty today. You can't have anything by mouth until after that, okay? Do you need something for the pain?"

"Yes, please."

"I'll get it for you right after I assess you real quick. Take some deep breaths for me." I continued my examination and as I gently pushed down on his lower belly, Mr. Biemers yelled out in pain. I could feel the outline of the bowl. *This is fucked up.*

I retrieved the morphine that had been ordered for him and gave him a good dose. I hoped his evening of fun was worth all this. Hopefully, they'd be able to get all the pieces and close him back up without problems. He'd be fine in a few days and back to doing strange things in the bedroom . . . or kitchen . . . or pottery store. Wherever.

Right before Mr. Biemers' surgery, his wife came to visit. Very thin, wearing a long denim skirt with a white, ruffled shirt buttoned up to her neck, and holding a bible, she screamed religious extremist. On her head she wore a tiny, white bonnet. *You've got to be kidding me. What are they? Amish? Mennonite? This is getting even more bizarre.* I walked into the room to introduce myself and answer any questions his wife had. I prayed she didn't ask me anything about the bowl.

"Hi, I'm Natalie. Can I help you with anything?" I clasped my hands together.

She sat at his bedside, holding his hand. I still couldn't get over his dark tan. And those teeth.

"I'm Joanne. Sam's wife," she said softly, looking at Sam the whole time.

"Nice to meet you, Joanne. Do you have any questions for me?" I asked, taking a deep breath and holding it.

"No, not right now. Thank you."

*Phew.* I exhaled. "Okay, well, I'm just outside if you need me," I said, pulling the curtains closed behind me. I decided to look through Sam Biemers' chart for details. I learned he was a minister in the Mennonite church and he and his wife had no children. That was it. Nothing more interesting. Just two religious people who liked to do strange things when the sun went down. Oh well. Made for a great story. Jason would be grossed out by it, I was sure. But Joel . . . *I have to tell Joel. He'd love this!* I'd leave out names and personal details, of course, but he'd love it.

An hour past Sam's expected surgery time, the OR called to say they were finally coming to get him. Better late than never. I unhooked him from the machines, taking off his heart and oxygen monitors, and clamping his IV. Sam touched my wrist as I leaned over him, which caught me off guard.

"Please. Do not judge me. I am a man of God." He stared straight ahead.

"Mr. Biemers, my job is to be your nurse. I'm here to take care of you, no matter what the problem." I patted his leg.

He seemed like a nice man. His view of sexual toys made him a little different than most people, I guess. No biggie. I tried hard to suppress any humor in this, though. I mean, a man had put a bowl up his ass. But he didn't need to know that I found that hilarious. I was sure he'd been humiliated enough. I told him I'd be seeing him soon and as they wheeled him out, his wife kissed him gently on the lips and held onto his hand until she no longer could. The surgical team planned to bring Sam back to the ICU after surgery so I left his belongings on the counter and told his wife I'd call her once he arrived back in his room.

Three hours later, Sam returned. I received report from the OR nurse. They'd taken a chisel and hammer to the bowl, broke it into tiny pieces, and sucked the fragments up through a catheter. They'd opened him up from sternum to pelvis in order to get the chisel and hammer in. With the bowl smashed to pieces, there was no guarantee the shards could be contained in one area so the surgeon had needed the room to explore and make sure all parts were recovered. Hundreds of sutures were used to close up both the inside of the abdomen and the incision itself. Mr. Biemers would have a large vertical scar once he healed, and would forever be reminded of his misfortune every time he took off his shirt. How sad.

I only had Sam to worry about because no new patients had been admitted. He recovered well from the surgery and slept for the remainder of my shift. I let his wife back in and she stayed at his side, holding his hand, her head on his chest. The night nurse arrived a few minutes early and I updated her on Mr. Beimers' status. Luckily, she listened without cracking any jokes or asking too many questions.

I signed myself out and began the short walk back to the hotel. Despite my desire to be nonjudgmental, I wanted to tell someone about my patient. Someone . . . medical. I found it fascinating that a man had been able to shove a whole bowl into his rectum. I needed to share it. I couldn't tell Jason, he wouldn't appreciate it. The second I explained how the bowl got in there he'd stop me; I just knew it. But, Jason was Jason. Fun, adventurous, honest, and . . . temporary. I didn't really need more than that right now. Did I?

# 15

*I'm falling. Water is all around me. No, wait! I'm ... drowning?
How can I be drowning?* I looked for the surface. Who is that?
A wavy figure, obscured by the bubbles and water, loomed above.
A woman? *My breath is running out. I need air!* I kept my eyes on
the figure standing above me. *Mom? Is she watching me drown?
Just standing there? I refuse to die like this! I've got to ... get ... air!*

My eyes opened and I sucked in all the air my lungs could
take. I looked around. I was in my bed, in my room, with my
luggage still on the floor. I was still in Australia. Safe, and dry. I
clutched my chest to steady my breath. Why would I dream about
drowning? And why was a woman watching me? What did this
mean? *My mom is supposed to have my back.* After a few minutes, I
caught my breath and went into the bathroom to splash some cool
water on my face. I felt so alone. Leaning over the sink and looking into the mirror at my frightened appearance, Betty entered
my mind. I thought about her narrowed eyes as she'd walked out
of her murdered husband's room. God, why had I ever covered for
her? It continued to haunt me. *Okay, stop.* Betty was not trying to
kill me. My subconscious is reminding me what I did by rearing
its ugly head and gnawing at me for not reporting her. Next time
I see Jason, I'll ask him if he ever heard anything more about the
dead blonde in Belize. Maybe he can put my worries to rest.

I splashed more water on my face and went back to bed but I

couldn't sleep. Grabbing my laptop, I checked my e-mails. *About time he reached out to me.* My dad had finally decided to check in.

> *To: naticurn@cable.com*
> *From: UlsterMD@umc.org*
> *Subject: How are you?*
> *Natalie, are you all right? It's been a while since we spoke and I don't even know where you are. Are you in the States? When you can, please let me know how you are and where you are. I'd appreciate it.*
> *Dad*

Just what I needed to deal with halfway across the world. Selfish asshole. *Now he decides to worry about me? It's been months! His own guilt overtook him to a point that he's clueless to anyone else around him. He can wait and wonder where I am. I'm not responding right now.* I slammed the laptop shut and pushed it away. I rolled over in bed and forced myself to get back to sleep. I needed to be at the hospital by six thirty and I didn't want to show up with dark circles and bags under my eyes. I flung the covers over my head in an attempt to hide from anything else this shitty night would throw at me.

On my second day at St. Vincent's, I felt like I had been there all week. I knew exactly what to do and where everything could be found on the unit. Everyone, so far, had been good to me and made me feel at home. I had Mr. Biemers again and another open bed for admission. Biemers appeared to be recovering well and the doctors wanted him transferred out later in the day. Nurses were making photocopies of his pelvic x-ray, blacking out his name, and putting it in their pockets to take home and show their friends. He'd become the joke of the ICU. I felt guilty about participating in that behavior, like I'd be betraying him as my patient. I wanted to be his advocate, as nurses are trained to do, but becoming a whistleblower didn't sit well with me. It would look bad, as the American here for only two weeks, to become a party pooper and tell the nurses to stop. I wasn't going to do that. Besides, I myself had brought home stories of unique patients. It's how we decompress. Making copies of a man's pelvic x-rays, though ... Hopefully, Biemers would keep improving and get out of here soon.

Heading into my patient's room, I heard the charge nurse say, "Natalie, you're up for the next patient. A fifty-four-year-old male, status: post-cardiac bypass."

"No prob. I'll get the room ready," I told her. I decided to start my morning assessment on Mr. Biemers, then I'd get ready for the admit. Mr. Biemers looked better. Sitting up in bed, he asked me to hand him the cup of ice chips.

"Good morning, Natalie," he said, fiddling with his sheets as I handed him the cup.

"How are you today? Do ya think we can get you out of here? I do."

"I'm ready to go. I know I've given everyone here something to talk about for years," he said, looking up from his bed but not quite making eye contact.

"You know we can't discuss our patients' conditions out in public. That's a breach of patient confidentiality. Nobody's talking about you out there." I hoped it didn't sound as much of a lie as it felt saying it. I continued to busy myself untangling his monitor wires and the IVs.

"Nice of you to say that, but I know it's not true." Mr. Biemers briefly met my eyes then looked out toward the window.

I didn't know how else to reassure him. "Let's just concentrate on getting you out of here, okay?" I placed the stethoscope tips in my ears to stop any further conversation and get on with my assessment. I felt awkward. Regardless of what had brought him here, he'd just had major surgery and would be in pain for a while due to his actions. I pitied him. Yeah, he'd done something completely stupid and reckless, but who was I to laugh at his suffering?

Marion, one of the nurses, sat down next to me as I diligently charted. The charge nurse had pointed her out to me yesterday, describing her as a very seasoned and knowledgeable nurse. It's helpful to know who to ask questions when you're new on a unit. Marion had earned her nickname, "Militant Marion," because she had once been an army nurse and was married to an army general. She had very short, gray curly hair, a roundish body, and a husky voice. She had been around the block a few times and evidently she took no crap from anyone. A real tough-ass.

"So, did you find out why your patient shoved a bowl up his ass?" Marion asked with her chest thrust out.

I stopped typing and turned to look at her. "We didn't exactly go into a detailed discussion about why he did it," I snipped. *Here we go.*

"Come on, American. You can tell me. What is he? Some gay porno dude with a fetish for clay?"

"What? No. He's not gay. His wife has been in here. He's a guy who got a little crazy one night, okay? Let's leave it at that." I turned back to the computer and resumed typing.

"Yeah, right. They should check him for AIDS and other STDs. He's sick. In all meanings of the word." Marion got up and started to walk away.

"You know what, Marion? You don't know anything about this guy. Leave him alone. He's suffering enough."

"Pussy American," Marion scoffed as she walked off.

I leaned back in my chair and folded my arms. What a bitch. And I was a pussy? She was talking about AIDS and shit right on the unit and spreading rumors about Mr. Biemers when she didn't know anything about him! She was the pussy. Couldn't find enough interesting stuff in her own life, so she had to go make up shit about other people's lives. Damn.

"Hey." The nurse manager, Martha, put her hand on my back. "Marion can be a bit curt at times. Ignore her."

"She's going to start spreading rumors about Mr. Biemers. He's a good patient, not giving me any problems. And he's in pain from his surgery. He doesn't need us talking smack about him. He told me he knows the nurses are talking out here. I feel bad for the guy."

"I know; it's a delicate situation. I'll talk to the nurses and reinforce our patient confidentiality policies. Violations like that will get you in big trouble. Between you and me, Marion is a jaded lady. For years we've been trying to get her to stop being so cynical, so negative all the time. I guess her time in the army wasn't all rainbows and lollipops."

I laughed. "Yeah, that's gotta be hard. But she shouldn't be spreading rumors about stuff she doesn't have a clue about."

"Rumors, gossip—it's all a way to deflect a person's own negative feelings. It gets directed toward one individual they feel they can talk about, to take the focus off of themselves. That's all."

I nodded, agreeing with what Martha said. People are always starting rumors about nurses and doctors, or who a nurse is sleeping with. It's like we don't have anything else in our lives to talk about. I used to think the television show *General Hospital* was bullshit. But a lot of it is true! Whether it's because medical people are overworked or because of the fact that we spend so much time together, a lot of sleazy stuff does happen. And the minute you look at someone differently, or talk to a guy—whether casually or not—people want to make more of it than it is. Just like back in Arizona when the nurses were making assumptions about Joel and me. And what did I do? I listened. I took out my insecurity and anger on Joel that day in the stairwell. Stupid.

The PA system, alerting me that a nurse wanted to give me report on my new patient, interrupted our conversation. Mr. Peyton, a fifty-four-year-old admitted with chest pain, had been taken immediately for a cardiac catheterization, where a cardiologist places a catheter through the groin to the heart. Then, an attempt is made to unclog the arteries of the heart, restoring blood flow. Similar to Roto-Rooter. Apparently Mr. Peyton's occupation and lifestyle caused him to have high stress, with significant blockage in his coronary arteries and uncontrolled blood pressure. He owned several businesses and worked non-stop—drinking caffeine, smoking, and always traveling. During report, the nurse lowered her voice a bit, as if afraid someone would hear her. She told me the cardiologist "may have perforated his artery, but it looked good when they closed him up." Great.

The minute they wheeled Dave Peyton in, I knew the shit would hit the fan. "Goddamn it. Get this crap off me!" he yelled. He squirmed around, pulling on his IV and hospital gown.

After catheterization, a pressure dressing is applied to the groin site and the patient must keep that leg absolutely straight so as not to pop the dressing off, risking hemorrhage. Mr. Peyton didn't care about keeping anything still, much less his leg. The nurses had applied a leg restraint tied to the end of the bed.

"Mr. Peyton, you need to relax. You're in the ICU. We'll take that restraint off you soon. You have to relax," I urged him.

"Fuck off," he said, pulling on the restraint.

"Good luck," the nurse told me as she handed me the paperwork and wheeled the empty gurney back to the cath lab. The other nurses and I situated the patient in his bed.

*Great, here we go.* I quickly checked the chart and looked

over the orders. Yes! The cardiologist had ordered an anti-anxiety medication. Just one dose? I needed more than that.

"Mr. Peyton, I'm Natalie, your nurse here in the ICU. We can take that dressing off your groin in about eight hours, but until then, I need you to keep your leg still. Understand?" I gave him the medication and would work on getting an order for more later. My nursing gut began to gnaw at me. Something didn't feel right.

"Get me up, I need to pee," he said, trying to sit up by himself.

"Whoa. You can't get up. I'll get you a urinal, hold on." I ran out of the room and saw my charge nurse walking around the unit. I told her I might need her help soon. My stomach turned rock hard as I prepared myself for the worst.

Seconds later I came back into the room with a urinal and showed my patient how to use it. After he finished relieving himself, he shoved the full bottle at me so hard urine sloshed over the sides of the container onto my hands. "Do something with this, would ya?"

I rolled my eyes and went to dump the urine out, forcefully washing my hands. If he didn't watch out, I might accidentally slip and empty some of it in his bed. With the med coursing through his system, Mr. Peyton appeared to be calming down. He lay back in bed and shut his eyes. I took that opportunity to exit the room and start charting. I would not stay late tonight due to this asshole.

Typing away at the computer, recounting Mr. Peyton's exam and recent behavior, I was interrupted by "Agghh!" and ran into the room. An emesis basin, blankets, and his IV were flying across the room. My patient had managed to free his restrained leg while pulling everything off himself, including the monitor wires, IV, and his gown!

"I need help in here!" I yelled to anyone within earshot. "Mr.

Peyton, please. You need to calm down!" Dangling his legs off the side of his bed, my patient tried standing.

"Go fuck yourself! And while you're at it, go back to the US!" He started to stand but fell back against the bed.

Two nurses, one huge guy, and a petite female nurse ran into the room. I felt relieved to see the male nurse. I'd probably be needing some muscle and protection. All three of us stood in front of Peyton. "Mr. Peyton," I said, "We're going to get you back in bed now. This is not an option. Lie down!"

He seemed to cooperate but, as we were lifting his legs onto the bed and raising the head of it, he shot straight up. Vomit flew at me, hitting me square in the chest, splattering my cheeks and dripping down onto my clogs. Shit! I ran to get a washcloth from the cabinet behind his bed and one of the other nurses informed me more help was on the way. What the hell was going on? For the next three minutes, Peyton kept spewing vomit. Then he turned extremely pale, beads of sweat formed on his forehead and upper lip, and his eyes rolled back in his head. He fell back against the pillows.

"His pressure's dropping!" I yelled. "Get the crash cart!"

The male nurse who had been trying to straighten Peyton's left leg and replace the pressure bandage looked up and ditched that effort. He ran out of the room to get help. For the next twenty minutes, we coded my patient, finally reestablishing a heart rhythm and stabilizing his blood pressure. In the middle of the trauma, we intubated him to establish a good airway. Trash lay sprawled throughout the room and vomit coated my clothes. Mr. Peyton lay comatose and on life support. I still didn't understand what had happened. He had seemed to be stable all morning—an asshole, but stable.

The cardiologist decided to show up as I was placing all the dirty linens in the hamper. I'd taken care of many post-cath patients and nine times out of ten the patient had come to the ICU somewhat stable with a little understanding of what they needed to do. Not this one. I couldn't understand what had gone wrong. Maybe they should've held him in recovery longer before dumping him on me.

"Nice scrubs. You always come to work like that?" he said, pointing to the vomit stains on my top.

*Douchebag.* "It's from your patient, Doctor. Right before he coded," I said, still cleaning up.

"Why didn't you call me if you saw him in trouble?" the doctor said as he placed his stethoscope on my patient's chest.

"I gave him the relaxant and he seemed to calm down. I was charting when all of a sudden he started thrashing around. I didn't have time to call you. We started the code."

"Well, this isn't typical of your standard cath. Something must have happened that you didn't see."

*That I didn't see? What the fuck? This is not my fault, buddy. Hell no! Typical doctor behavior. The minute the shit hits the fan, the nurse gets blamed.* Total bullshit. Maybe he hadn't done such a bang-up job in the OR as his ego allowed him to believe. Maybe the punctured aorta wasn't as patched up as they'd thought. I couldn't think of anything else that would have caused his sudden mental status change, his pressure dropping, and the vomiting, other than the fact that my patient's bleeding had never stopped. Period.

"He was stable, then he started getting angry, he vomited, and then crashed. That's all I can tell you. Unless something happened in the cath lab that I don't know," I said, walking out of the room. I didn't want to hear his bullshit answer and I figured he wouldn't admit to anything anyway.

The cardiologist finished writing orders and slammed Mr. Peyton's chart closed right in front of me. "Call the OR and tell them I'm coming. He needs to be opened up." He skulked out of the unit without waiting for my response. *Jerkoff.*

Shift change would be in the next fifteen minutes and I welcomed it. I looked for Martha to update her and to cover my ass. I'd done nothing wrong and I'd followed the appropriate protocols when my patient's status took a dive. I've taken care of a ton of heart patients and they're usually straightforward. Nothing I did caused Mr. Peyton to code. Risk management or whoever needed to look into the actual cath and see what went down. The guy had probably come to me bleeding out. They'd thought they had it fixed, but they didn't. Now, Dave Peyton lay intubated and unconscious, and who knew if he'd even survive surgery. *Why did I get this shit? I'm here only two weeks!*

I arrived back at the hotel and showered off the rank smell of vomit, climbed into bed and turned on the TV. I felt so tired, yet my mind kept racing. What could I have foreseen with Peyton? Something I could've caught earlier? Did he act like an ass because he knew something was wrong? I went over everything in my head again, from the minute he'd come to the ICU until the code. I wouldn't have done anything differently. God, I hated this. Feeling responsible for someone nearly dying when I knew I'd done nothing wrong. All this guilt weighed me down. Guilt over the Betty cover-up, guilt about my father, guilt about Joel, and now this. *I feel so alone right now. I could call Jason, but he wouldn't understand.* I pulled out my computer and the inbox messages appeared. I read Joel's e-mail again. It would be nice to talk to him. I really missed him. My heart ached. Why had I ever left? He'd understand my feelings, from a medical standpoint. He'd probably understand my emotions too, from a personal standpoint. Longing came over me.

*To: jlansy@yahoo.com*
*From: naticurn@cable.com*
*Subject: Re: What's up*
*Hi Joel. Thanks for the heads up on the job opportunities. Austra-*
*lia is pretty cool! You should come here :)! I haven't been swimming*
*since I left but will have to find a pool soon. I need to de-stress! This*
*traveling thing is starting to wear on me. I kinda miss you. Anyway,*
*hope you are well.*
  *Natalie*

# 16

D ave Peyton died. When I reported for work the next day, the night nurse told me he'd gone into cardiac arrest for a third and final time. They tried to resuscitate him for over twenty minutes, but were unsuccessful. At fifty-four years old, he died. When I left my shift, he had seemed somewhat stable. Still on life support, but stable. I wanted more details. I was told that his family was very upset and risk management had been called. They'd probably want to talk to me since I'd received him fresh from recovery.

I wanted to talk to the nurse manager about Mr. Peyton. I needed to be assured I hadn't done anything wrong. My own feelings weren't enough. I needed to hear it from someone else. I figured he'd probably bled out, lost too much blood, and then died. But I needed to know there wasn't anything I should've done differently. Anytime I lost a patient, I always blamed myself first. I felt as if I'd failed them. I've never messed up so badly that one of my patients died, but somehow I try to blame myself whenever one does, no matter what the cause. Maybe my own insecurities allow me to worry so much about what other people think of me. Why do I feel the need for validation and approval?

The night nurse seemed relieved as I sat down across from her, ready for report. I had arrived a few minutes early and, judging by the tapping of her nails on the counter, she seemed more than ready to go home. We had finished report on my first patient of the day, and were just starting report for the second when the ward clerk interrupted us.

"Natalie, there's a phone call for you on line six. Some guy, says it's important."

Who the hell was calling me here? "Okay, thanks." I told the night nurse I'd be right back. She gave me a pissed-off look, but I ran to the phone before she could say anything. Because of my phone call, she'd have to stay five minutes longer. Poor baby. Picking up the phone I said, "Hello?"

"Hey Nat, it's Jason."

"Oh, hi, Jason. I don't think you should really call me here. I'm in the middle of report. Can we talk later?"

"No. I just need an answer real quick. I have to go to Cairns the day after tomorrow for a photo shoot for the website. They want me to dive the Great Barrier Reef. I can bring someone for free and I want you to come, but the dive shop needs to know right now. What do you say?"

"Um, isn't Cairns, like a two-day drive? I can't do that on such short notice. I mean, how long will we be gone, where will we stay?" Why did we need to talk about this right now while I was at work? The glare from the night nurse seared into my brain.

"It's an hour-and-a-half flight. No driving. You can come back later the same night if you want. I have to stay a few days. It's all paid for. Come on, say yes and I'll get off the phone. The Great Barrier Reef, Natalie!"

I wanted to hang up before the charge nurse scolded me for personal phone calls, so I answered fast. "Oh, what the hell . . . okay." I knew I had the next few days off. To dive The Reef, as experienced divers called it, is a once-in-a-lifetime opportunity. It's one place all divers want to experience. The clarity of the water, the millions of species of fish—it's one of the Seven

Wonders of the World. I'd be an idiot to turn that down. And besides, I could use the fun.

"Great," Jason said. "I'll give you the details tonight. Cheers!"

"Wait . . ." He hung up. How had he known how to get hold of me? I still had too many questions about the trip. Staring quizzically at the phone, I hung it up and went back to the night nurse who, I swear, had smoke coming out of her ears. Her laser eyes squinted at me just enough to let me know we'd better get on with report. Jeez, God forbid she stayed one minute longer than she had to.

"Okay, sorry about that. Carry on." I forced a smile. *Screw her, soon I'll be diving the Great Barrier Reef!*

The rest of my day went smoothly. No difficult patients and nobody dying. I had a chance to speak to the nurse manager, who explained that Peyton had coded due to his recent heart issues. She reiterated the risks involved with heart surgery, which include rupture of an artery, and gave no indication that I'd done anything wrong. Management didn't think so either and the cardiologist hadn't complained—probably because he knew he'd be under scrutiny if a full investigation were opened. Peyton's family decided against an autopsy because the consent form had clearly outlined the risks of surgery, including death. As far as they knew, his death had not involved foul play. The nurse manager told me not to worry; these things happened. As if I didn't know that. Still, I welcomed the reassurance. It would make the dive trip more fun and I could relax with a clear conscience.

Jason e-mailed me that night with the details for our day trip. This dive is definitely worthy of a Facebook post. *Natalie Ulster is ready to dive the Great Barrier Reef tomorrow! Cairns, here I come!* I met him at the dive shop the next morning—much too early for my taste—so we could catch a bus to the airport. With half of my venti extra-bold coffee sparking up my brain and a blueberry muffin in my hand, I waited for Jason to gather his stuff while I quietly sucked down the rest of the caffeine load.

"Ready to go?" he asked, all perky and energetic at six o'clock in the morning.

"Yeah," I said, readjusting my big black sunglasses.

After a short bus ride to Kingsford Smith Airport in Sydney we boarded the Jetstar, a small express plane, for the hour-and-a-half flight to Cairns. The plane was a little puddle-jumper with one seat in each row. Were the propellers held together by rubber bands? I had never seen a smaller plane nor ever been in one. No door to the cockpit; only a seat for the captain and a clear view for us out the front window. *Oh God, if this thing goes down we were definitely goners. Why am I doing this?* We found our seats and I leaned my head back, sunglasses still on, thinking I'd try to get more sleep. Jason sat across the aisle from me. He couldn't stop talking about the different sharks, fish, coral, water temperatures, water depths, different lenses he would use, and so on. I reached across the small aisle and touched him on the arm, interrupting his explanation of megapixels and zoom lenses for his Canon 360.

"Do you mind if I just chill for a little bit? This plane makes me a little nervous and I had a rough shift yesterday. My patient died, the family got pissed, and it wasn't fun. I want to hear about all this, but just give me an hour to wake up, okay?"

"Ugh, how do you watch people die? That's got to be the worst thing ever." He fiddled more with his lens.

"Well, I didn't really *watch* him die; he died during the night shift. You get used to death after a while. I'm kind of numb to it. It just sucks, that's all. I feel like I let him down. But this guy, he acted like an a-hole and threw up all over me . . . It was a crappy assignment from the get-go."

"Oh my God. You got thrown up on? Blech!" He stuck out his tongue and turned to look at me as if I still had fresh vomit dripping from my clothes.

"If you knew what kind of bodily fluids have been spilled on me during my nursing career, you'd want to jump out of this plane," I said jokingly.

"You're probably right." Jason sounded serious. "I can't stand seeing gross things like that. Much less talk about them. I mean, dead animals and fish guts are things I'm used to. But people guts . . . yuck!" He started playing with his camera again, looking through the lens, adjusting it, and then looking through it again.

I couldn't help what I did. Nurses like to talk about their jobs a lot because most of the time, we love it. It's not as if I constantly talk about shit or piss while eating or anything. It's stuff I encounter during a day's work. If he couldn't stand to hear about my job, did I have to spend the rest of our time together talking about his? We needed to have more to talk about than that. When we'd first met in Belize, it had seemed so easy. So casual. Now I felt like we were trying too hard to find things we had in common. There's more to life than diving and fish.

"Sorry, Jason. Nursing is a huge part of who I am and some-times I don't know how to leave my job at the door. I'm a nurse all of the time. I check out people's veins to figure out what gauge IV they would need. I assess someone's limp and try to diag-nose them as they walk down the street. It's like I'm always on. I promise I'll try to stop being so medical all the time." I touched his arm and gave him a soft smile. Not everyone wanted to hear about what goes on in the hospital, and I needed to respect that.

"No worries, I'm just not into that stuff, you know. Can't stand the sight of blood and talking about puke is the one thing that actually makes me want to do just that. Puke. Anyway, you'll stop thinking about that stuff after our dive because your brain will be too full of all the cool fish you saw. It's going to be awesome!"

A man grunted and hocked up some mucus, spitting it on the floor behind me. Disgusting. I turned around in my chair and a large, hairy, acne-scarred face grinned back. I glared at him. *I'm not in the mood for you, asshole.* He leaned back against his seat with that dumb smile on his face, tilted his head upwards, and closed his eyes.

I turned toward Jason and gave him a soft smile. "I'm just going to close my eyes for a little while, okay?"

"No prob." He went back to his camera, and I leaned my head against the tiny window.

*Lord, please don't let me die in this thing.* I tried to relax, closing my eyes. It bothered me that Jason never asked about my family, or more importantly, my mom. I remembered how good it felt when Joel had asked me about her. Talking about her honored her memory and I needed to do it more often. Maybe I should start with my dad. She'd be ashamed of what he'd become: a drunken, lonely man who's found comfort in his scalpel. *Each new skank he brings home covers up his pain until there's nothing left. He's become so empty, drowning out reality with his alcohol.* Not being religious, I didn't take comfort that my mother was "in God's hands" or "one with the angels." My own spirituality led me to believe that she was with me, all around me, and she'd be upset with me if I let Dad continue on this way. I envied Joel and his big family, yet I hadn't been doing anything to save mine. I continued to look out over the ocean, searching for an answer.

Finally we landed in Cairns and went straight to the ship. The weather looked a little cloudy. Sprinkles of rain were leaving spots on my sunglasses. Jason saw me looking at the sky and reassured me that, even if it stormed, it would be much calmer out at sea. I began doubting him when I saw our boat bouncing up and down in the waves. The ropes holding the boat at dock were being pulled around like the strings on giant yo-yos. I looked around the dock. There were mostly people from the plane and a few workers. The gross guy who'd sat behind me had vanished. *Good riddance.*

"You sure we should be going out? It looks rough up there." I pointed to the boarding area.

"It'll be fine, Natalie. Come on." Jason led me up the plank.

We entered a main room with red velvet movie theater seats. A tanned guy in his late forties with a beer belly greeted us and told us to have a seat. His white shirt, bearing the logo *Reef Tours,* had sweat stains at the armpits and he smacked his gum. He handed us forms to sign and started his spiel about where we would be diving and safety precautions, etc. I tried my best to pay attention, but the rocking of the boat turned my stomach in flips and we hadn't even started yet. Forward and backward, forward and backward—I gripped both armrests to keep myself in my chair.

Mr. Sweatypits directed us to the back of the room where a huge spread of food lay atop a large table. The staff had set down huge platters of blackened chicken, red beans and rice, shrimp cocktail, and rolls. I couldn't even think about eating. My stomach wouldn't stop lifting up and then falling back down inside me. I started burping, holding my hands over my mouth, and as the boat pulled away, I told Jason I needed to get some air.

Grabbing any side rail or wall to steady myself, I made my way to the bow. Ocean water splashed the wooden planks and the white mast up front swayed back and forth with the wind. The boat pitched and rolled with the waves, and with each lift and dip my stomach turned more sour. The swells were getting so big that the bow heaved upward and then dove down fast, breaking the surface of the water. I held on to the rails tightly so that I wouldn't fall overboard.

With each dive down, I could almost make out the fish underwater. Then the rain let loose and I began to shiver from the cold. I couldn't keep it in anymore. I grabbed the rails at the front of the boat and hurled my undigested muffin into the water. Fish food. Each time the boat flung forward under the surge of the waves, I threw up. Oh God, I'd never felt so sick. Not even in college after drinking all night. I hurled again. Wiping the mucus and vomit off my chin and trying to catch my breath, I noticed several passengers making their way outside to do the same thing. I wasn't alone. All around me people leaned over the rails and heaved.

The clouds covered any trace of the sun as the weather continued to worsen. Freezing from the torrential rain, every so often I'd get a sprinkle of warmth from the salt water getting tossed up on deck. *Where the hell is Jason? I could use some support right now.* On cue, Jason came running toward me.

"Oh God, Natalie. You okay?" He rubbed both of my arms with his hands, trying to warm me up.

"Jason . . . I feel . . . so . . . "—another hurl over the side—"sick," I finished, wiping my chin. There couldn't be anything left in there. Fearing that the next time I vomited would bring up vital organs, I tried holding back the nausea.

"I'm so used to boats and dive trips that I don't get sick at all. I never thought it would be this bad for you."

The boat lurched forward with such strength that Jason grabbed the back of my shirt to keep me from falling forward. The winds were blowing so hard, there had to be at least two inches of water on deck. More seasick people were filtering their way outside to empty their stomachs into the sea.

"Oh God," I said, exhausted.

"Natalie, I'm going to go find you a slicker or something. You're freezing. Can you hang on here until I get back?" Jason said, putting my hand around one of the rails.

"I'll try," I said. *Oh no . . . not again.* Nothing but bile at this point. The boat heaved forward again, the warmth of the waves splashing onto my face. Jason ran back inside.

The captain came on the overhead system and announced that although we were in rough waters, it would be calm on the reef. They were going to continue on. How much longer? I didn't think I could take much more. And I certainly didn't feel like I could dive.

Just as I thought things were settling down with my stomach and the storm, a huge wave lifted the boat up and out of the water and then the bow came crashing down. I flung forward with such force that I lost my grip on the rail and toppled over the front of the ship. I screamed and reached for anything to hold onto. I found a rope secured to the mast above me.

"Help! Help!" No one could hear me over the clanging of the bells and the sound of the boat crashing in the swells. Everyone on deck was faced toward the ocean so all the vomit would go overboard. Nobody saw me.

It had happened so fast. I couldn't go down like this. Not halfway across the world, not this way. Someone would help me, wouldn't they? Jason would know I'd disappeared. He'd look for me. If the goddamn boat would be still for a second, I could try to climb back up.

Nature must have heard me because the boat stilled. My fingers were losing their grip when a huge, hairy hand reached down and took hold of my wrist. I looked up and saw the man from the plane. The repulsive scarface guy behind me! He leaned down and held onto my wrist. I focused on his pockmarked face and glanced at the star tattoo on his hand. Relief spread over me.

"How ya doing?" the man said, smiling. American. He sounded American.

"Oh, thank God. Pull me up," I pleaded.

He laughed. *What? Why is he laughing? Pull me the fuck up!*

"You're making this too easy on me, little girl. I shouldn't even charge her for this one." The words oozed out of his mouth. He chuckled before he lifted my hand and began peeling it finger by finger off the rope. My wrist held prisoner, I dangled off the boat like bait for a great white. Then, he let go. My eyes opened wide as his face faded from view. I plunged into the water, back first. Water filled my ears and lungs. I righted myself and brought my head out of the water, watching the boat barely miss my head as it coursed by.

Surfacing, I spit out the salty water and gasped for air. Treading water, the nausea almost overwhelmed me. Spinning my head around to orient myself, I looked in all four directions. I spotted an atoll about three hundred yards away. An easy swim for me, even with a shitty stomach and rolling waves. There were several anchored boats in the distance. There had to be divers and tourists all around the place. I would be saved, I knew it. Thank God. What the hell had just happened? Who was that guy? Why had he tried to kill me? Oh no . . . it had happened again! Someone *was* trying to kill me. "I shouldn't even charge her," he'd said. Betty! There was no other explanation. She'd maliciously killed her husband and had a grudge against me! *She certainly is capable of something like this. I can't explain it any other way. I'm not imagining it. The drink in Belize, the shrimp, Ozzie— now this. Shit!* How did she keep finding me? Only my family and the nursing agency knew my whereabouts.

*Oh Fuck! My Facebook page! Goddamn it!* I had posted all my locations. And I'd never un-friended her. Stupid! The guy she'd sent was a real idiot. What did he think would happen to me?

I'd die from the fall? That no one would ever know I'd fallen and they'd all sail off? There were too many people around to not see me. And Jason, well, he'd tell the crew and they'd come find me for sure. Pockface thought he'd kill me this way? Bullshit! "Wrong girl, buddy!" I yelled as I turned on my stomach and began my swim toward the atoll.

Lying on my back on the sand, I could still feel the ship rocking forcefully up and down with the rough motion of the waves. If anything had been left in my belly, I would definitely have been throwing it up right now. My esophagus and mouth burned from the acidic remains of my vomit.

The sun finally peeked through the clouds and the rain completely stopped. Sure, *now* the weather turned perfect. Leaning up on my elbows, I took in my surroundings. Crystal clear, blue water surrounded me. I sat on a mound of sand bordered by coconut trees. I felt safe on the atoll. Alone, but safe. Not the way I'd wanted to experience the Great Barrier Reef, but . . .

This sucked but I needed to figure this out. There had been too many close calls since I'd been traveling, and all of them seemed suspicious. Now, I knew as soon as I got off this atoll, the police were going to get involved. I knew Betty was responsible and I wanted to end this. Ms. Watson was going down.

Several minutes after I landed on the atoll, a little dinghy pulled up on the shore and interrupted my internal tirade. I collapsed back down to my back in relief.

"Natalie! Oh, jeez. Thank God! Are you okay?" Jason jumped out of the boat onto the sand with two other guys. He had found me. He knelt before me on the beach and scooped me up in his arms. I buried my head against his chest and fell apart.

"I want to go home, Jason. Please, take me home. There's someone on the ship trying to kill me!"

All three men exchanged confused looks. "Natalie, come on. No one's trying to kill you. I've got to finish my job here. I can't leave yet. Let's get you back to the boat and into some dry clothes. We'll make a plan, okay?"

"You don't believe me, do you? I swear, Jason!" He continued to help me to the dinghy, ignoring my accusations. Jason put a large towel around me. *All I want is to close my eyes and sleep.* The sun shone bright, no sign of any more storms. And damn it, I'd lost my sunglasses in all the craziness. I'd loved those Ray-Bans. Those big black rims covered half my face. Now everyone would see me crying. I took a deep breath and wiped my cheeks. *Get yourself together, Natalie.*

A while later, we were back on the dive boat and the smell of food brought the acid up into my throat again and the nausea back into my stomach. A fat couple who had just returned from diving the reef, while I'd played survivor and swam for my life, were attacking the shrimp cocktail and loading up the fixings on their huge silver plates. They were stuffed into their black wetsuits so tightly I had no clue how all that food was going to fit in their rotund bellies. I wanted to puke . . . again.

"How bout a roll, little Sheila?" the pit-stained guy said to me. "It'll fill the gap!"

"No. No, thank you," I told him, swallowing down some bile. What the hell did "fill the gap" mean, anyway? Stupid statement. I'd heard that in Belize too. Must be divers' lingo. "Look, a man on this boat tried to throw me overboard! Shouldn't someone be looking for him?" I scouted all the exits I could find.

"Natalie, I told the captain what you told me. Try to relax," Jason said, coming to my side. I watched as the other man walked away, shaking his head.

"Why doesn't anyone believe me?"

Jason helped me change into the dry clothes we had brought for after the awesome dive I'd missed out on. "Captain will come down to the cabin to talk to you soon, I promise," he said. I had a feeling everyone on the boat thought I was a real loon.

I decided to spread myself out across the same chairs we'd sat in when we first boarded. I needed to lie down. My muscles felt tense and my nerves were raw. I wanted to file a police report when we docked in Cairns. Jason told me that after the captain met with me, he'd take a statement and then they'd want me to be checked out at the local hospital. Totally unnecessary, but too tired to fight, I complied. So far this trip wasn't turning out at all like I'd planned. "Jason, we should be looking for this guy. He had a tattoo . . ."

Kneeling on the ground so he could touch my face, Jason tucked the blankets around me. "The captain sent some crew members to question other passengers. They're investigating. You just lay still. I'm going to try to go down and get some pics for the other divers. I'll come right back. Sound good?" He moved a strand of hair from my face. "The staff and captain will be keeping an eye on you. Not to worry."

I nodded and closed my eyes. "Yes," I whispered. "Thank you." I wanted to do my own search of the ship, but I could barely move. I needed sleep and waved to Jason as he left for the Great Barrier Reef. My gut told me the guy who'd thrown me overboard wasn't on the ship anymore. No one would believe me.

"I'm sorry, ma'am. Nobody who fits that description stepped foot on that boat or the plane," the policeman said as nurses and techs were hooking me up to the monitors at Cairns Hospital.

"What? Well, I don't know what to tell you. He was there. He had me, then let me go. Right into the sea. I didn't imagine it! Check the goddamn flight records! He sat right behind me!"

The words were flying out of my mouth. Neither the captain nor Jason had seen anybody fitting my assailant's description. He'd managed to sneak onto the boat unnoticed, attacked me, and then disappear. How was that possible?

"Maybe all your seasickness did something to your mind," said one young, stupid cop. "I mean, maybe you were—"

"What? Hallucinating? Yeah, I hallucinated that some scar-faced guy with a star tattoo on his hand had me dangling over the front of the boat and then dropped me into the sea. I imagined a man trying to kill me because of seasickness? Get the hell out of here!" I threw a box of tissues that had been on my bedside table at him.

"Natalie, calm down." Jason put his arm around me. "They're just trying to understand what happened. Nobody saw this guy. We're all trying to help you."

"Jason, it happened, I swear it. This is the third time. Remember Belize and the blonde dead woman? That was no mistake. Someone is trying to kill me!"

"Okay miss. Let's take a break here," another policeman said. "My name is Detective Rich and I'll be handling your case. We can finish this conversation down at the precinct and I'll take your formal statement there. Okay?" The detective was tall and thin, with sandy brown hair and a mustache. His eyes were bright blue and warm. I felt like I could trust him. But lately, who *could* I trust?

"Oh, what's the point? It all sounds so stupid." I leaned my head against the pillows and didn't acknowledge the ER doctor who walked in.

"Would you men please excuse us? I need to examine Ms. Ulster." He flung the curtain open and everyone left, including Jason. "Just like your father. Full of passion and pissed off at the world."

I opened my eyes and turned my head. "What? How do you know my father?" Embroidered on the left side of his scrubs read the name William Greene, MD.

"He and I worked on a case together about ten years ago. The woman from the U.S. Army who'd been shot in the back while on her tour in Afghanistan. Remember?" Dr. Greene pushed his wire-rimmed glasses up on his nose and ran a hand over his graying crewcut.

"I remember. You guys made national news. The heroic Dr. Ulster and Dr. Greene, who saved a United States hero from becoming a paraplegic. My dad hadn't fully lost it then. Still had his head in the game." I fiddled with my heart monitor wires and untangled the oxygen gauge attached to my finger.

"He and I have kept in touch ever since. I know things aren't great, but he is a good guy. Does he know you're here?"

"Hell no. He and I only speak out of necessity these days. Ever since Mom . . . well, he's never been the same."

Dr. Greene sat down next to me. He placed his stethoscope on my chest and shined a light in my eyes. "Everything looks good here. What do you want me to do?"

"I want to get out of here. Please." Dr. Greene seemed like a nice man and I knew I was being a pain in the ass.

"Can I call him? Your father? He should know, Natalie."

"I don't care. Just discharge me, please." I wanted to cry even though I felt fine. I had shit to do.

The doctor smiled. "You're a lot like him, you know that?" He stood up, flipped through my chart and scribbled something in it. "All right, you're free to go. Wait until they come and unhook first, okay?"

I stopped pulling the tape off my IV. "Fine," I said, crossing my arms over my chest.

After the hospital and a quick stop at the precinct, I boarded a plane back to Sydney. Alone. Jason had stayed with me through most of it but his job didn't end for another two days and I wanted to get as far away from that place as I could. I wanted to leave Australia. Now. I had been scheduled for three more days at the hospital and I didn't know if I could get out of it. I had signed a contract and it would cost me a fortune to change my plane ticket. So I was stuck.

Detective Rich listened to my story. I told him about everything from the beginning, starting with Betty, back in Denver, up until today. He took notes and didn't ask too many questions. He told me they'd look into her whereabouts, but without firm proof that the guy I described knew Betty, they couldn't do much. They'd keep a lookout for the scarred guy, but he had probably slipped out of the country as anonymously as he'd boarded the plane. None of what he said gave me any comfort. They wouldn't be able to find Betty or this guy and I'd be looking over my shoulder forever, everywhere I went. If only I hadn't lied to cover up Betty's mistakes. She would've gotten fired and moved on to another hospital. Far away from me. I never would've taken care of her husband and we both would've gone our separate ways. But no. I had to have some sort of drama around me all the damn time! Why couldn't things just be normal for a change? I leaned my head back against the seat and closed my eyes. Only in sleep could I escape this shit for a little while.

I decided I'd honor my commitment here in Australia, but then I needed to go. I needed to call Peggy and let her know I planned to apply to Marisdale for a permanent job. I wanted to go back to Arizona. My feelings for Jason weren't strong enough to stay and my travel bug had already fizzled out. I'd deal with Jason later. Right now, Peggy and my future were my priorities.

Peggy told me they could assign me to a temporary travel

spot back in the ICU until I could secure a permanent place. That way, I'd have a place to stay while I got things finalized. *I don't want to do this anymore, Mom. Death has been looming over me ever since you left. I don't know how much time I have, but I know for the last several months, I've stared mortality down and defeated it. Who's to say I wouldn't be able to do that with cancer? I've been running from a diagnosis I've yet to be given, instead of nursing the one I already have. Grief. It's time to start healing.*

# 17

I sat down for report and looked at my patient's face sheet, the front page of the chart with all the patient's personal information on it. I was surprised at how young Mrs. Joan Irwin was. I wasn't used to a forty-eight-year-old being on a ventilator in the ICU. She was way too young. The night nurse had told me the patient preferred to be called Joan, not Mrs. Irwin; otherwise she felt old. That made me laugh, grateful for a patient with a sense of humor, especially after caring for Mr. Peyton. Poor Mr. Peyton. I didn't want to think about him anymore. I needed to get through these next few days without any crap.

Joan, a yoga instructor, had been here almost three weeks, two of them spent in a coma. She had been brought in with a severe case of pneumonia. Normally, this could have been treated with antibiotics and resolved over a few weeks, but for some reason, Joan had continued to get sicker. After her husband had brought her to the hospital in severe respiratory distress, she was diagnosed with Staphylococcus pneumonia, which is very resistant to several antibiotics and can potentially be fatal. Her kidneys had shut down and the infection got into her bloodstream.

Whenever a patient is in the ICU for more than one week, it is in everyone's best interest to maintain continuity of care, meaning the management tries to assign the same nurses to a patient as much as possible. When the same nurses familiarize themselves with the patient and their family over a period of weeks, the patient is more comfortable. The family is more trusting, there are not as many errors in communication to other healthcare providers, and most importantly, the patient feels a bond to the nurses that improves his or her overall well-being. Unfortunately, most of Joan's nurses were either sick or had gone on vacation, so I became her new nurse. Before I went in to care for her, I wanted to make sure I knew all the details of her history, as if I had been caring for her all along.

Reading her chart, I learned that Joan had overall been very healthy. She had no underlying medical issues and she taught yoga five days a week. She was married with one son. She had gone to see her primary care physician a month ago for a cold and was given antibiotics. She worsened over the next week and her breathing began to suffer. When her husband brought her to the ER, her oxygen levels were so low that she required an oxygen mask. Things went downhill from there. With low oxygen, her organs began to fail—first her kidneys, then her heart—then infection took over and went into her blood. When her kidneys shut down dialysis was started to remove the excess waste from her blood. Then her heartbeat became irregular putting her at risk for a heart attack or stroke. In order to reduce the strain on her lungs and heart, she had been placed into a medical coma.

After two weeks on a respirator, Joan had finally begun to stabilize. Her heart rate returned to a normal rhythm and her kidneys started to function on their own again. It was time to wake Joan up. But when a patient has been on a ventilator for more than two weeks it's standard procedure for doctors to give the patient a tracheostomy. The breathing tube is removed from the mouth, an incision is made through the trachea, and an opening is made in the neck. This allows more mobility for the patient and they can begin to get out of bed. It is also easier to clear away secretions and reduces the risk of infection. Although the trach is usually temporary, it's a bit scary for patients and their families to see a huge hole in the patient's throat. They can't speak and there is a significant amount of pain.

Over the past two days, Joan had started improving. Her pneumonia had resolved and the doctors wanted to begin weaning her off the ventilator. I would be responsible for getting Joan ready to have the trach removed. I imagined myself in her shoes. How frightening it would be to wake up with a tube down your throat in unfamiliar surroundings with medical personnel all around you. Then, after the tube was pulled out of your neck, having to relearn swallowing, talking, and breathing on your own. I was determined to make her feel as comfortable and unafraid as I possibly could. I wanted to be the best nurse I could be for her. I don't know if it was because she was so young or the fact that she had been used to a core group of nurses and I would be new to her. I just wanted her to have my all and I wanted to end this horrible stay in Australia on a positive note. Then, I'd be out of here.

I walked into Joan's room and saw her husband sitting in a chair holding both her hands, with his head on her lap. She was sound asleep. The humming of the IV pumps and her heart monitor were the only sounds in the room. I pulled the curtain around the bed and Mr. Irwin lifted his head.

"Good morning, sir. My name is Natalie. I'm your wife's nurse today."

"You're American. What a nice change. Please, call me Jim," he said as I smiled at the similar dialect.

"A fellow countryman, nice. Where are you from?" I asked. It felt good talking to someone from the homeland. I missed being back in the U.S. even more. With just that little conversation between us, I felt comforted and among friends.

Mr. Irwin stood up and stretched. He looked tired. He had on a wrinkly white polo shirt with khaki shorts and white tennis shoes. His graying brown hair was disheveled. He must've stayed the night with her. "We're from California but have been living out here two years now. My job brought us to Sydney but Joan's been wanting to go back."

"Me too. I'm originally from Colorado. I'm a travel nurse, here two weeks, and I'm ready to go home. It's killing me." No pun intended.

"Well, nice to have you. Joan will love the fact that you're from the U.S. I'm going to go home for a bit and get cleaned up. She's a fighter. I know the plan is to get the trach out. She's ready for that. We both are. I'll be back in a bit for some moral support." Jim moved toward the door, winking at me. "Take good care of her; she's my Joan," he said to me as he left.

"Will do. I'll be here when you get back." I waved from the computer monitor at the head of Joan's bed. Nice man. I needed a little niceness.

I flipped on the lights and opened the blinds to let the sun stream in. Joan slowly opened her eyes. There was a collection of sputum and mucus around her trach.

"Good morning, Joan. My name is Natalie. I'm your nurse today. I'm going to suction you out real quick and get you cleaned up. We've got to start working on getting that trach out. Okay?" I asked, leaning over so she could see me clearly.

Joan nodded, and I could see her smiling. Jim was right; she was happy to see and hear me. I opened the sterile wrapping with the cannula in it. Trachs are not my favorite things to take care of. They're messy with all the secretions oozing around the incision, and the skin underneath can be broken down from the constant moisture. It's very cumbersome for nurses and the patient. But we were going to get Joan's trach out. I was determined. I slid the suction catheter down the trach and all sorts of vacuum sounds filled the room. Joan coughed silently, as anybody would when a tiny tube is being shoved down your throat. When I was done suctioning, I removed the gauze that was soaked with mucus and blood, cleaned the surrounding inflamed, red skin, and then placed a fresh, dry piece of gauze around the tube.

I went to Joan's side and started explaining to her what we were going to do. She had been on a couple of liters of oxygen to help her out when she was asleep. We were going to stop that and see how well she did on room air. Then we could start with extubation. I asked the ward clerk to page the respiratory therapist and let them know we wanted to get this done as soon as possible. Joan's eyes opened wide and were darting all over the room as I relayed the plan. After several weeks of being supported by an artificial airway, she was probably scared to have it taken away.

I took her hand in mine. "I'll be right here with you the whole time. You can do this. I need you to stay with me and do what I say, okay?"

Joan took a deep inhale and nodded, yes. She squeezed my hand, then pointed to a whiteboard lying against the countertop. I walked over and grabbed it, handing it back to Joan.

*Want stupid tube out*, she scribbled. Not only had Joan lost her gross motor movements, but her fine motor skills were gone as well, so her handwriting had suffered. She was in for a long recovery consisting of physical and occupational therapy, but at least she was alive.

I laughed at what Joan had written and told her I agreed. We'd work on it all day today and if she did well, she'd be ready to go tomorrow morning. I finished the rest of my assessment and stepped out of her room. I told Joan and the respiratory therapist that we'd take off her oxygen in a little bit.

An hour later, Joan's husband returned and we started the

room air trials. Joan was holding her own and remaining calm. The pulmonologist didn't want to rush things because if a trach is removed too early and the trial fails, the tube goes right back in and they don't try again for another few weeks. We were going to keep her off oxygen supplementation during the night, and if she remained stable, we'd take everything out tomorrow. I let the charge nurse know I wanted to be with Joan for the remainder of my stay. I liked her and wanted to be the one to get her talking and eating again. I wanted to be her hero. After what had been going on with me lately, I was feeling very vulnerable and I needed to succeed with Joan. If Superman wouldn't come to my rescue, then I needed to feel like a superhero myself. I couldn't take another failure, not in my personal life, and certainly not in my professional one.

My mother had been a little younger than Joan when she died. I didn't want Jim and his son to suffer as my family had. Not if I could help it.

Back at my hotel, I only wanted rest. Jason had been leaving me messages. I tried calling him but he didn't answer. Probably on a dive somewhere. I'd try again tomorrow. My incoming e-mail binged and I clicked on my inbox. Joel. A smile came across my face. Perfect timing. Someone to talk to.

*To: naticurn@cable.com*
*From: jlansy@yahoo.com*
*Subject: You*
*Hey, you. If the traveling thing is starting to wear you down as per your last e-mail, then maybe you should stop. I've been looking at other options myself. Private practice maybe. I'm getting tired of the hospital thing. And I'm not working out as hard as I used to. It's more fun when you're in the water with me.*
*See ya, Joel*

I had one hand over my mouth, covering my smile. Should I tell him I was thinking about permanently coming back? He had a right to know. I chose my words carefully and replied.

> *To: jlansy@yahoo.com*
> *From: naticurn@cable.com*
> *Subject: Re: You*
> *It's good to hear from you, you have no idea. Just wanted to let you know I've got an interview next Thursday with the nurse manager of the ICU. I'm looking at staying in Marisdale. I'll try to find you when I come in. We shall see what happens . . . Until then, Nat*

That should get me through the next few days. I would be going back to the States where I could get my shit together. I needed to find the detective's card from Denver and let him know what my thoughts were about Betty and my near-death episodes. I couldn't live like this—always looking over my shoulder, moving from place to place. I wanted it all to stop.

My second day with Joan was devoted entirely to getting the trach tube out and getting her up and moving. The minute I walked into her room she waved at me and smiled. The night nurse told me Joan had had a great night and had remained off oxygen. All things were a go. As usual, the room had been left a mess. Cleanliness is not a high priority among night nurses and I started tidying up so we would have room to work. The respiratory therapist came by and told me we were going to pull the trach by ten o'clock. The lung doctor would be making rounds then and it would give me some time to get ready.

"You ready for this?" I asked Joan.

She gave me a thumbs-up and picked up her whiteboard to write. *Can I get cleaned up? Feeling gross. Want to be clean when I get up to walk.*

I smiled. This woman couldn't wait to get out of bed. How refreshing! Most times I have to push patients to start moving because they can become such slugs. Not Joan. I grabbed the washbasin, some washcloths, soap, and lotion. I filled the basin with warm, soapy water and dropped some cloths in there. I brought it over to Joan and wrung one out, ready to start on her face. Joan touched my wrist and shook her head no. She wanted to do it herself. I handed over the wash stuff and let her go at it, thinking, *I love this woman. She is the symbol of strength.*

By ten o'clock, we were ready. I sat Joan up high in bed and told her husband he could sit by her side and hold her hand. Someone from respiratory and speech therapy, plus the pulmonologist, came into the room. The pulmonologist was a big, tall, balding man with bright blue eyes who actually smiled as he introduced himself to me. Nice. Most doctors would come in, bark some orders, and not give a rat's ass what their patient's nurse's name was. But not Dr. Townhouse, or Dr. T, as the other nurses called him. He reminded me in a way of my dad. When I used to go on rounds with him as a kid, he'd always introduce himself to the nurses and then proudly introduce me. I missed that.

Dr. T gave the signal and I grasped Joan's hand and got right in front of her face. I explained that they would be pulling her trach out and her breathing would be a bit weird for a little while but we would all help her through it. For the last three weeks, Joan had had something in her mouth or throat doing the breathing for her. Soon she would be on her own. The respiratory therapist told Joan to blow real hard as he pulled the cannula out from her neck. I quickly grabbed a four-by-four gauze and covered the gaping hole. I looked at Joan to see how she was doing. Once again, she gave me the thumbs-up.

I stepped out of the room with Dr. Townhouse once we

knew Joan was doing okay and walked with him to the nurse's station. He told me I would have to watch her very closely and then try to get her out of bed and moving around. I told Dr. T that would be no problem. He closed the chart and put a hand on my shoulder.

"You're a very attentive nurse, Natalie. You're going to be great for Joan. We need to get her out of here before she starts getting 'ICU-itis'." Being cooped up in an ICU for several weeks can drive anybody crazy. Just look at Betty. *Not funny, Natalie.* Dr. T continued, "She's too young to be going through this and I know you'll do real well with her. Call me for anything."

Wow. I don't take compliments very well, but this made me feel good. "Thanks. I'm only being good to her because she's American," I said over my shoulder, winking. Dr. T left, laughing a deep, barrel laugh.

On my last day, my goal was to get Joan to dangle her legs off the side of the bed and eventually start walking. Her husband had brought in some pajamas that we put on her in place of the hospital gown. If a patient can begin to feel human and more functional instead of like an invalid, the recovery process goes much faster. I was grateful I had been given the opportunity to be Joan's nurse through all of this. If we were successful in keeping her off the trach and could transfer her out, all our work would be worth it. I would be going home tomorrow and I wanted to be the one to send Joan off. Both of us would move on to bigger and brighter things . . . hopefully.

After about three rounds of dangling off the bed and Joan getting too fatigued to go on, I laid her back down and told her I'd be right outside charting. She could always try again tomorrow. Joan asked if I'd be back tomorrow and I told her no. She asked that I give her an hour to rest and we'd try again, right before shift change. I was fine with that, but told her she didn't have to.

"She likes you," Jim said. "She wants to do this with you."

"Okay, no problem. I'm all yours. Just tell me when you're ready." I closed the curtain behind me and sat down at the computer. For the first time during this whole trip, I felt content.

An hour later, Joan was on her feet. I had my arms linked underneath hers and the two of us were face to face, practically dancing. We smiled at each other and I walked with Joan slowly, to a mirror. I wanted her to see her progress up close. Even though most people would be horrified to look at themselves after almost a month of hospitalization, I wanted Joan to see how far she had come and how tall she was now standing. I moved to the side of her and let her look. She smiled through her tears and turned to look at her husband. He too, was tearful. He came to the other side of her and placed his arm around her shoulder. The three of us stood there looking at Joan's reflection. Empowerment filled the room. For a brief second, I had to remind myself that these were not my parents.

"Well, there you go. You are one beautiful woman," I said. "In no time, you'll be doing sun salutations and downward-facing dogs. You're going to have your life back."

Joan put her head on my shoulder. "Thank you," she whispered. The three of us stood there basking in her radiant glow. She closed her eyes, relishing the moment. Joan's son walked into the room.

"Mom! Oh my God!" He came running over to her. I loosened my hold on Joan and handed her over to her son and husband. They needed some time alone. Family time. As much as I wanted to be included, it wasn't my place. I had my own family I needed to go home to, no matter how fractured we were. I briskly strode out of the room, blinking the tears away.

After I gave the night nurse report, I poked my head back into Joan's room to say good-bye. We hugged each other a little longer than necessary.

"I'm so glad I had you as my nurse," Joan whispered. Her voice's full potential would not come back for several months. "I miss America so much and you gave me a little piece of it. Thank you."

"It's been a pleasure, Joan. You and your family are so kind and loving, I needed that. It's been lonely out here. You're going to be fine and by this time next year, it'll be as if none of this happened."

We hugged again, and I waved to her as I left her room. After all that had happened, at least I could leave Sydney knowing I had started this woman on her way to recovery and that felt pretty damn good. I could walk out of St. Vincent's with my head held high.

Back at my room, there was a message from Jason. He wanted to take me to dinner tonight before I left in the morning. I liked Jason. We'd had fun together and it had been nice knowing someone in these foreign places. But over the last few days I had decided I wanted stability and I knew that Jason was not the one for me to be with. A big piece was missing from our relationship. I hopped in the shower and threw on some jeans and a T-shirt. We'd planned to meet at a little bar outside the hotel with views of the Sydney Bridge and Opera House. One last look at this gorgeous city.

Jason was sitting at the bar when I walked in and I sat on the stool next to his.

"Hi. Is this seat taken?" I smiled, sidling up to him.

"Hey, you. What do you want to drink?"

"Just a beer, thanks. How are you?" I asked, putting my hand on his shoulder.

"I'm good. Just got another assignment in Thailand. Awesome waters. Can't wait." Jason took a sip of beer. He kept bouncing one knee, avoiding eye contact.

"That sounds fun," I said, sprinkling salt on my cocktail napkin so the beer bottle wouldn't stick to it.

"What about you? You're leaving tomorrow." He finally looked at me.

"Yeah. I'm leaving."

After an awkward moment of silence, Jason said, "So what's going on with the attack? Have you gotten anywhere with that?"

"No. I'm going to get some help when I get back home, before my next assignment. I'll get to the bottom of it. Somehow."

More silence. What had changed? Was it because of the whole boat incident or something else? It was like Jason didn't know how to act with me anymore. There weren't many words between us. Then again, there hadn't been many words between us since we'd met. I put my beer down and looked at him, waiting for him to speak.

"Natalie, I . . . I want you to know that when I first met you, I thought you'd like traveling around the world and playing around with me. But I don't think that's what you want anymore, is it?"

"What makes you say that?" It was true, but how had he seen it?

"You're bothered by your family and things at work. You don't let things go. It's like you have unfinished business back home and until you settle it, you won't be happy. When you're with me . . . you're not really with me."

"You're right. I realize I don't want to spend my life traveling from one place to another. I thought I did, but I don't. I can't keep running."

"Yeah, got that." He motioned for another beer.

I raised my hand and turned Jason's face to look at me. "Look, don't feel like you're dumping me. We both know this isn't going to work. It's okay; I had fun."

Jason silently nodded. I wasn't feeling very hungry anymore and thought this would be a good time to leave. It would be too uncomfortable eating together half in silence, the other half making small talk—not after all that had happened between us. I kissed Jason's cheek and whispered "thank you" in his ear. I was thankful he had been there when I needed a friend, and for the experiences I might never have had if I hadn't met him. Who'd have ever thought I'd see manatees in Belize or visit the Great Barrier Reef? I slid off the barstool and grabbed my purse. Jason reached for my hand and held it to his lips for a very long time. I flashed him a wide grin and walked out of the bar and out of Jason's life.

The captain came on the loudspeaker and notified us we were arriving in Los Angeles. One more plane trip to get home. I began to cry. So many years I've been running from my mother's death, running from my father, and keeping everybody at a distance. It's hard to try to take on the world alone. I didn't want to do it anymore. I was tired. Smearing away the wetness on my cheeks, I knew where I wanted to be. I had been happiest in Arizona. The climate was beautiful, the hospital was great, and so were most of the people. There was nowhere else to run to, and no reason to look. It was time to start living.

# 18

Two weeks later I met with Detective Harris in Colorado, the guy who'd taken over Betty's case after her husband died. Judy had tracked down his number for me. I had put together my own summary of events, starting with the day I took over the care of Mr. Watson and finishing up with the day Pock-Face had thrown me off the boat into the Great Barrier Reef. I wanted Betty and the goons she'd hired to get caught and be locked up forever. I didn't want to live life on the edge anymore, always wondering when the next attack would be. Or if they'd try again to kill someone or something I cared about. I couldn't wait to find out. The police had to help me.

"I'm sorry, Ms. Ulster. We're still looking for her, of course, but we haven't had any good leads for several weeks now. She's ... elusive." Detective Harris frowned.

"So what am I supposed to do? Wait until the next hoodlum finds me? The next time may be his lucky day! I'm tired of this!" I threw my hands up in the air.

"We're doing everything we can," the detective said, placing a hand on my shoulder.

"Well, that's just not good enough. Let's hope the next case you're on doesn't have me, covered by a white sheet, in a morgue drawer." I grabbed my messenger bag and flung it across my shoulder so hard I knocked over a cup of pens on his desk. I sat there looking at the pens spilled all over the floor, then looked back up at the detective, fighting back tears. I had to get out of there.

"I promise to call you the minute something comes up," he said as I fumbled for the doorknob. My nerves were shot.

I turned around and glared at him. "Whatever." I shut the door firmly behind me.

Sitting in my car with my hands and head on the steering wheel, I started crying. The police weren't going to do shit. I had to do it myself. If only I could hire someone to help me . . .

Then I remembered. Karen, my good friend from Porter's, had once told me she'd hired a private investigator to find her ex and get her child support payments. She'd told me the investigator was real shady, but had done a great job.

Taking out my phone, I dialed Karen's number with shaking fingers. "Hey, Nat," she said. Good ol' caller ID.

"Oh, I'm so glad you answered," I said, wiping my face and sniffling.

"What's wrong? What happened?"

"Nothing. Well . . . a lot." My voice trembled. "Look, I'm going to be moving to Arizona soon. I don't have a lot of time, but I need to ask you something."

"Whoa, whoa. You're moving? For good? What happened with the travel thing? Natalie, what's going on? You're scaring me."

Taking a deep breath, I calmed down. "Karen, a lot has happened since I started traveling . . . " I didn't know how much I should tell her. Screw it. I needed to tell someone. "Do you remember Betty?"

"Yeah. You were taking care of her husband when he died. The police arrested her, but then she skipped bail. Haven't heard anything about her since. Why?"

*Here we go.* "Betty's after me, Karen. I can't prove it, but I know it's true. I implicated her by going to Judy and somehow Betty knows it. She saw me walk into his room after she did whatever she did to him. Now she's after me and the police are worthless."

"What do you mean, *after* you? Are you in danger?"

"Three separate times, all while I've been traveling, suspicious accidents have occurred. I won't go into detail, but trust me, Karen, I'm not wrong."

"Okay, I hear you. What can I do to help? And why aren't the police helping you?"

"They're good for nothing," I said. "But you, on the other hand, once told me about a private investigator. You said he helped you."

"Sonny Merchant? Oh Natalie, are you sure you really want to go there? Working with someone like that makes you feel . . . dirty. You know what I mean? He's kinda slimy and I was desperate."

"And I'm not?" My voice rose. "Sorry. Karen, please. I'm running out of options."

"Okay. I'll get you in touch with him. But I'm coming with you. Let's meet at the Fourth Avenue Café, by the hospital, and we'll go together tomorrow. I'll call and let him know I'm bringing you by, okay?"

Breathing a sigh of relief, I said, "Thank you so much. See you soon."

So it had come down to me taking matters into my own hands and contacting a private investigator. How had I gotten to this point? Where the hell is *Magnum, P.I.* when you need him?

The next day Karen and I drove downtown to meet Sonny Merchant. Tom Selleck, this guy was not. Sonny made my skin crawl. His office resided in a two-story brick building with torn yellow awnings out front. A liquor store and an STD clinic flanked the building. Karen and I climbed the stairs, my flip-flops sticking to the gunk on each step. I could hear the suck of my feet lifting out of the grime. Disgusting. Where had Karen found this guy? It appeared that other tenants in the building had paid a few extra bucks to make their space more presentable, displaying a welcome mat or an even coat of paint, but not Sonny. Standing outside his office it appeared to me that he didn't give a shit about decor. His office door had a crack in the glass and part of his name had peeled off. Walking through the half-open door, Karen tapped a knuckle on the glass to announce our presence. I gently pushed through and noticed one window that let in streaks of light between the bent, cockeyed plastic blinds. A big wooden desk with a small wooden chair on four wheels stood empty, and behind it hung a huge collection of newspaper articles describing solved cases. I could only assume Sonny had helped solve them. There were murder cases, kidnapping cases, robbery cases—you name it. Maybe this guy did know his stuff.

Karen whispered, "He should be here. I called him right after I hung up with you. Sonny?" The two of us looked at each other. Karen shook her head as I ran my fingers through my hair.

"Yo ho ho! Be right out," someone shouted from behind a closed door. Karen took my hand and squeezed it.

A few minutes later, Sonny came out, rubbing his nose and a thick, brown mustache with his thumb and forefinger. A puff of white dust flew into the air. What the . . . ? Who was this guy?

"Hi, Sonny. It's me, Karen. I called you yesterday? You snagged my son-of-a-bitch husband a few years back."

"Karen! How the hell are ya?" Sonny reached to hug her and Karen responded halfheartedly, barely touching him but relaxing in his embrace.

"Um, hi," I said, clearing my throat to get his attention. Sticking out my hand to shake his, I said, "I'm Natalie." *Do not hug me, please.*

"Right, right, right. Karen mentioned you needed some help. You're a tiddle early, little ladies." Sonny sat down at his desk, still sniffing and wiping his nose. He reached down and pulled out a flask, took a swig, and put it back. I stared at him. Karen cleared her throat. He had a long braid down the back of his head, a huge potbelly and wore army-fatigue cargo shorts, a wife beater undershirt, and a black, satiny jacket with a scorpion on the back. Total class.

"Well, don't just stand there. Sit your asses down." He motioned to two bridge chairs, both with torn cushions. Eww. Did we have to?

We both sat down gingerly. "I brought this for you to look at. It outlines what's been going on over the past few months with descriptions of the nurse who's after me and descriptions of the guys she's hired to kill me." I handed the portfolio across the desk.

Sonny breezed through the papers, then slammed it shut. He sat there, both hands on the folder, staring at me. Karen nudged my elbow and nodded, urging me to press him.

"Do you think you can help me?" I leaned forward toward his desk.

Sonny let out a barrel laugh. "Oh, little missy, I know I can help you. I've got connections. Bad connections. Some good, but most of them bad. Anyhoo, I've heard of Mr. Watson before. Gangsta," Sonny said, making some kind of gang sign with his hands.

"I just want this to stop. I never did anything to deserve this, other than cover up her fuck-ups. It was just my bad luck that I took care of her husband the day she killed him. That's it. Now she wants me dead."

"Wrong place at the wrong time," Sonny said, tsk-tsking with his tongue. "I don't do this shit for free, you know."

"I know. What are we looking at?"

Karen interrupted. "I hope you'd be as generous and fair to my friend here as you were to me."

Sonny leaned back in his chair and folded his hands behind his head. My God, those wheels were going to bust right off. The chair squeaked as he began to swivel back and forth and back and forth. "I felt sorry for you, Karen. You too . . . Naomi, is it?"

"Natalie," I said.

"Right. Because you're a friend of a past client, let's say . . . thousand bucks now and then we'll talk. If you'll excuse me, I've got a lady friend waiting for me." He glanced sideways toward the door he'd come out of.

"A thousand? Shit." I didn't have that much. "Will five hundred work for now? I'll get you more soon. Please, Sonny." I'd have to figure how to come up with the rest.

"The number grows bigger as I get closer," Sonny said, in a Vincent Price sort of way, lifting his eyebrows up and down like a crazy person. I looked at Karen, wondering how the hell she'd come up with this guy.

"Sonny," Karen interjected. "Settle down. Take the five hundred. I promise, she's good for the rest. What happens next?"

I didn't wait for him to answer. "Should I call you or what? How will I know what's going on?" I hesitated about handing him the money. If not for Karen, no way in hell would I ever put my trust in Sonny Merchant. But I loved Karen, and if she said this guy was good, I believed her.

"Give me a week to gather some 4-1-1," Sonny said, folding a stick of gum into his mouth.

"4-1-1?" I asked.

"Yeah, sweets. Information. You know, 4-1-1."

"Oh. Yeah, right. Okay. Well, I'll give you a week and then I'll give you the other five hundred. I'm moving to Arizona tomorrow and I've got to know how I can reach you."

"I'll find you, 'cuz that's what I do," he said, smirking.

*Oh my God.* "On that note, Mr. Merchant, we're out of here." Karen and I stood up. Luckily, I'd brought with me the cash I'd withdrawn after closing my bank account. I shelled out five hundred bucks and set it on the desk. "One week!" I yelled over my shoulder as I grabbed Karen and booked it out of his office.

"Bye, Sonny! Nice to see you again," Karen said, telling me to slow down.

I locked the door to my old apartment and began walking down the stairs with the last of my cartons. My stuff covered the back window of my car and a long drive to Arizona lay ahead.

For the most part, Colorado had been good to me. I'd had a happy childhood, for a little while, and my parents had given me everything, but now I needed to move on. I'd gotten everything out of Colorado that I could. I placed the carton in the car and, just as I slid into my seat and put on my seat belt, my dad knocked on the window, startling me. I debated whether to drive off or get out of the car. I rolled the window down halfway. Better to keep up a barrier.

"What?"

"Can you get out of the car, please? So we can talk?"

"We haven't 'talked' in years. Why now?" I turned the key in the ignition.

"Please, Nat. I got a call from Dr. Greene, in Australia. You're in some trouble." His hands were gripping the window.

"Nothing I can't handle." I revved the engine simply for the purpose of being a smartass.

My dad reached in and put his hand on the wheel. "Wait. I want to help you. Please."

"I don't need your help. You've done nothing for me for the last thirteen years. Alcohol and self-pity were the only things you were interested in." I looked up at him, angry at myself for my stinging eyes.

"Natalie, please. Can you at least give me your address or let me call you when you get there? I can't bear to lose you, too. Please," he pleaded.

I stared at him. I didn't even recognize him anymore. He looked tired, stressed, and much older than I remembered. His hair was more gray and there were wrinkles and dark circles around his eyes. Grabbing the notebook I kept in the glove compartment, I ripped off a piece of paper, wrote down my new address, and stuck it through the window opening. He reached for the paper but I didn't let go. We just looked at each other and I saw the pain in his eyes. The same pain I've seen in mine. I wanted to rip his head off, but then I remembered he was my dad, and it hadn't always been like this between us.

"I need some time to get settled. I've hired a private investigator. I'll know more in a few weeks. You can call me then," I told him, letting go of the paper.

"Thank you. Please be safe. I love you, Natalie."

I rolled up the window and floored the gas as he backed away. I glanced in the rearview mirror and saw my dad standing in the same spot, watching me drive away. Both our hearts breaking for the second time, together.

Even at six-thirty in the morning it was hot as hell, like breathing in a four hundred-and-fifty-degree oven. Why had I moved to Arizona in the summertime?

Before I could start full-time in the ICU at Marisdale, I had to go through two days of orientation. Yawn. The good news was, I'd get paid for it, but I couldn't wait to start working on the floor.

Luckily I found a nice apartment close to the hospital, similar to the one I'd stayed in when I worked for the travel nurse company. Lots of water features, palm trees, Spanish architecture, with red roofs and stucco.

My little one-bedroom apartment had a view of the courtyard. A large, three-tiered water fountain splashed continuously outside my balcony. It made a nice, relaxing sound, like a slowly running stream. I left the sliding glass door open so I could hear it. The kitchen was small but modern, with stainless steel appliances and black and gold granite countertops. Saltillo tile and soft beige carpets covered the floor. All I needed were a few live plants and time to totally unpack my stuff and this place would be mine. Knowing me, I'd get everything done in the next few days. For now, though, with all my boxes and nothing on the walls, my apartment felt temporary.

Driving to the hospital, I decided to focus on getting my apartment fixed up. Then I'd get back to swimming and get familiar with my new city. I thought about Mary and Ozzie. Poor Ozzie. *Maybe I should get a dog when I get settled. Hmmm.* Something to think about. I wanted to contact Joel. But first things first: I needed to get through orientation.

I checked in at the reception desk and an elderly volunteer directed me to a conference room. There were several rows of tables and chairs and a PowerPoint slide on a screen with the title "Welcome to Marisdale." I found an open seat next to a pretty Asian girl who was reading through the orientation packet. Appearing to be about my age, she had long black hair tied loosely in a low ponytail and her perfect skin showed off her pretty face.

"Hi. Mind if I sit here?" I asked her.

"Of course not. I'm Mallory."

"Nice to meet you. I'm Natalie. New ICU nurse." We shook hands.

"Really? Me too. What unit?"

"Two, I think. You?"

"The same! How funny. Guess we'll be seeing a lot of each other." Mallory smiled.

"Awesome. Maybe on our break we can go upstairs and look around a bit. I'm glad I found you. It sucks being the new chick. Gets lonely."

"I hear ya. We'll help each other through it."

My anxiety about starting somewhere new again got easier. Mallory seemed nice enough. We'd see if we became friends. Right now, I didn't trust anybody.

Mallory and I got through our two days of orientation and were free to start on the unit. For the next two weeks, we each would be paired with an experienced nurse who would familiarize us with the unit. I didn't need much help because of my travel stint here, but every new nurse needed to be signed off by another nurse before getting set free.

"Hi Natalie, welcome back!" Deb, the charge nurse, said as she met Mallory and me on the unit.

"Thanks! I'm happy to be back." I clutched my critical care reference book to my chest. "Where do you want us?"

"Let's get you two lockers and then I'll pair you with Sally and Emma," Deb said, leading us toward the staff room.

"Can I put in my request for Sally, please?" I said. Mallory looked at me and tilted her head. "Emma and I had some run-ins the last time I worked here."

"Oh, Natalie, I told you not to worry about her. She's a good nurse," Deb said, showing us our lockers.

"I know. I'd rather not deal with her right now." I fiddled with my cuticles.

"So you're going to make me work with her?" Mallory whispered.

"She's never met you before. Me, she met. We don't get along," I whispered back.

"I'll put you with Sally, Natalie. Mallory, you'll be fine with Emma. She's great, just a little sassy at times, but you'll be fine. She likes to orient new nurses to the unit."

*Really?* I didn't remember her like that. She'd wanted to bite my head off. Oh well, Mallory seemed a lot sweeter than me so I was sure she'd do fine with Emma.

"Come on, ladies. Let's get you out there," Deb said as we put our stuff away and headed out to the unit.

My shift ended and it had been a good day. Unfortunately though, I never saw Joel. Sally and I had one stable post-op patient and a transfer from the med-surg floor. I got the hang of the computer charting and Sally pretty much let me do everything. She'd answered questions I had, but otherwise, I did everything. Sally had been at Marisdale for thirty years. An older, overweight woman with a blonde pageboy haircut, Sally wobbled when she walked due to "years of abuse on these knees," and let me do most of the work. She wore white scrubs and the old orthopedic white nurse shoes. She meticulously bathed her patients and their rooms were always spotless, which I loved. Those things seem simple, but it makes the job so much easier and the families like to see their loved ones neat and smelling good.

"We're getting a forty-six-year-old male, pancreatic cancer, into room eleven," Sally told me.

"Ugh. It's almost shift change," I told her, pretend-whining. I didn't mind the admit, but coming so close to shift change, it meant I'd be staying later this evening to tuck him in—which meant getting him into the room, onto our bed, and hooked up to all the machines. It had been a long day and I wanted to go home.

"Come on, let's get to it," Sally said as we went to room eleven to prepare.

Rob Hatcher had just been diagnosed with pancreatic cancer and transferred to us from the OR. He'd had surgery done to remove parts of the pancreas and small intestine. Surgeons say this procedure can buy the patient a few years, but in my experience, with a diagnosis of pancreatic cancer, no matter what is done, death is inevitable. I'd never seen these patients walk out of the hospital and death always seemed a slow and painful process.

Mr. Hatcher remained sedated and on the ventilator when they brought him to the ICU. He had a huge bandage over his abdomen and several IVs running: one for fluid hydration, one for sedation, and one for an antibiotic. Sally placed several heated blankets over him while I hooked him up to our monitors. I labeled all the IV pumps and checked his meds. His sedation would continue throughout the night through tomorrow morning, when they would try to get him off the ventilator. I had two days off after today so I hoped all would go well. The OR nurses told us he had a very nice family and had been very cooperative. It hurt to see this happening to someone so young.

Sally listened as I gave report to the night nurse. I saw Mallory waiting for me. Finishing up fifteen minutes later than shift change I wanted the hell out and felt tired. I had a ton of stuff to do at home.

"Thanks for waiting for me; you didn't have to. We got a late admit," I said to Mallory, grabbing my bag and slinging it over my shoulder.

"Oh, don't worry about it. I've got to wait for my fiancé. He's finishing his rounds upstairs."

"You're engaged to one of the doctors?" I said, grabbing her arm.

"Yeah, Dr. Berkley. A urologist. Why do you sound so shocked?"

"I don't know. Isn't it hard to be with a doctor in a major hospital like this? Aren't you worried about what people say?" We started walking downstairs.

"Why would I care what people say? We're not doing anything wrong. He was single, I was single, and now we're dating. We fell in love and the rest is history." Mallory shrugged her shoulders.

"But don't people talk shit about it? People who don't know anything about you two?"

"If they don't know anything about us, then why would I care if they talk shit? Do you have a problem with this?" Mallory said, stopping and looking at me.

"Oh, God no. I'm sorry. I think it's great; I didn't mean for it to come out that way. I'm friends with a doc here and when we went out once—casually—I became the talk of the ICU. It pissed me off."

"Natalie, this is a hospital and a bunch of the people working here don't have enough going on in their own lives so they bullshit about other people. Who cares? Do what you want to do and stop worrying about what others think." I beamed at her. She sounded so down to earth.

"I've heard that before. Sorry. I didn't mean to put you on the defensive. Sometimes I don't think before I speak. It's a major problem of mine."

Mallory laughed. Thank God. I didn't want to alienate her. I needed a friend and she and I fit together pretty well.

"There he is," she said, and pointed to a tall, young-looking doctor walking down the stairs. "When are you back?"

"I've got two days off. You?"

"I've got tomorrow off, then I'm back. So far Emma's been

okay. We'll see what happens as the week goes on." Mallory nudged me with her elbow.

Her fiancé walked over. He was nice-looking with a great smile and wore jeans and a button-down oxford. He'd hung his stethoscope over one shoulder, not in the usual position around the neck.

"Hey babe, you ready?" he said to Mallory before greeting me.

"Honey, this is Natalie. She started this week with me. We're both on two. Natalie, this is my fiancé, Don Berkley."

I held out my hand. "Nice to meet you," I said, shaking his.

"You too. I'm glad you found a friend," he told Mallory, wrapping his arm around her. He looked a full foot taller than she. "Mallory was hesitant about coming to Marisdale but I thought it would be cool."

Mallory rolled her eyes. "He wants me with him all the time. Probably wants to keep tabs on me," she said, getting on her tiptoes and giving him a kiss on the cheek. "I don't mind too much, actually."

"You were miserable at the other place. So why not come here?" Berkley added.

"Yeah, why not?" I said, agreeing. They seemed like the perfect couple.

"Don't encourage him, please," Mallory said. "Come on, I wanna get home. I'm exhausted."

"Me too," I said. "It's very nice to meet you, Dr. Berkley. Mallory, I'll see you later," I said, leaving them to head toward physician parking while I walked the extra mile to the staff lot.

"Please, call me Don. Nice to meet you, too," he yelled over his shoulder as Mallory waved good-bye.

Nice people. They were making it work. It would be nice to be with a guy who could understand the ins and outs of my job, the patients, and the stress. Someone who wouldn't get grossed out at the mention of bodily fluids. Someone to bounce ideas off of, who I respected, who made me feel safe . . . someone like Joel.

# 19

Sonny stayed true to his word and contacted me one week after our visit, only to tell me he hadn't found out anything yet and would be in touch. He also wanted the other five hundred dollars. He reassured me he'd be working on my case and he'd have answers soon. I couldn't do anything but wait. I told him I'd send the check out that day. Despite my uneasiness about Betty, I forced myself to worry about things I could control and ignore the things I couldn't.

After a few weeks at Marisdale, I settled in. The heat didn't go anywhere but I didn't care. Mallory and I had become close and were spending a lot of time together outside of work as well as working the same days together. Often I felt like a third wheel with Don and her, but she wanted to include me whenever they hung out. They were both so nice and genuine I felt comfortable tagging along.

I thought it strange that I hadn't seen Joel around the unit since I'd arrived. I worried that maybe he'd moved away. I never got his cell phone number so I'd e-mailed him a week after arriving but still hadn't heard anything back. I didn't want to seem needy by sending him another one. He hadn't even been to the pool.

One day, I got up the courage to ask the ward clerk, Lynda,

what had happened to him. She'd worked at Marisdale for so long that they could name a wing after her, and I figured she'd have some information. I prayed he hadn't left.

"Hey," I asked, "so whatever happened to Dr. Lansfield? He seemed pretty cool. There're nothing but stuffed shirts around here lately." That sounded innocent and casual. Harmless question.

"Oh, you didn't hear? He went out on his own and joined a practice right across the walkway. He still comes here to round on his patients when they get admitted." Lynda continued typing away at her computer screen.

"Wow. Good for him." Out on his own. I probably wouldn't see him very much now. Maybe I'd e-mail him and let him know I'd heard about his new job. Maybe he didn't get the first e-mail.

After stopping at the grocery store after work, I returned to my apartment with my arms full of grocery bags. My father was sitting on the steps waiting for me. He wore a suit and his black leather attaché case rested next to him. I stopped halfway up the stairs, shook my head, and then kept walking right past him to my door. I unlocked it, almost lost the bags, caught them on my knee, then pushed the door open with my foot. Setting the groceries down on the counter I turned around.

"You coming in or do you want to stay on the steps all day?"

He got up and came into my apartment. "It's good to see you. Nice place."

"Yeah." We both stared at nothing for a while. To break the silence, I turned toward the kitchen and offered him a drink. "And no, I don't have any Jack Daniels."

"Water will be fine." He started looking around. He picked up my mother's picture and wiped his fingers over the glass. After gently placing it back on the counter, he went to the couch.

"Here you go." After putting my mother's picture back

exactly as I had it, I handed him the glass and sat down next to him. "Why are you here, Dad? The phone works too, you know."

"I wanted to see you. I don't like this . . ." He turned toward me.

"You don't like what? The fact that you and I haven't really spoken in years, or the fact that you let me grow up pretty much on my own, or . . ."

"Natalie! I don't like hearing you're in danger." He sipped the water.

"Okay. Why are you so concerned about my welfare now? Run out of liquor and floozies?" I rubbed my arms.

My dad pinched the bridge of his nose and rested his forehead on his hand. "I'm sorry. When your mother . . ." He looked at the window, right past me.

"Died, Dad; the word is 'died'."

"Damn it, Natalie! I'm trying."

"Look," I went to the front door, my hand on the doorknob. "I spent my whole day caring for sick people, trying to help them overcome illness and avoid death. I don't need to do it with my own father, too. You're supposed to be the one to fix everything, to make it all better. You let us all die, as far as I'm concerned."

"You blame me for your mother's death?" He stood up and came to the door. This conversation needed to end.

"Not for her death. I know you couldn't help her. But you let Jennifer and I go too. You gave up. We were alive, Dad. We were right in front of you. And you chose to hide."

Grabbing my shoulders he said, "Then let me make it right. Let me help you. Please."

Through tears, I yelled, "I haven't needed you in thirteen years and I don't need you now!" I flung the door open and took a step back.

Dad reached for me, then pulled back. "I'm here for a trauma

conference and staying the next few weeks. I'm at the Fairmont."
He walked through the door with slumped shoulders and walked
down the steps. I slammed the door shut behind him.

Three weeks later, I was trying to get through a last shift before
I could get my much-needed three days off. I took care of Rob
Hatcher again but he'd continued to get worse. He had been
in the ICU more than three weeks now and had had several
more abdominal surgeries to fight the spreading pancreatic cancer. Get-well signs and pictures of his family and his Harley
crowded his room.

His parents brought the nurses bagels, muffins, candy—you
name it. The best way to get really good care out of your nurses
is to give them food. We love it. We're being acknowledged for
what we're doing and we're being fed. Awesome.

Rob's parents were in their late sixties and devoted to their
son. They came every day and sat at his bedside, watched TV
with him, and brought him books. They were cornbread, plain,
down to earth, flannel-and-jeans-wearing, nice people. Gladys,
his mom, wore no makeup and had let her short hair go completely white, like her husband Tom's. They reminded me of
characters from the movie *Fargo*. I couldn't understand how they
could sit and watch their son dying day after day and still smile
and be pleasant to all of us.

By the end of my shift, the hospitalist had finally agreed to
consult hospice, for comfort care only, after the last surgeon had
told the family nothing else could be done. Rob's pain would
get worse, and the cancer had grown out of control. His insides
were hollow. His pancreas, spleen, intestines, and half of his liver
were gone. He would need thirty or more pills each morning,
vitamins and hormones his body no longer produced among
other medications, like insulin, to keep his blood sugar under

control. Without a pancreas, diabetes is imminent. But it's all just a Band-Aid. Rob couldn't be fixed and he had no fight left in him. On several occasions he had asked his nurses to give him a "mercy dose of morphine." None of us wanted to see Rob go, but we all knew he and his family were ready. Hospice was called in to make him comfortable and I had a feeling Rob would not be alive by the time I returned in three days.

Once Rob and his parents realized comfort measures made sense, I began shutting off the IVs and removing the EKG pads from his chest. "You okay with all this, Rob? You understand what's going on?" He looked like shit. His skin had turned yellow, his lips were cracked, and his eyes were glazed. He had lost more than forty pounds since being admitted. Gone were the days of riding his motorcycle and wearing leather. His mother came to his side and took his hand.

"I thought you might need this," she said as she tied an American flag bandana around his head like a do-rag. "Now, there's my son." Rob's dad came to her side and wrapped his arm around her.

"Thanks, Mom, Dad. I'm tired. I'm just so tired." Rob leaned his head back down and closed his eyes.

"I'll give him a little morphine right now and then we've got orders to keep giving it around the clock. He won't be in any pain, I promise."

"You've all been so good to him. Thank you," Gladys said, hugging me tight. "He is such a kind, nice man. I know wherever he is going he will be fine. Anything is better than this." How could she do this without falling apart?

"I'm so sorry," I said. "If there is anything else I can do, please let me know." I got a fresh blanket out of the heater and laid it across his body. I then placed my hand on his chest and held it there, sending any positive energy I could right to his core.

It was my way of sending him off, to what I didn't know, but I knew he'd be at peace. I looked at Tom and Gladys, nodded and smiled. I admired how strong they were. Then I walked out of Rob Hatcher's room for the last time.

I had my head down as I walked to the bridge on my way to the parking lot. Saying good-bye to Rob had been hard. The loss of some patients bothers you more than others. I don't know whether Rob's young age had upset me or the fact that he and his family had been so kind. Either way, I felt sad and sorry to see him go. Cancer. Fucking. Sucks. *How much longer before I experience the same fate? That is, if Betty doesn't get to me first. What do I do? Sit around and wait for something to happen?*

"Well, look who the cat dragged back," said a deep, sexy voice. A slow smile came across my face.

"Joel. I mean, Dr. Lansfield. Hi," I said, sighing but trying to remain professional on the hospital grounds. I felt relieved to see him. Fate had finally decided to show her face and I couldn't be more grateful.

"When did you get back?" He leaned against the railing, crossing his ankles and folding his arms.

"A few weeks ago. I tried e-mailing you. I heard you'd gone to private practice and I didn't know whether I should bother you. You haven't been to the pool or in the hospital."

"I've been busy with the new practice and changed my e-mail address. I should've told you. Sorry. Haven't had much time for myself. You look . . . tired. Everything okay?"

"Thanks, thanks a lot." I looked up at him. Falling into his chest seemed like the right thing to do, to have him hold me, but I couldn't bring myself to get any closer. "Can we maybe go out later? I could use the company."

"Yeah, I think I can manage that. I've got a few people to do rounds on here but I can meet you somewhere when I'm done. I've got family in town so I'd have to bring them, too. That okay?"

"Totally fine," I nodded.

"How about that bar around the corner in an hour?"

"Sounds good. I'll run home and change." I stood there smiling up at him like a dork.

"You're crazy." Joel laughed. "I'll see you soon."

I got into my car and breathed. I hadn't realized how much I had missed him.

I had downed a shot of tequila and started sucking on the lime when Joel walked in. I'd needed something strong. Why wasn't Sonny calling me? I couldn't go anywhere in public without scrutinizing every person around me. Were they suspicious looking? Were any of them Betty? Did any of them want to kill me?

I felt like drowning my sorrows tonight. Unfortunately, I probably should've done so alone instead of inviting somebody to join me.

"What're you drinking?" Joel asked, taking a seat across the table from me. Without waiting for me to answer, he said, "Natalie, I'd like you to meet my sisters. Natalie, Rosie and Maria."

Oh shit, his sisters? I'd forgotten his mentioning his family was in town. "Hi, nice to meet you both. I'll have whatever," I told Joel.

"Pitchers of beer, then. You really do look bad." He smiled at me.

"Joel! *Cállate!*" Rosie hit Joel's arm and apologized for him. Maria brayed out a laugh.

"It's okay, I feel like shit. What's that word?"

"*Cállate* means 'shut up' in Spanish. You don't speak Spanish?" Rosie asked, pulling her chair closer to mine.

"You Mexican or what?" asked Maria. She reminded me of Rosie Perez, gum-smacking, loud-speaking, straight-to-the-point chick. Her orange-red dyed hair was gathered loosely in a banana clip while her painted-on, pencil-thin eyebrows rose up above silver eye shadow.

"Guys, guys. Let's not scare the poor girl. Jesus." Joel looked at me with apologetic eyes. "I had to bring them; they gave me no choice."

Laughing, I decided to address their questions. Looking to Maria I said, "I'm ... Jewish. Not Mexican." On to Rosie. "I don't speak any Spanish, sorry."

Rosie and Joel exchanged glances. "Come on, Maria, let's go play some pool." Rosie kicked Maria's leg and the two went off, leaving Joel and me alone.

I looked at him. Tears crammed into my eyes. *Come on, Natalie. Don't be such a wuss.* "It's really nice to see you." The waitress came over to take our drink order.

"We're having a special on Cabo Wabo tequila. Buy one shot, get one free. Can I bring you two some?"

Joel didn't hesitate. "Bring two, please."

"I've already had one. That's probably enough," I said, knowing I didn't want to be kneeling over the porcelain idol later.

A petite redhead with big fake boobs and a tiny T-shirt that had the Cabo Wabo logo on it brought over two shots and two lime wedges. Joel thanked her and handed one to me, raising the other in his hand. I raised my shot and with his free hand, Joel took my other hand and kissed it. "Kisses and shots!" he said, as we both downed the burning liquid.

"Ugh," I told him, forcing it down. "What is that for?" I looked at my hand, still in his.

"It's nice to see you, too."

"There's so much going on right now, Joel. I don't know

where to begin." He didn't say anything, offering me an invitation to continue. Taking a deep breath, I told him about Betty and Sonny Merchant. And my suspicions about Ozzie. And my dad.

"Whoa, whoa, whoa. Someone's out to kill you? And you think they killed the dog? Natalie, we've got to do something!" He started looking around the room as if the FBI were there, waiting for the call.

"Joel, relax. It's no use. I've already tried. The police can't do anything without evidence. They're supposedly working on it. That's what led me to Sonny."

"What about your safety? You're alone in your apartment. Someone needs to be with you." He leaned in closer to me, across the table.

"I'm fine, really. I figured out that Betty used to be on my Facebook and as long as I kept posting my destinations, she kept following me. I've deleted her now. There's no other way she can find me. She probably doesn't even know I'm here."

"Let your dad help you, Natalie. You're not going to be able to afford the PI much longer. It could take him months to solve this case for you. You don't have to do it alone."

"He hasn't been my dad since Mom died. I was a teenager, Joel! Left alone to grieve. I needed him then. I'm fine without him now."

Calmly, Joel took both my hands. "I get that, but he's making an effort. He's got to live with her death, too. And believe me, I know—as a doctor, he feels responsible."

I shook my head. "Would you let someone back in so easily? What if . . . what if *she* showed up at your door and apologized for . . ."

"The abortion? This isn't about me, Natalie."

I crossed my arms, frustrated. I could deal so much easier with this shit alone. There were too many voices swirling inside my head. I preferred only listening to mine, but somehow I knew that wouldn't be enough. Rosie and Maria sidled back to the table when they saw the waitress standing there, ready to take our food orders.

"Sorry you two, but we gots to eat!" Maria said, barking her order to the waitress.

"We'll finish this later," Joel whispered.

Throughout dinner, Joel and his sisters entertained me with stories of when they were kids and how Joel used to piss everyone off; spraying them with hoses as they sat on the porch, hiding up on the roof with eggs ready to aim at Rosie and her boyfriend, or stealing all of their father's attention by scoring touchdown after touchdown for his Pop Warner team. They all seemed so happy, so loving of each other. It was a scene I wasn't familiar with.

"Hey, what do you say we all go back to the house and chill?" Joel said, covering the entire tab.

"Thanks, but I'm going to head on home. This has been fun, really," I said as Rosie wrapped an arm around me.

"Come on. Come with us," she begged.

"I can't. Thanks, though." I picked up my wallet and the four of us walked out.

"I'll call you tomorrow, okay?" Joel said, both hands on my shoulders. I wanted to hug him so badly.

"Sure. Thanks for tonight. I'm glad I got to see you and meet the family." I turned and waved to them, then got in the car.

What a completely shitty day this had been. Back at my apartment, I turned on my playlist and hooked the iPod into the stereo. The familiar sound of the Eagles came on and I went to sit on the balcony and mope. Don Henley's voice sang "Wasted Time" and it echoed in my ears. I listened hard to the words. When I was little, my mom used to play this song over and over. Sometimes, life seems like a waste of time. So what that Rob Hatcher learned to ride a Harley and loved his dog? He was dying. Mr. Peyton had been a high-powered, successful businessman who wore out his heart. At fifty-four! Nicolina had been sixteen when she died. And my mom? My mom got married, had children, and lived happily until one day, gone. What was the fucking point? I envied Joel and his sisters. So happy and full of life. It had been a long time since I'd possessed that feeling. In fact, I thought I'd forgotten the whole idea of family.

I sat there and sobbed until my eyes became swollen and my throat hurt. I went to wash my face and, as I wiped it dry, I looked in the mirror. *Who is this pathetic girl?* One of the neighbors' doors slammed shut and shook the apartment. I heard a crash in the kitchen. My mother's frame had fallen facedown on the floor. I knelt down to pick it up. Luckily, the glass hadn't broken. Wiping away the dust, my eyes connected with my mother's. The hairs on the back of my neck prickled but a sense of calm came over me. *All right, Mom, I hear you.* I placed her picture back on the counter, kissed my fingertips, and pressed them to her face. I went back to the mirror. I hated this sad, tired face looking back at me and so did Mom. I needed to fix it. All of it. I decided to call Sonny and push him to get moving. Then I would call my dad. If he wanted to help, I'd let him. I had come back to Arizona for some stability and a sense of home. I'd do it for Mom. I couldn't give up now. *It's game time. Bring it on.*

# 20

Standing outside his office window, I waved from underneath the tree. It seemed very stalker-ish but I wanted to see Joel. We finally made eye contact and shortly after, he came out.

"What are you doing? Spying on me? You could've come in," he said, pointing to the door. "You okay?"

"Yes, I'm fine. I had to turn in a book to the ICU and wanted to stop by and thank you again for last night."

"The girls liked you," Joel said, crossing his arms in front of his chest.

"Maria's a little crazy but I liked Rosie. She's warm."

"Why don't you stop by my place today? We're having a barbeque. They'd love it if you came. More estrogen to beat me up with."

It sounded nice, but I couldn't. "No. I don't want to intrude on your family visit."

Joel placed his hand on my shoulder. "What other plans do you have?" He raised his eyebrow at me.

"I could have plans; you never know." I placed my hands on my hips.

"Just shut up and come. I'd feel better knowing you're with us. I've got to get back inside."

"I'll try," I told him, waving as he walked back into his office. Part of me really wanted to go. I liked being around him and his family. But I couldn't help feeling like an intruder. Joel didn't need all my shit. Why did he have to be so nice? Why couldn't he leave things as they were and not worry about me? We should be acquaintances and nothing else. Saying no became quite the challenge. Maybe because I really wanted to say yes.

Joel texted me directions to his home, a two-story condo in a quiet little neighborhood. I walked in and noticed how masculine his place looked: black furniture, leather couch, stainless steel appliances. No touch of femininity here. Until now. Rosie came running up and hugged me tight, her huge shelf of breasts squishing my entire upper half. Joel stood outside by the grill with Dr. Winger and Maria was in the kitchen cutting vegetables.

"Here, come get the limes ready with me," Rosie said, pulling me to the kitchen.

"I should probably tell Joel I'm here."

"I'll tell him," Maria said, yelling at the top of her lungs, "Joel, Natalie's here!"

Joel turned around and waved to me through the glass door. I had to hand it to these two; they made me laugh. "Fair enough. What can I do?"

"Cut these for me," Rosie said, handing me a bunch of limes and a knife.

I started cutting the limes in circles. "What's he making out there?"

"Natalie, no!" Rosie ran to me, laughing. "Wedges, silly. Not wheels! Can't fit wheels into beer bottles. Like this," she started cutting the limes in quarters and then in eighths. Maria tsk-tsked in the background.

"Sorry. Maybe someone else should do this?" I put down the knife.

"Nope. You're fine. Go ahead." Rosie stirred the huge pot of beans she had cooking on the stove.

"Hey, there you are. Glad you made it," Joel said, kissing the top of my head.

"Yeah. I've been getting lessons on lime cutting." I showed him my perfect pile of the citrus slivers.

"Let's eat!" Dr. Winger said, bringing in a huge plate of beef.

We sat together outside: Joel and Winger, his two sisters, and myself, drinking beers and laughing. I couldn't remember laughing so hard. His sisters were a kick. Crazy, but very entertaining. Dr. Winger and Maria excused themselves to the bedroom and Joel went outside to clean the grill.

"What's that about?" I whispered to Rosie.

"Oh, them? We've known Winger a long time. Maria likes to get her fill every time we come."

I laughed. "This has been fun."

"It has," Rosie touched my hand. She took a swig of beer.

"Do you have any kids?" I asked.

"Two. They're both grown up now. I lost one son when he was eleven."

"What? How?" I scooted closer to Rosie.

"Leukemia. He died less than a year after being diagnosed."

"I'm so sorry, Rosie. I was a teenager when I lost my mom." I peeled the label off my Bud Light bottle. How did she do it? "You seem so . . . happy."

"Well, what else is there? The pain never goes away but I know he's in a better place."

"Why do people say that? 'In a better place.' He's not with you. That doesn't make sense to me." I leaned back against my chair, folding my arms in front of me and breathing fast.

"God has a plan for us all. He knows what he's doing."

"Sorry, Rosie. I don't buy that."

"Well, sweetie, it gets me through the day. Don't get me wrong. It's the worst thing any mother, or child, should have to go through. My heart will never be the same, but I have to go on living." She swallowed hard and blinked away some tears that caused her eyes to shine.

I softened my tone. "I didn't mean any disrespect. Really. I don't understand why people we love—good, innocent people—are taken from us so young. What did they do to deserve it?"

"It's not that simple, sugar. There's a reason for everything. Your mother's death has probably made you who you are. Correct?" She pointed a finger at me.

"It's why I became a nurse." *This chick really gets me. Almost, like . . . a sister.*

"See," she said, nudging my arm and smiling.

"There are better reasons for becoming a nurse, Rosie."

She let out a huge laugh. "Yes, there are. But, Natalie, your mom's always with you. Death isn't the end. It's a gateway to something else. Something better." Rosie winked at me. I swallowed hard, my mouth dry and my heart pounding. I had to get out of there.

Joel walked in, sliding the glass door behind him. "How are we doing here?" He sat down next to me.

I stood up. "Thanks, Rosie. I could get used to talking to you."

"You're not going?" Joel asked. "I just sat down." Anger banked in his eyes.

"Sorry. I need to." I patted him on the shoulder and waved to Rosie. She had gotten so raw with me. Torn into my soul and exposed my pain. I refused to cry in front of Joel, especially at a goddamn family barbeque! Walking out, I heard Joel ask Rosie in a harsh whisper what the hell she'd said to me.

Back at my apartment, I changed into my swimsuit, grabbed my equipment bag, and left. I drove a little too fast to the pool and prayed there'd be an open lane. Luckily, not many people were there. I stripped down to my suit, put on my cap and goggles, and dove in. By the speed at which I swam, you'd think I wanted to try out for the Olympics. My arms were slapping the water like propellers, my feet kicking with the speed of a powerboat. I let my anger out with every stroke and cut through the water like a pissed-off dolphin on steroids. Rosie thought she had it all figured out. *God has a plan, my ass. How does she do it? Put on such a well-adjusted, normal face everyday, knowing her son is gone? Really gone.* Not an ounce of anger in that woman, and so loving and nice. I slammed my hand into the wall and stopped to catch my breath. Truth was, Rosie's words made sense and I wanted to believe her so badly. She seemed to handle things a hell of a lot better than I did. I don't think I'd ever talked about losing my mother so much since meeting Joel. Over the years, I had pushed her down so far, muting her, that now, with Joel's encouragement, my mother wanted to speak.

A few days later I spoke with Sonny. He said he had tons of information for me. And another bill. Great. He would fly out to meet me. My dad was still in Arizona with his conference and I decided to accept his offer to help. I also needed the money. He agreed to come with me and find out what Sonny had to say.

We met at a Chinese restaurant across from Dad's hotel, near the hospital. Sonny hadn't arrived yet, so it was just the two of us.

"I'm glad you called, Natalie. Thank you." Dad scooted his chair closer to the table.

"I guess I'm having a hard time understanding why you're taking such an interest in me now." I took a swig of water.

"The night that doctor in Australia called me, telling me what had happened to you, something strange happened."

"Okay . . ."

"Your mom wrote a book when she got sick. A journal, so to speak, recounting your and Jennifer's childhoods, our wedding, trips we took together. Basically, the story of our family."

"I didn't know that."

"Well, when she died, I took it and hid it. I couldn't bring myself to read it, but she used to write in it all the time. She would laugh at parts she wrote and she would cry. I think it brought her back to us each time she took to the page."

I looked down at my hands. Tears were coming down. "Where did you put it?"

"I hid it high on one of my shelves in the closet and over the years, stuff accumulated on top of it. I had completely forgotten about it."

"So. Did you find it?"

"It found me. I got upset after hearing about you in the hospital and I started drinking, heavily. I got so drunk I stumbled into the closet, getting ready for bed, and fell against the shelves. Your mom's book came tumbling down on my head, along with a bunch of other stuff."

I laughed. "Mom always thought you could use a good bonk on the head."

"It wasn't funny. It hurt like hell. But here's the weird thing: the journal landed flat, pages open. The last page exposed."

Sighing, I stretched my neck. "Dad, get to the point."

"The words said, 'Take care of my girls, no matter what.' Even blitzed beyond recognition, I could read that."

"And you took that as a sign?" I gave him a condescending smile. "Sounds a bit far-fetched, Dad."

"That's what happened. Even in death your mom looks out for you. And me too. And now I'm here." He shrugged.

Before I could express more skepticism, Sonny walked in.

"Hey there, sugar muffin. This must be your father. Pleasure's all yours." He held out his hand to shake my dad's, who cleared his throat. Sonny had his hair loosely pulled back in a ponytail. He had on the same scorpion jacket, but this time with a clean undershirt and baggy jeans. His black aviators hid his squinty eyes.

"I want to thank you for what you're doing to help Natalie," said my dad in his best bedside manner.

"Have a seat, have a seat. Lots to go over." Sonny opened his satchel. Papers poured out of the bag's sides. He flicked his sunglasses on the table.

"Something to drink?" Dad asked.

"Whiskey will do." He kept rummaging through the papers.

I quickly filled my dad in on everything that had happened since Mr. Watson's death. The waitress took our order and Sonny waited until he could take a swig of his drink.

"So what did you find out, Sonny?" I couldn't wait while he made love to the liquor.

He smiled up at me, then after a long pause said, "Well, here's the thing. I spoke with that Mr. Petronoff dude you told me about a while ago. Remember?"

Actually, I had completely forgotten. The last time Sonny and I spoke, he'd asked if I could tell him anything unusual about Betty. Mr. Petronoff and his fear of her came to mind. "Yeah, what about him?"

"Their daughter was one of Betty's girls. Or should I say, *Dominika's* girls. Liliya Petronoff had been brought to Dominika's strip club. Betty—because I get tired of using her other name—sold Liliya to a high-powered Russian official. Two days later, she was found in a dumpster, strangled."

I covered my mouth with my hand. "Oh my god." My father wrapped an arm around my shoulders.

"Mr. Petronoff was a Russian opposition politician. He had

a lot of enemies and had to flee the country. There is a Russian community in Denver where a bunch of them immigrated."

"So how did he end up in the same hospital as Betty? Coincidence?"

"I guess Porter's is a hotspot for Russian immigrants."

I gave him a pissy look. "Sonny."

"Okay, I haven't gotten that far. But, who cares? Petronoff knows who Betty is and called in a few favors. He went to his guys from back in the day, and now they're on to her."

"Interesting," I said. "So where does that leave things?"

"The police and agents from the US Treasury have tracked down her counterfeit money, the money her husband manufactured. See, nobody these days can successfully counterfeit money anymore. Watson and his goons came close. They used the "washing off the ink trick" where the ink is removed with lye from one-dollar bills and then replaced with one-hundred using updated software."

"What?" I placed my hands alongside my head.

"Yeah. Then, the money is printed off using a color laser printer that leaves tiny yellow dots on the fake cash, making it easily traceable. She's got a lot of pissed-off henchmen now. The feds have frozen all her assets, her funds, everything. Any time she's tried to use that money to pay someone, say, for the attempts on your life, the feds traced it back to the printer and to any hands that touched it. Those guys that worked for her have nothing now. Most of them have been arrested."

"But Sonny, why is she after my daughter?" My father banged his fist on the table.

"She thinks Natalie turned her in. That's it. She's running for her life. Plus, she knows Petronoff spoke to Natalie and maybe feels she's helping him get to her."

"This is bullshit, Sonny." I threw my napkin down. "She's

trying to *kill* me. Because I took care of her husband. Fucking bullshit!"

"No, Natalie. She's going after you to save herself."

"So what do we do, Mr. Merchant?" asked my father, pronouncing each word very clearly.

"Here's the thing. Betty can't hire anyone anymore. She's going to have to come after Natalie herself. No one will work for her because she's got nothing to pay them. The best part is, we were able to trace the money back to her hit men. Well, all but one: he's still out there."

"Which one?" I asked, praying I didn't already know the answer.

"This one." Sonny pushed a picture of a scummy man in front me. I immediately recognized the star tattoo on the inside of his right wrist.

My hands flew to my mouth. "That's the one from the boat! At the Great Barrier Reef. He's the one who . . ." My dad leaned in to get a closer look.

"I know, but he won't come after you without *mucho dinero*. Hired killers only kill for the money. If this guy uses any of Betty's cash, odds are he'll be found. There's too much anti-counterfeit technology out there, and guys who've been in this game for a while know that. Betty's a dead end. The Feds are on it. If anything, this guy's gonna be pretty upset with you-know-who so he may go after her. That's how they work."

"So you're telling me that all I have to worry about now is Betty? Look what she's capable of! She found me in Belize and Arizona and Australia from my Facebook page. I've taken her off but she could still manage to find me! She was associated with the Russian Mafia, Sonny! She's bad. Very, very bad. That doesn't give me much comfort, that all I have to worry about is Betty." My voice rose a few octaves and my arms flailed about.

"She's been out of the mafia for years. They think she's dead," Sonny said.

"But she's got skills, does she not? Jesus, Sonny. You act like she's a normal bimbo."

Sonny cocked his head at me but my dad interrupted his response. "Why is this woman so difficult to find? Why can't the police do something? This woman is after my daughter!"

"Okay, on to the bad news. I hope you're ready for this. Actually, I don't care if you are or not." Sonny leaned back in the chair and brought his fingers together to form a triangle with his hands. "I started looking at the people in Natalie's life. Dr. Ulster, does this woman look familiar?" Sonny pushed forward a picture of a red-haired, tanned woman in a bikini, wearing bright red lipstick. My dad rose up halfway and leaned over the table, taking the picture in his hands.

"She looks a bit familiar." His voice lowered.

"You met her at a hospital party, no?" Sonny said.

"Sonny, what's going on?" I grabbed the picture. Holy shit, I know that face.

"Natalie." Sonny took a deep breath. "I have a daughter about your age. She don't talk to me anymore but I'd do anything for her. That's why I took your case. You remind me of her. And if this was my kid . . ." He looked directly at my dad, shaking his head. "I'd set things right."

"What are you saying?" Dad stood up, hands formed in tight fists at his side.

Sonny took the picture from me, stood up, and shoved it in my dad's face. "While you were boinking Betty in the coat closet, she stole your phone and got Natalie's numbers. She's been tracing her!" He turned to me. "Once she couldn't find you on Facebook, she needed to try something else. She found you through your father."

My father stood up, looked down at me, and walked out of
the restaurant without a word. "Typical, Dad. When the going
gets tough, you get going!" I yelled after him.

I couldn't believe it. Through meaningless sex with Betty, my
dad had given her access to me, putting my life in further danger.
Yeah, she'd colored her hair and probably given herself a fake
name, but it was Betty.

"Look, you need to work some shit out and I've done enough
for today. Truth is, Betty is a calculating, murderous bitch and
can pretty much manipulate anyone into helping her. That's how
she's made it this far. If this were my daughter, I'd do anything to
keep her safe. Forever. Sorry, little one." He gathered his things
and held out his hand to me.

"Here's my Dad's number. He has your money." I couldn't
look Sonny in the eyes.

The next two days I got through work on auto-pilot. I followed
the orders in the charts, didn't question anything, and only gave
my patients what they needed, nothing more. No chatting, no
extra attention. I felt numb. I came in on time, punched in, and
then punched out. Mallory tried to talk to me about what was
going on, but I didn't want to involve her. Who wants a friend
with all this drama? It would drain the friendship. I'd deal with
this on my own, somehow.

"Boy, you're really looking happy these days," Emma scoffed
as I brought some meds over to her that had been mistakenly
put in my patient's box.

"Go fuck yourself, Emma," I said, dropping the meds on the
counter. A respiratory therapist snorted back a laugh.

"Damn, such words. You're really a mess." I looked up. Joel
was standing in front of me.

"Hi," I said quietly.

"Here." He handed me a CD. "Take this." He turned and walked toward the door.

"Wait, what's this?"

"Just play it." And he left.

I shoved the CD in my bag and finished up my shift.

With all the events in my life recently, I'd gotten used to carrying a can of mace in one hand with my keys poking through each of my fingers on the other, like sharp brass knuckles. I walked from my car to the apartment, ready for anything, my senses heightened. I'd left my lights on in my apartment when I went to work so I wouldn't come home to darkness. *Sonny better do his job because I can't stand living like this, always afraid.* Inside, surrounded by my things, I felt secure. After turning off some lights and pouring myself a glass of wine, I took the CD out of my bag and knelt in front of the stereo. Track five had a sticky note attached to it. Staying on my knees and resting against my heels, I listened. I wasn't sure what I was supposed to be hearing, except for the fact that I recognized the group as Coldplay and the title of the song read "The Scientist." I needed to hear it again, something about a man's love: he'd screwed up, and now wanted to go back to the start. Who was Joel referring to? My father? Two people who were apart but shouldn't be, and the man wanted her back, even if it would be hard. He wanted her back.

*How the fuck does Joel Lansfield know so much about me? He knows more about me than I do!* I don't want to bring him into all this shit. Who wants a friend with five thousand pounds of baggage? I'm too complicated. He doesn't need this. How many times do I have to keep pushing him away? I want him at a distance. I've gone through my adult life dulling any emotions, staying strong. Preventing patients from dying alone or making sure their loved ones know that the patient is at peace. Seeing death all the time and ensuring patients don't feel the same fears and doubts I have. Making sure they're not going to end up like me. Hiding from my grief. It's a hell of a lot easier to hide than to be found. No matter how hard it would be, I needed to reveal myself.

"This is Dr. Lansfield."

"Hi, it's me. Natalie."

"Hi. Sorry, I didn't recognize the number."

"It's okay." A long silence filled the space between us. "Thank you."

"For what?"

"That beautiful song. I got it." Again with these goddamn tears!

"Oh, that. Yeah." More silence.

"So what do we do now?" I asked.

"You want to meet somewhere? Or, how about you come over?"

"Okay. Give me a couple of minutes and I'll be there."

"See you soon."

"Bye." I hung up and went to my closet and grabbed my big silver tote. The clock said eight o'clock and I had a feeling I wouldn't be coming home tonight.

I drove to Joel's house, unsure how to handle things. Allowing myself to want him as more than a friend frightened me. Jason had been easy. Love 'em and leave 'em. Like the ER: treat 'em and street 'em. I had no idea how to keep 'em.

"I'll take a beer if you have one," I said, coming through the open garage door.

"Of course I have beer. This is a bachelor pad."

I stood up straighter as he came over with the beer. He had a good eight or nine inches on me so his sculpted pecs were at eye level and I could see through his thin, white T-shirt. I wondered if Joel had gotten used to being alone and had now decided he no longer wanted to be. Was he really willing to take a chance with me? Why? Without taking the beer, I threaded my arms under his and lay my head against his chest. Oh God, being so close to him felt good. All the tension and stress I had going on inside me melted into nothing as I stayed molded against him. Joel, beer in hand, wrapped his arms around me. We stood like that, holding onto each other for comfort, not speaking, just standing there. I felt my knees wanting to buckle and Joel moved us apart as I looked up at him. He set the beer down, took my face in both his hands and kissed me. Warmth travelled upward from my toes and spread to the tips of my ears. My entire body, including the hairs on my head, tingled. This felt so natural, so easy. Worrying about how I looked or what he thought about me didn't even register. I had never felt such a response in myself, with anybody else I had ever kissed. *This is what I've been waiting for my whole life. This!*

A flurry of clothes quickly obscured the living room floor. Shorts, shirts, shoes—everything flew all around as we hurried to undress. We couldn't keep our hands off each other and Joel couldn't stop kissing my body. We were filled with such urgency and passion; we were almost on fire, starving for one another. Out of breath, Joel held me at arm's length, which made it difficult for me to fold mine in front of my body in order to cover myself like I usually did. He stood there staring.

"Joel, please," I hunched a little, trying to hide.

"No. Let me look at you." I wanted to let him, but . . . "No more hiding. You're absolutely beautiful." He started kissing my neck, my shoulders, my breasts, everything. I yearned for him. How could I just stand there naked in front of the man and not move? We sank to the floor, Joel on top of me while my legs easily separated.

"Wait, what about . . . ?" I asked.

"Oh, shit." He relaxed on top of me, moving the hair out of my face. "I don't have anything. I'm clean, though, I promise. What about you? The pill?"

"Yeah, I'm on it. I know I'm clean; I've never been unprotected." I wanted him so badly.

"What do you want to do?" Joel gave me a light kiss on the mouth.

"I'm okay with it if you are. I never skip the pill. And I trust you."

"You sure?" Instinct told me it would be okay. It wasn't the most responsible decision, but it felt right. I nodded.

He eased himself in and I felt his hardness fill me up completely. My pelvis rubbed against his with such vigor that I went crazy. Sex had never felt this good to me before. Within seconds, I had orgasmed and screamed so loud Joel had to cover my mouth with his so as not to scare the neighbors. He finished quickly after me and we both lay there laughing.

"I'm going to call you quick-draw McGraw," he said. "Damn. What was that, thirty seconds?"

"Sorry. I didn't mean to be so quick. I don't know what happened there."

"It's okay, I like it. I don't have to work as hard," Joel said, winking.

"Where did you get that tattoo?" I asked, slapping him on his left butt cheek.

"What? The four-leaf clover? Back in medical school. I needed luck."

"Did it work?"

"Not until just now." He kissed me again and began to trace the outline of my eyebrows, my lips, and my chin. I touched the scar on his face and kissed his nose. We spent the rest of the night wrapped around each other, gossiping about people in the hospital, sharing tales of patient cases, and talking about our childhoods. He loved the pottery bowl story and empathized when I told him about Rob Hatcher's death.

"So what now?" I asked.

"Come with me to Vegas. I have a convention to go to, but I never participate. I just sign in, get some handouts and leave. It'll be fun. Three days, you and me. I'm supposed to leave the day after tomorrow."

"Okay," I replied without any hesitation.

# 21

I couldn't get off work until the day after Joel left so we decided he would meet me at the Vegas airport and we'd drive back together after the conference. That would leave us two days to play. Fancy hotels, restaurants, and nightlife seemed so romantic. I'd always thought of Las Vegas as a couples' retreat and I couldn't believe Joel wanted me to join him. I prayed he wouldn't change his plans. It all seemed too good to be true.

Exiting off the highway towards the airport, my phone rang. *Damn it. He's calling to cancel.* "Hello?" I cringed.

"Hey you, it's me. There's been a change of plans," Joel said.

*I knew it.* "Oh. What's the matter?" *Should I pull over or keep driving?*

"The convention hotel is a dump. I've booked us at Mandalay Bay. I'll see you in a couple of hours, okay?"

I exhaled. "Yeah. Sounds good. You scared me for a second."

"Why?"

"I thought you were calling to cancel." I lowered my voice, ashamed of myself for saying it.

"Never. I can't wait. I'll meet you at baggage claim."

I felt my smile spread so big my cheeks hurt. "Me, either. I'll call you when I land." We hung up and my heart lifted. I couldn't wait to get on that plane.

- - -

Two hours later I arrived at McCarran Airport. I heard the *ding ding* of the slot machines and personal poker games as I stepped into the terminal. I pulled my carry-on behind me as I made my way to baggage claim. *Please let him be here.* Coming down the escalator, I read signs advertising Cirque du Soleil, Cher, Blue Man Group, and other shows that all sounded good to me. Maybe we would see one. Scanning baggage claim, I didn't see Joel anywhere. I stopped, surrounded by all the carousels, and called him. No answer. I tried him again; no answer. *Shit, I knew it!* I turned around and headed toward the exit, not sure what to do.

"Natalie!" Joel came running toward me. "So sorry, I have no reception in here. Did you call me?"

I relaxed my shoulders. "I tried a few times." We hugged and kissed.

"Let's get out of here," Joel said, taking my carry-on.

I took his hand and my steps bounced. I must have looked like such a dweeb, but I was glad to be in Vegas. To be there with Joel.

Joel had reserved a room on the seventeenth floor. Walking into the room I froze, shocked. I had never seen such a beautiful place. A king-sized bed took over the room and the bathroom contained a Jacuzzi tub and a glass shower. The large glass window revealed a beautiful view of the Vegas strip. I had been so nervous on the flight over; the minute I saw the bathroom I rushed to use it. When I came out I saw Joel facing the window and admiring the scene. Across the street was Paris Paris; to our left, the Luxor; and a ways down, we could see the dancing fountains of the Bellagio. Could this be any more perfect?

"Are you blind?" Joel asked.

"What?" I turned to look at him. And then it clicked. Sitting right behind him on the desk were two dozen red roses, baby's breath, and purple lilies surrounded by greens in a huge, square glass vase. "Oh my God." *Do not cry, Natalie!* I put one hand over my mouth. I took the card stuck in the middle of the bouquet— *You are so beautiful. Thank you for joining me.*

"You act like you've never gotten flowers before." Joel wrapped his arms around me.

"You . . . you shouldn't have done all this. It's too much." I looked up at him.

"Most women would say thanks, like it's no big deal. It's nothing, really. Just flowers." He kissed the top of my head as I leaned against him.

"They're absolutely beautiful, and this room . . . It's amazing."

"Well, you deserve it." Joel brought one hand under my chin and lifted my face to meet his lips. "You're way too easy to please," he teased.

We began kissing each other passionately and with such wanting. His touch lit me on fire. He brought out the need in me—the need for intimacy. It wasn't forced or one-sided. Both of us wanted each other. Equally. He tilted my head back as he kissed my neck and my shoulders while unbuttoning my pants and then his. He pulled his shirt off and then both of us separated to finish undressing. I reached over and gave a good-luck rub to his tattoo. Stepping out of my undies, Joel moved back and said, "Stop. Let me look at you." How many times did he need to see me? Reading my mind, he said with a smile, "I'm very visually oriented, so deal with it."

Naturally, I folded my arms across my body. Joel reached over and gently moved my arms out of the way. Here I was, standing in front of a glass window on the seventeenth floor, buck naked, the Las Vegas strip as a backdrop, while Joel examined me with his eyes. And I let him. He dropped to his knees and started kissing between my legs. I thought my knees would buckle. I ran my fingers through his dark hair and threw my head back, moaning. Joel's hands proceeded upward and cupped my breasts while his mouth stayed down below. I grabbed his hands as he continued to caress me. I couldn't stand the anticipation. I wanted him inside me so fucking bad. No one had ever been this attentive to my body and I couldn't stand it. Every inch of me was aflame. Everywhere his hands and lips touched, my skin singed. When I couldn't take any more, I knelt to his level and nudged him up. I remained kneeling and began to kiss his manhood. Joel was the definition of a perfect specimen. Tall with chiseled muscles, trimmed hair over his body in all the right places, and beautiful tanned, dark skin. He gently put his hands on my head and helped me take him in and out of my mouth. When he couldn't take anymore, he lifted me up and brought me to the bed, laying me down gently. Our pelvises rubbed together and Joel began sucking my neck, my breasts, my shoulders, anywhere he could find. Our lips finally met, and as our tongues played with each other, Joel entered me. I gave out a loud moan and placed my hands on his ass, pressing him harder into me. We began rubbing against each other with so much friction, I thought my skin would rub raw. But it felt so good, like heaven. Sex had never been like this for me. Never. And I wanted more. Moan after moan, expletives and prayers, and we both started to sweat. Then Joel stood up and pulled me to him. He picked me up and I wrapped my legs around his waist as he penetrated me again. Lifting me up, he placed his forearms under my butt. I bounced up and down, almost as if I could touch the ceiling, my legs tight against his back so he stayed buried in me. I screamed in ecstasy. He propped my body against the huge window overlooking the city and my eyes opened wide. Could people see us?

"Don't worry, love. They can't see in." He continued to move his pelvis into me, forward then back, forward then back. Hearing my sweaty ass screech off the glass, Joel brought me to the desk and set me on it. He pulled my legs toward him as I felt him again inside me. I crossed my ankles behind his back and pushed my pelvis into his, rubbing that little area that stimulated my inner soul. I began to claw at his back, feeling the orgasm rise within me. I threw my head back and yelled, "Joel!" but just as I did, he lifted me up and brought me back to the bed. His face burrowed into my neck and I wrapped my arms tightly around him, and we moved faster and faster with him in me. The headboard banged against the wall and the bedsprings squeaked in perfect rhythm.

"Oh God!" I yelled.

"Here it comes," Joel said. And together we climaxed.

Coming down from my sexual slice of bliss, I wasn't sure if I could ever feel like that again; it was too good. "That . . . oh wow." I needed to catch my breath.

"Welcome to Las Vegas." Joel rolled off me and lay on his side, propped up on his elbow. He moved some hair out of my face and traced the curves of my eyebrows with his finger.

"Don't ever leave," I said without thinking. As soon as the words came out, I shut my mouth. *Nice, real nice, Natalie. Dumbass!*

Joel laughed. "I don't intend to." He kissed me again.

"Sorry. I shouldn't have said that. I just . . . I'm . . ."

"Yes?"

I hugged him so I wouldn't have to look at him. I wasn't good at this. Letting someone in. So close. Had I gotten caught up in the moment, in the incredible lovemaking? No, I knew what I felt but I couldn't say it. "I'm in . . . deep like . . . with you." That's all I could say. I felt it, I knew it, but I couldn't say it. Not yet. What if it wasn't returned?

Joel held me tightly against him and whispered in my ear, "I love you too."

"What?" I quickly let go of him so I could face him. Panic bubbled to the surface.

"You heard me," he smiled. I couldn't do anything but cry. I'd sworn I'd never let anyone get this close to me. It wouldn't be fair: falling in love, planning a life together, and then . . . I could be gone. I couldn't bring him into this. There was Betty, the possibility of me becoming sick, and the fact that I simply suck at relationships. *How did I let this happen? He loves me, and the worst part is, I truly love him back.*

After finding a cute little deli at New York, New York, Joel and I had lunch and walked around the hotel. I decided to enjoy this while I could and worry about the consequences later. Our conversation never lulled. We talked about places we had been and what we were going to do for our last day in Vegas. Joel asked me questions about the countries I'd visited, what the food tasted like, how the hospitals were, what the doctors were like. He seemed interested in everything I had to say and we ended up in long discussions about different societies, the medical field, and life in general. Our conversations started out casual and became more cerebral, each of us learning so much about the other. *So this is sharing. Sharing experiences, feelings, and having the other person respond in turn.* Reciprocity. I liked it!

Joel pointed out a woman with so much plastic surgery he called her Cruella de Vil. My phone rang, interrupting my laughter. "Hello?" I said, clearing my throat.

"Natalie, it's Sonny. Are you okay?" He sounded worried.

"I'm fine, why? I'm in Vegas," I looked at Joel. He gave me a wink with a smile.

"I lost her. I had her nailed down to this dump in New

Mexico. I had the police so close to catching her and bringing her in. Then, out of nowhere, I lost her. I had her phone tapped but I think she's on to me because I couldn't make anything out of her last call. Why aren't you in Arizona?"

"Can I not leave whenever I want to? Do I need to ask permission every time I want to go somewhere?"

"Natalie, I'm trying to help you here. Don't forget who you're talking to, little lady."

Sonny was right. Calming down, I started over. "I'm sorry, a friend asked me to join him in Vegas and I said yes. Sorry I didn't tell you." Joel looked at me with furrowed brows.

"Just be on the lookout, okay? At least when I had her I knew she couldn't do you any harm. But now that I've lost her . . ." I heard him take a deep breath. "Be careful. I'm going to try to get out there tonight."

"Sonny, we're leaving the day after tomorrow. You don't have to come. Don't worry. I'll be fine. I'm with . . . someone." Joel reached across the table and took my hand in his.

"Whatever. I'll feel better when I can pick up her scent again, if you know what I mean. She's a slippery broad, but I found her once. I'll find her again."

"I know you will, Sonny. Thank you for everything you're doing. I'll talk to you when I get home, okay? Please don't fly out to Vegas just to check on me." We hung up.

"You all right? Was that the PI? What did he say?" Great. Now Joel seemed worried. I hadn't wanted to bring all this bullshit with me.

"He's lost Betty's trail and he wanted to make sure I was fine. That's all." I took a sip of water, waving my hand in the air. Why couldn't the bitch be caught? Then I could get on with my life and she could get what was coming to her, whatever that might be.

"Should we go back home? What do you want to do?" He looked toward the exit.

"Joel, we're not leaving. I'm not going to live life always worried about Betty. It's enough that cancer is lurking in the shadows. There's no way for her to know where I am. Relax. The only thing I want to do is more of what we've been doing." I leaned across the table and kissed him.

"I don't want anything to happen to you. Knowing someone out there wants to hurt you, makes me want to . . . kill that person. Not literally, but you know what I mean. If Sonny thinks you should go home, then we should do it."

"He didn't say that. Please, Joel. Stop worrying. Nothing's going to happen here. Now can we please go walk around some more? Vegas awaits!" I stood up, stopping the conversation.

"You are one stubborn woman you know that? Let's go." He took my hand as we walked out of the hotel.

Joel's arm around my shoulder felt comforting and safe. I didn't want him to feel as if he had to rescue me. I could hold my own. I needed to stay strong. We went back to the hotel to lie out by the pool and a few hours later, returned to the room for some more lovemaking. We fell asleep for about an hour and both of us woke up famished. We decided to eat at the Bellagio. Joel opened doors for me, pulled my chair out at the table, and once again paid for everything. I had never been treated so well and I started to get depressed, knowing that tomorrow would be the last day of this lovefest.

After dinner we stood outside watching the dancing fountains in front of Bellagio. The lights underneath the huge pool in front of the hotel lit up in beautiful colors as water sprayed in rhythm to music. Some of the sprays went as high as four hundred and fifty feet. It was beautiful; the fountains and the music were perfectly in sync. An unusual song played and I couldn't make out the lyrics. Sung mostly in Italian, the only English words were in the chorus, and in the title of the song, "Time to Say Goodbye." How depressing was this? I didn't want to think about saying goodbye. I looked up at Joel, who had his arms wrapped around me. "These lyrics suck," I told him.

A tall, dark-haired woman stood next to us. She overheard me and commented, "It doesn't mean what you think. She's singing about the places she's never seen or experienced with her love and now she will. She'll sail with him across the seas. They're both saying goodbye to loneliness, not to each other."

Warmth radiated through my body. This was all too perfect. "How do you know that?" I asked her.

"Just picked up some Italian during my travels. It's really a beautiful song, isn't it? You two have a wonderful night," the woman said, walking away. Strangely, she turned to look at me, nodded her head, and then held her index finger over her mouth as if to shush me.

*What the? No. No. It can't be.* "Holy shit! That's Betty! Joel!" I frantically tapped his chest. "That woman, it's her!" I pointed down the street.

"What? Who?" He pushed me behind his body and stuck out his chest. "Betty? You saw her?"

"Yeah. That way! Come on!" I took off running.

Joel caught up to me, pushing people out of the way. There were too many of them. I dodged my head around looking for her dark hair. The smell of fuel and alcohol emanated from the road and sidewalks.

"Do you see her?" Joel asked.

"No. Come on! We need to keep going." I ran faster, chasing life—mine and the woman's.

After a mile or so, we came upon a crowd gathered around a street performer who was juggling on a unicycle with fire sticks.

Our only path was obstructed. I shoved through the mob with Joel right at my heels. Once we came to an opening, we were near the end of the strip. I stopped and looked in all directions. The woman had vanished.

"Come on, baby. Let's call the police. I don't see her anywhere."

"They're not going to do anything. Maybe I'm being paranoid. I want to go back to the hotel." I hyperventilated and my body trembled.

He hugged me in silence, then took my hand to lead us back to Mandalay Bay.

I kept looking over my shoulder as we walked, looking for anything or anyone unusual. Had I imagined that the woman nodded at me? Was I seeing things?

"Can I do anything for you? Do you want me to call someone?" Joel asked, holding me tight as we lay in bed later.

"No. I just want to sleep." But my mind was too frazzled to rest and my eyes did not want to close. This could never work out. Not now. I'd screwed myself by telling Joel my true feelings. I had let everything fall into place and all the signs were there. *This is meant to be. But I can't accept that. I'm incapable of giving myself to someone. I'm better off alone. That way no one gets hurt.*

"We should head home." Joel said.

"No. I'll have to deal with this shit there, too." I rolled over, leaving my back to Joel.

He leaned over me and kissed my cheek, wrapping his muscular, comforting arms around me. "I'm not going to let anything happen to you. I promise." His words tore at my heart. *How do I end this?*

"Where do you want to have dinner tonight?" Joel asked, gently waking me up from a nap after a full day in the sun, lounging by the pool. I needed the rest after tossing all night due to my neurotic thoughts about our relationship.

"Wherever. It's your choice." My chest felt heavy. I sat up in bed and started flicking through channels, staring directly at the TV.

"You okay? What are you thinking about?" He moved a hair from my face.

"Nothing. I'm fine," I said. He reached over and cupped my face in his hands. How could I do this? He didn't deserve to be punished. He deserved so much more than me.

"Come on, love. What is it?"

*Okay, here we go.* I sat up, propping a pillow against the headboard. "I never expected this to happen. I really didn't." The words got stuck in my dry throat.

"Okay . . ."

"I don't think I can give you what you want."

"And what would that be?"

"Me. Marriage. Kids."

"Um, well. You're a little too late, Natalie. You've pretty much given yourself to me already. Lots of times. No one's asking you for more right now. Can we just enjoy each other? We're only getting started."

"I know, but . . ."

"No. I understand we've got a huge problem with Betty, but Sonny's looking out for you and she will be caught. I know it. But don't start making dumb decisions, Nat." He stood up and started picking out clothes for dinner.

"Dumb decisions? I don't want you involved in this shit, Joel!"

"Too bad. I already am. Now get up; we'll talk about this later."

"When, Joel? I can't . . ."

"No one is asking you to do anything except to get your ass up. Let's go, I'm hungry." He lightly slapped my feet and went to the closet, abruptly ending our discussion. I knew I shouldn't have said anything. I should've waited until the drive home.

We showered together and got dressed, our conversation sparse. At the restaurant, we ordered a bottle of wine and steaks. Joel also asked the waitress to bring two shots of tequila. "Kisses and shots," he said.

Two tiny glasses were set down in front of us and we both leaned across the table toward each other. I pressed my lips to Joel's and inhaled his feel, his smell, his touch. I lingered there savoring the last taste of his love. I threw the tequila down my throat and sucked the lime. My eyes were wet. While we were waiting for our food, the awkwardness overwhelmed me. Joel kept shifting in his chair. I'd let this happen. I nervously tore the crusty bread to shreds, leaving crumbs all over my plate and the tablecloth. The meal came and we ate in silence. The ride home would be torture.

"Natalie, there's something I want to say." Joel put down his utensils and placed his forearms on the table.

I stopped eating and leaned back in my chair. *Brace yourself.* "Joel, please . . ."

"I meant what I said earlier. I do love you." He looked down at his hands. "But you've got to stop this bullshit."

"Excuse me?"

"You're scared because you think that what happened to your mother will happen to you. Am I wrong?"

I looked directly into his eyes. "We both know there is a huge chance of me getting breast cancer. I watched my mother suffer for over a year, Joel. It spread to her lungs and her brain. We all watched her, screaming in agony, vomiting, seizing. I begged my father to bring home a syringe filled with anything to end her pain. I refuse to let you or anything in our future go through that."

Joel threw down his napkin. A vein on his forehead pulsated. "You're like a terminally ill patient who curls up in a little ball, waiting for death to come. That's weak, Natalie. You think you're so strong, but you won't even fight!"

"I've spent my whole life fighting!" I yelled, unleashing my tears. People were starting to look and whisper.

"You've spent your whole life avoiding, Natalie. Two different things." I didn't know how to respond. Joel lowered his voice. "I don't know what happened to you. One minute you were in love, and the next, you're done."

I took my napkin and dried my eyes. "Don't you get it? This is too good, Joel. The sex, the love, even that fucking fountain music! All the signs are there."

He reached over and took my hands. "So what's the problem?"

"I . . . I can't." I let go of his hands and hung my head, the tears falling, snuffing out any remains of a blazing fire.

Joel asked for the check, paid it, and then stood up, motioning for me to follow. We walked back to the hotel in silence, Joel a few feet ahead of me. When we came back to the room, I immediately grabbed my swimsuit and went into the bathroom to change. I came out, towel in hand, and went to my luggage to look for my goggles.

"Where are you going?" Joel asked angrily, lying on the bed.

Gesturing to my body, standing there in a swimsuit, I said, "Swimming."

"The pool's closed. And you shouldn't be going anywhere alone."

"There's an indoor one down on the ground floor. I need to clear my head. And guess what? I do better when I'm alone." I threw on my cover-up and started to turn the door handle, grimacing at my own words.

"Natalie, don't!" Joel yelled as I shut the door.

I walked quickly downstairs. This was supposed to be the end of a great weekend, our weekend. And I'd fucked everything up. I couldn't wait to get home. *I know I'm doing the right thing. To hell with it. I don't need this crap. I have enough issues going on with Betty.* I had my career and my apartment and I liked it that way. Joel was the one who wined and dined me. Told me he loved me, seduced me. Introduced me to his goddamn family. His loving family . . . He started all of this; I'd never wanted it to happen. So why was I in so much pain?

The workout pool was located at the far end of the ground floor near the fitness center and laundry room. I knew I'd be alone since not many people went for a swim this late at night. I did my best thinking in the water and it was the one place I felt strong, powerful, and confident besides the ICU. I believed I had the power to do anything when I swam. Slipping out of my flip-flops, I threw my towel on a nearby lounge chair and dove in, feeling the warm water wash over me, rinsing away the tears left on my cheeks. Nothing could be heard underwater. Only pure silence. No painful words, no crying, no phones—just silence. I began swimming fast and hard, racing against imaginary competitors. Before I knew it, I had done forty laps. Calming down, I switched from freestyle to breaststroke. The warm temperature of the water caused mist to swirl around the pool area, making it hard to see. At one point I thought I heard a door open, but couldn't see much with my fogged-up goggles. I kept swimming. Then I heard a splash.

Coming to the deep end, someone jumped in almost right

on top of me. Reaching for the wall and stopping so I could yell at that person to be more careful, I lifted my head up out of the water and took my goggles off. Where'd they go? I could have sworn I had seen someone . . . Then I got pulled under, hard, like that woman at the beginning of the *Jaws* movie. *Oh God! What the hell?* Someone gripped my ankle, dragging me down to the bottom of the pool. Kicking ferociously to escape, I managed to shake loose the hand that gripped me, allowing me to swim to the surface. There were bubbles everywhere! I turned my head, frantically trying to see anything or anybody. Breaking the surface, I spit out water and put my goggles back on. *I'll find you before you find me.*

Just as I was about to go under, someone popped up. It was her! Her fake blond hair stuck to her face and that fucking lipstick stained her lips. Black mascara left skid marks down her face, reminding me of a very scary clown. How had she found me?

Betty lunged at me. She threw her arms around my neck as I treaded water. I grabbed her wrist as she brought a syringe, with a large needle attached, to my neck. I treaded faster, bringing my other hand around, using both of them to fight her off. She kept lurching forward, trying to stab me with the needle. I brought my knees up and kicked my left foot into her crotch. Betty doubled over and lost her grip on the syringe. It floated passed me and I grabbed it, swimming for the surface. Hurling my upper body out of the water, I threw the syringe and heard it land on the tiled deck. Betty grabbed my feet again. Gathering my senses, I knew exactly what I had to do. I gulped in all the air I could and let her take me down. Betty looked comfortable in the water, but I was better. There is no way she could hold her breath as long as I could. I'd trained for years to be able to stay under for one hundred and twenty seconds. *This is my turf, bitch, and here I own you!* Using all the strength in my legs, I whipped them into a strong frog kick and pushed my arms upward, keeping us at the bottom. *I can stay down here all day, you psychotic skank.* Once at the bottom, I sculled the water in an upward motion with one arm, keeping us toward the bottom while using the other arm to break her stifling grip around my neck. We must've been down there less than thirty seconds when I felt Betty's clutch loosen. Her need for air had overcome her need to kill. She was wearing down and running out of time. Constantly twisting and squirming, all the while keeping us at the bottom, I wriggled free. But I wasn't ready to go up yet.

Betty struggled to breach the surface; she needed that life-saving gasp of air. Tiny bubbles escaped her mouth and she raced up.

*You're not going anywhere!* I reached up and grabbed her ankle so tightly I thought I could break it. All my adrenaline now left me feeling invincible. She tried kicking me with her free foot, but I dodged her and rested my knees comfortably on the pool floor, blowing out more bubbles to keep me down while still having plenty of air left in my lungs. She floated above me, suspended in the water with my arm as the tether. *Come on, a couple more seconds. Give up, you sack of shit!*

And then she went limp. One last bubble came out of those red lips. I let go of her ankle and Betty floated up, with me easily swimming to the surface beside her.

"Natalie! Oh, thank God!" Joel kneeled by the edge and extended his arm to me. Sonny stood right behind him. I passed on Joel's hand and reached for the wall myself. I propped an elbow up on the gutter as Betty, face-down, drifted into me.

My nursing instincts and lifeguard senses made me reach

around her chest and position her where I could get her arms out of the water so Joel and Sonny could pull her out. I couldn't let her die. I wanted to, but I couldn't. It's not me. Betty lay motionless on the pool deck as I jumped out of the water and positioned myself above her. Without saying a word to Joel or Sonny, I readjusted her head to access her airway and leaned over her, pinching her nose. I started to give her rescue breaths when Joel put his arm across my chest, holding me back.

"What are you doing?" he asked me. "You don't have to save her. She tried to kill you."

I tilted my head at him, like a dog cocking his ears to hear better. "Really, Joel? I'm not going to let her die."

"But ..."

"And you're not, either. Now start CPR." He didn't argue, placing both hands on Betty's sternum.

Together we worked on Betty for about five minutes until she began sputtering water and coughing. Rolling her on her side so she couldn't aspirate her own vomit, I heard Sonny on the phone and then sirens. He found the syringe I'd thrown and pulled a tissue from his pocket. Kneeling down, he secured the syringe within the tissue and held it in his hand.

"Looks like anti-freeze." Sonny turned the syringe over in his hands. I could clearly see the neon green fluid in the chamber.

"Why did you save me?" Betty whispered. "I'm better off dead." She coughed and sputtered.

"Because unlike you, I have morals." I stood up and spit on Betty's weak, pale body.

"You turned me in! You did this!" Betty yelled with venom.

"You killed your husband! You think I asked for that assignment? I've done nothing but cover up your bullshit, more than once!"

"Your stupid suspicions about what happened to him—why

did you have to tell Judy? Why?" Her crumpled body shook on the cold tile.

"Why? Are you fucking kidding me? Jesus, Betty." I shook my head in pity as I glared at her.

"And you were so nice to Mr. Petronoff," Betty pushed herself to her knees, sitting up straight. "He went to Sergeiv! They're after me now!" Betty grabbed my ankles, not to harm me, but to beg. Beg for what, I didn't care.

"Sergeiv Lovevich, the Russian mobster. Her old boss," Sonny said.

"You made this fucking bed. Now lie in it!" I peeled her off me like chewed up, used gum off a shoe. Police and paramedics rushed in.

Joel wrapped a towel around me and despite our earlier conversation, I collapsed against him. My legs felt like jelly. He cradled me and smoothed my hair. The police stood over Betty while the paramedics worked on her. My nightmare finally over, I broke down, shaking and crying while Joel held me close and Sonny stood next to us.

"I'm sorry I couldn't get to you sooner. I tried to warn you," Sonny said. "Why weren't you answering your goddamn phone!"

My phone. I'd left it behind because I'd wanted to be alone. I hadn't even thought about it.

"How did you find me?"

"It's a long story. Not the time right now. I'm just glad we got the broad."

"Ma'am, we'll need you down at the station," said a police officer. "Or do you need to get checked out at the hospital first?"

"Yes, the hospital. Can we take her?" Joel said. "I want her checked out."

"No! I'm fine." I pulled away from him. "I want to go to the station. I'm not going to the damn hospital."

"Come on, we'll get you in dry clothes and we'll go. Babe, what if you're hurt?"

"Are you no longer a doctor? You can look me over later."

Both Joel and Sonny exchanged glances with the police officer, not knowing what to do.

"All right then, let's go," the officer said, leading us to his cruiser.

I spent the rest of the night at the police station, giving all the details of my experience with Betty. Sonny shared file after file—explaining all the characters involved, the crimes, and the locations where the crimes had been committed. The Feds were alerted and then my dad. He ordered Joel to take me home, and Joel told my dad we'd be leaving shortly. Sonny said he'd meet me at my apartment the next day. I was sure he wanted to collect his final balance, but I knew he cared about me too. The guy had grown on me. He'd worked hard on my case. I needed to let him know how much I appreciated it once all this was over.

The ride home with Joel hurt. Five hours of painstaking torture. We spoke here and there. He asked if I wanted to talk about what had happened, but I told him no. Mostly, I leaned my head against the window and watched the desert landscape. When Joel pulled into my apartment complex, I couldn't look at him. I put my hand on the car handle and held it there.

"So, you're going to leave and not say anything to me?" Joel asked.

I didn't respond. I got out of the car, zombielike, staring straight ahead, moving slowly. I opened the back door of the car and took out my suitcase, closed the door behind me and turned toward my stairwell. *Don't look back, Natalie.*

"I knew I never should've trusted you!" Joel yelled as I slowly walked away. "You're weak, Natalie. Fucking weak. You survive numerous attempts on your life by murderers, yet you can't deal with me? Fuck you!" He slammed the car door shut and I heard the screech of his tires as he sped out of the parking lot. His dark words caused my heart to shatter into a thousand pieces, held up by only organs and bones that physically supported it. No emotion, love, or joy lay among the ruins.

# 22

Two days after I returned from Vegas, I had to go back to work. I still hadn't heard from Sonny. I had spent those two days sitting on the couch, still in jammies, flipping through tv channels, on auto-pilot, comatose.

A knock on the door brought me back to Earth. I briefly hoped it would be Joel but then, remembering how I had treated him, dismissed the idea. I got up and went to look through the peephole. My father waited outside. *He's here. For me.*

Opening the door, I squinted against the sunlight. "Hi, Natalie." He walked into my apartment and set his luggage down, walked over to me as I shut the door, and shrouded me in his arms.

"Thank you," I blubbered into his chest. The Betty ordeal had left me vulnerable, wanting comfort and protection. But after pushing Joel away, I didn't have the energy to do the same thing to my dad. His presence had now somehow begun to compensate for his years of absence.

"Oh, Natalie. I'm so sorry. I . . . I almost lost you because of my stupidity and self-interest."

Pulling away from him, I grabbed a tissue and started drying my face. "It's not all your fault, Dad. Trust me. Betty would stop at nothing to find me." I didn't know if my tears were from relief, from him being there, or because Joel wasn't.

We both went to the couch. Dad put a hand on my knee. "Look, I know I wasn't there for you and your sister. I know that. I'm the worst father."

"So why are you here now?"

"Natalie, after I got that call from Australia, everything changed. When your mother died, I felt like a failure. I mean, people knew me as the 'World Renowned Surgeon', right? The 'Great Dr. Ulster,' yet I couldn't do a damn thing to save her. She was my world, Natalie. And so were you and Jennifer."

I stood up and went to my mother's picture. "We never blamed you."

"You didn't have to. I blamed myself. And I shut down. Booze and women were an excuse, a place to hide. Whenever I got loaded or in the sack with some bimbo, I didn't have to be Dr. Ulster. In fact, he was nowhere to be found."

"I think I do the same thing with my patients." I looked down at the floor. "I hide behind them, making sure their deaths are easy and peaceful. Making sure they're comfortable and their families are comfortable, because I didn't get to do that with Mom. I guess taking care of people is my outlet." I was confused by my own realization. *Holy shit.*

"I think it's time we both stop hiding, before we lose someone close to us again."

"It's not that easy, Dad." I went back and sat down beside him.

"Life's not easy. Anything worth having requires work. You and your sister were definitely worth having, but I wasn't willing to do the work. Until now." He draped an arm around me and pulled me close.

I began to cry. Again. "I gave up someone so important to me. Someone . . . I loved. It's too late." Head in my hands, I slowly recalled the story of Joel and me to my dad.

After my tears dried and I could breathe again, my Dad tilted up my chin and made me look at him. "I dismissed my own family as if another could replace them. I was selfish. You gave me a second chance. Don't you think you deserve one, too?"

"He'll never forgive me, Dad. He's so angry. I don't blame him."

"Natalie, don't give up like I did. Don't wait fourteen years to realize what matters. You're better than that. You're better than me."

I threw my arms around him and hugged him tightly. I didn't want to let go. In all the years of growing up, I'd never thought my dad was proud of me. I became a nurse instead of a doctor, my mother and I were closer than he and I, and I always felt he favored my sister. Never would I have imagined we would be having this conversation. It made me happy. A little piece of my heart started to twitch with life.

The phone rang, pulling me from the warmth of my dad's arms. "Hello?"

"Hi, doll. Sonny. I'm in town. We need to talk."

*Oh shit.* "Okay. My dad's here at my apartment. Can you come here?"

"Sure thing. See ya when I see ya." He hung up.

Thirty minutes later Sonny arrived. "Sit down," he told me.

"Well, hello to you, too. Can I close the door, please? Yeesh!"

"Natalie, I have bad news." He took off his shades and tossed them on the coffee table.

"What?"

"Betty escaped."

"What? What the hell, Sonny?"

"Hey, don't yell at me, missy! She escaped from the hospital. Those incompetent assholes." He paced the room with his hands on his hips.

Dad stood up. "What happened, Sonny?"

"Betty was having a procedure done, an x-ray or CAT scan or something, and the shackles and handcuffs had to be removed."

"And what, she just took off? No one followed her?" I asked. How could this be happening again? *I swear, the only cancer in my life is Betty, and I want her out.*

"Kinda. She smooth-talked the radiology tech into letting her go to the bathroom. When she didn't come out they called the police in, but by then, she'd disappeared."

"Son of a bitch!" I went to the window. "So what now, Sonny? I'm supposed to be on the lookout again? When will I be able to get on with my life?"

Dad stood up and put both of his hands on my shoulders to calm me down. "What else do you know, Sonny?"

"She jumped into a car that had been left running outside the hospital. Maybe the driver went to take a patient in or something, I don't know. Anyway, a highway patrolman spotted the stolen car parked along I-215, outside of Temecula, California. She may have hitched a ride from there."

"You think someone picked her up?" I asked.

"Don't think so. She's been on her own for a while. I don't think any of her goons would help her. Most of them want her dead."

"Where the fuck is she going?" I asked.

"If she's trying to leave the country, Tijuana is south of where they spotted her last. It's the first border city into Mexico," Sonny speculated.

"Sonny, have you been able to locate any of her henchmen?" Dad asked.

"I'm still working on it. Why?"

"Maybe you and I should step outside and talk," my dad said.

"Whatever you have to say, you can say it here. It's my life we're talking about!" I yelled.

"And I'm determined to preserve it," my father said sternly. "Sonny, may I speak to you outside, please?"

Sonny jumped up. "Sure thing, boss."

Dad looked at me. "Honey, I need you to trust me. This will all be over soon." He kissed me on the top of the head.

Sonny and my father never came back in. Dad later called and told me he and Sonny "were on it," whatever that meant, and he would stop by sometime tomorrow. I wanted to get out of the house and take a walk. One bad thing kept happening after another. The sun began to set and it felt pretty warm walking outside, but I could care less. I took off, grabbing a bottle of water. The sidewalks were empty and I savored the silence. Around the corner from my complex there's a lake surrounded by huge, gorgeous houses. The lake's a mile around and there are several picnic benches and tables to sit at. Stopping to look at the ducks and sit a while, I felt a little ball of fur rubbing against my legs. Looking down, I couldn't tell what it was. A stocky, white thing with short legs, a long tail, and completely matted fur. The dog's hair looked so snarled and dirty that I couldn't tell where its ears began and where they ended. The fuzz around its muzzle looked like a Fu Manchu mustache. He appeared part-lion, part-dog. The furball stood on its hind legs and placed its front paws on my lap. I could see he was male. He had no collar, and I didn't see anyone who looked like they could be his owner anywhere in sight. Was he a stray? He looked hot and very sad. His little dark eyes looked at me, pleading, *Please, take me home.*

"I can't take you home, little guy. Let's see if we can find your owner." I stood up and he followed right at my heels. There was nobody around. Shit. No way in hell could I just leave him here. "Okay, come on," I kissed the air and he followed me back to my apartment.

I drove to the vet around the corner and carried the dog in. "Hi. Um . . . I have a problem here."

"Oh my," said the receptionist. "And who is this?"

"That's my problem. I don't know. He came up to me at the lake. There was no one around and he doesn't have a collar." The dog's tail wagged wildly back and forth as the receptionist cooed and petted him.

"Well, it looks like he hasn't had a bath in a while either. Let's take a look." She got a scanner gun from her drawer and ran it over the dog's neck, looking for a reading. "Doesn't seem to be a microchip in there. Must be a stray. Let's just clean him up and get him checked over and then you . . ."

"Oh, I wasn't going to take him home. I just didn't want to leave him alone at the lake. Can't you guys adopt him out or something?"

"Well, we can, yes. I assumed . . ."

"No. I can't. I can barely take care of myself, much less a dog. Thank you, though. Do I owe you anything?"

"Nope. Since he doesn't belong to you, he's not your responsibility. You saved him, though. We'll try to find a good family for him. Thank you."

I turned to leave and had my hand on the door, the dog trying to follow me. "No, little guy. You need to stay. They're going to take care of you." I tried leaving again. The dog put his front paws on my legs and made a whining sound. It killed me. "Sorry." I looked up at the lady for help. She came over and picked him up, shutting the door behind me. Stupidly, I looked back and saw the dog watching me leave through the glass door. Guilt tore at my heart. I couldn't take this dog home. What would I do with him when I had twelve-hour workdays? Who would watch him? Having a dog was a long-term commitment. No, it wouldn't work. I would just go back home and forget him.

Back at my apartment I flipped through the channels trying to forget the stray. And Betty. And my father and Sonny. And . . . Joel. I hoped the little dog would go to a nice family. I hoped he would be okay. Then I saw a commercial. "Ozzie says, don't let your muffler get the best of you. Come to Ozzie's Auto Parts in Phoenix." A pug, looking exactly like the Ozzie I had known, sat on a guy's lap. The man said, "And if you come down today and let us fix your car, we will donate one dollar to the local pet rescue. It's a win-win!" His offer was followed by a "woof!" from the pug. Poor Ozzie. He had been such fun, so loving. I really loved having him around, providing constant companionship and unconditional love. I missed that. I missed him. Goddamn it! Turning off the TV, I sat there in silence. Another door in my complex slammed and my mother's picture fell to the floor again. I looked to the ceiling. *I hear you, both of you. I owe it to Ozzie.* Shaking my head, I stood up, grabbed my car keys and drove my ass back to the vet's office.

"Hi. It's me again. Any chance I could see the dog I brought in? I'm having second thoughts."

"Of course, one minute," said the same lady as before.

In the back room, I could hear an electric razor and a dog yelping. I hoped that wasn't him. It sounded like he was under-going torture. After several minutes, a vet tech brought him out. He didn't look anything like the same dog. His fur was sheared very short over his pink body and I could see his spot-ted tan and white skin on his underbelly. He looked like a mix between a Westie and a Bichon. They had combed out and cut the fur around his muzzle to look like a fluffy mustache. He was absolutely adorable. The minute he saw me, his tail wagged fero-ciously. He stuck out his tongue and his mouth opened to look like a smile. I guess he knew I would come back for him.

Hearing I would take him with me, the vet came out to speak with me. She wore a white coat over scrubs and looked tall and thin. "Hi! I'm so glad you're going to take him. He's a doll! Such a happy puppy considering what he's been through."

"Is he okay? Any ticks or fleas or anything?" I didn't know if I should pick him up until he got checked out.

"He's been on the street for a while, by the look of his fur and nails. I'd say he's less than a year old. He's awfully skinny, too. We killed and removed two ticks but didn't see any fleas. I'm going to give you a medicine for *Giardia* and something to put on his cuts. His fur was so matted we had to cut pretty close to the skin. He'll heal fine, though."

I reached down to pick him up. He looked so cute with his new haircut. He reminded me of Falcor the Luck Dragon from *The Neverending Story*. Round face with perky ears. Maybe he'd bring both of us some good luck. He leaned his head into me as I held him. It felt good. We needed each other. I waited for the meds and a license, trying to think of a good name for him. "You look like a Farley. That's what I'm going to call you, Farley."

I couldn't sleep that night because Farley's excitement filled my apartment. He would lie in his bed for a few minutes then get up to sniff around some more. He wanted to go on the balcony, down the stairs, in the closet, and any other place his little body could explore. I loved having him. He warmed my heart. It was nice to feel again. I thought about what my dad had told me. *Don't wait. Don't give up.* I grabbed some paper and a pen and decided to write Joel a letter. I brought Farley down to the fountain so he could have free reign of the place. I wasn't worried about him running off. I knew he was where he wanted to be.

> *Dear Joel,*
> *Please don't crumple this up and throw it away. I need to explain. I'm not asking you to forgive me and I don't expect you to after what I did. But I need you to know this:*

*The more I was with you, the more I saw myself as normal, not as someone drowning in a pool of sorrow. I know people die all the time, Joel; we're in the field, but I never dealt with grief the way other kids could. No one was there for me. Now, I compensate for it with the care I give my patients. I use my pain as an excuse not to get too close to anybody. Doing that keeps my mom alive. She was always there because other people weren't. Until you. You listened to me, encouraged me, and introduced to me to the most warm, loving family. You resuscitated my heart and everything was perfect. The more I fell in love with you, the more I worried you would to have to go through the pain of losing me to the same disease as my mother. I wanted to spare you that.*

*I now know how stupid that is. I almost died, several times over the last year, and none of it was because of cancer. You were right. I wasn't living, I was eluding a disease called fear because it was easier than letting someone in. My mother's all around me, not just in my heart. I know that now. And if cancer does come looking for me, fuck it. I'll fight back. Just as my mom tried to. In the end what she lost, I have found. Hope.*

*I do love you. Natalie*

The day after writing my letter to Joel, I drove to his condo when I knew he'd be at work and dropped it in his mailbox. *Whatever happens, at least I've told him the truth.*

A week later, I picked Farley up from puppy day care and couldn't wait to get home. It had been a long day at the hospital and I wanted to get out of my scrubs and relax with a good movie. Farley gave me love, companionship, and someone to talk to. My dad and I had spoken a few times and he informed me he had been looking at property in Marisdale. A second home where he could visit me often. I curled up on the couch with the dog nestled next to me and turned on *Under the Tuscan Sun*, a movie about a divorced woman who goes to Italy searching for herself, and ends up falling in love with a divorced Italian man. *I can't do it.* Searching around for something else, I was startled when the phone rang.

"Hello?"

"Hi, it's me."

Joel. The pain of hurting him came back and I swallowed the lump closing my throat. "Hi."

"Um . . . I think you took home a shirt of mine when we were in Vegas."

I closed my eyes. *Hurry this up, please.* "Okay. I'll look for it and leave it outside for you to come get."

"Actually, I'm outside your door right now." I heard knocking.

Farley growled low and jumped off the couch. "Shush!" I told him. Placing one hand on the doorknob, I couldn't decide whether to open it. *You have to open it, Natalie. You have to.* I opened the door and immediately my eyes overflowed. I said nothing as he walked in.

"Who's this?" Joel said, bending down to pet Farley.

"Farley," I croaked, still holding the door open.

"Come here," Joel said, motioning for me to stand next to him.

"What?" I shut the door and we stood face to face.

"I didn't come here for a stupid shirt. I came here for you."

My muscles trembled and I couldn't bring myself to look at him. "Joel, I . . . I'm so sorry. You were so angry."

"Look, I haven't been the same without you. It sucks. You

and I go together. You're like the female version of me. We fit. I swore I wouldn't trust anybody for a long time, but you made it so easy."

"And I fucked it up."

"I read your letter and I understand. I'm here. I'm not leaving you. I miss you." Joel put both of his hands on my shoulders and continued, "I love you."

I kept looking at my feet. "I want to try," I said softly.

Joel took my face in his hands, tilting my head to meet with his. "Then let's try."

I took his hands off my face. "I know I'm a pain in the ass, but I'm working on it." I dabbed my hand over my cheeks.

"You are a pain in the ass and I love you anyway. And whatever comes with you. I don't like how I feel without you."

I studied his eyes for some sign of doubt. I couldn't find any. He was telling the truth. "You're sure?"

"Absolutely," he said without hesitation. "And I promise I'll never tell you to fuck off again."

I stood on my tiptoes and flung my arms around his neck. He held me to him and whispered in my ear how much he loved me. We pulled away enough to kiss and the tingling returned, filling my body. When I needed a breath, I pulled away and he wiped the sadness from my face. I gave a little laugh and apologized for being such a mush. "It's been a long week," I said.

"Get your shit," Joel said, gesturing to my closet and the dog, "and let's go." He winked at me.

"Back to your house?"

"Yes. Pack your stuff and let's go."

"Him too?" I picked up Farley.

"He comes with you, doesn't he?" Joel took the dog from me.

I looked back at the two of them—at Farley licking Joel's

face—and my heart beat steady and calm. I beamed and mouthed the words, "I love you" as I went to pack up.

Three weeks later, I received a certified package. Joel played tug-o'-war on the floor with Farley as I signed for it. I sat at the kitchen table. Inside, I pulled out a note from Sonny: "Thought you'd like to know . . ." A newspaper article from Mexico was stapled to the note and behind that were several pictures.

*TIJUANA, Mexico—A man was shot to death today by Mexican police seconds after he murdered a woman in the back alley behind La Cuva Bar in Tijuana. It appears the man strangled the woman with a bungee cord. An anonymous person tipped off police, who arrived seconds too late to save the woman, but in time to stop the man from fleeing. The police ordered the man to kneel with his hands up. The man refused, and when he tried to run, police fired their guns, killing him. Medical personnel attempted to revive the woman but they were unsuccessful. Both victim and murderer were pronounced dead this morning.*

*Police have identified the woman as Betty Watson, AKA Dominika Montov, a former member of the Russian mafia who posed as a nurse and was wanted in the U.S. for several crimes. They are still trying to identify her assailant.*

*Holy shit.* I put the article down and looked at the photos. One picture showed Betty with a white sheet over her body, leaving only her face visible. She had dyed her hair black but still wore her red lipstick. There were dark marks around her neck and she appeared pale. Totally lifeless. *I can't believe the bitch is dead.* The next picture had another body under a white sheet. This didn't tell me anything at first; the only thing sticking out was a man's arm. *I'd love to know who did this to her.* Then I took a closer look at the photo. Motherfucker! I picked the picture up again. On the inside of the right wrist, clear as day, I recognized the familiar star tattoo.

Joel came to stand by me at the table. "Everything okay?"

"I'm not sure." Then I saw more writing on the back of Sonny's note:

> *Just wanted you to know. You won't have to look over your shoulder anymore. And FYI, after knowing what your dad did for you, I reached out to my girl. She hasn't responded yet, but I made the first move. It's not much, but it's a start. Your dad and I worked together for weeks, tracking down the star-tattoo dude. We figured he would be after Betty for his unpaid services and your dad thought if he offered him a fat sum of moolah, he'd help us find her. Well, we found him and he did exactly what we asked after we dangled your dad's money in front of him like a slithering worm on a hook. Best part is, we set him up by tipping off the police, sealing both their fates. Classic. The old man and I should go into business together! Glad I could work this case for you! It's been real. And thank Boss for the huge check he sent me! This has been a most lucrative case! See you on the flip side~ Sonny.*

Oh, Dad. Something told me he and Sonny had been determined to stop Betty, no matter what. He'd put so much on the line for me. His career, his reputation . . . everything. When Rob Hatcher had died, his father had told me, "There is no greater love than the love a parent has for their child." I'd always thought my dad resented me after Mom died because I reminded him of her. He never stopped loving me. He'd reached out to me during all this crap more than he ever had since my mom died.

I admired his courage. He was at least trying and now, we had something to build on.

Joel read the note with me. I stood up from the table and went into his arms. He just held me for awhile. Finally he said, "Glad that shit's over with. Could you watch who you fuck with at this hospital, please? I may have to kill someone next time."

Laughing, I said, "There won't be a next time," and playfully tapped him on the chest. Mentally exhausted, I needed sleep. "Can we go to bed now?"

"After we celebrate. Kisses and shots!" Joel went to the kitchen to pull out the tequila and two glasses. Like the alcohol going down, Joel's love burned in me. We kissed, took a shot and laughed. Holding out his arm, he said, "After you."

Together, the three of us climbed the stairs to the bedroom; Joel and I arm in arm, Farley bounding ahead of us. Lying in bed, Farley at our feet, I knew that for the first time in a long time, I would sleep soundly. I touched the picture of my mom that now rested on the bedside table. I swear her smile had grown. I'd call my dad in the morning to tell him thank you. I turned on my side to face Joel and touched his face. We didn't say anything, just caressed each other with our hands and our eyes. Farley let out a huge sigh, curled up at my feet, and fell asleep. A wave of peace came over me.

"Hey, remember when you asked me why I got that four-leaf clover tattoo and I told you I got it for good luck?" Joel asked, kissing the top of my head.

Gazing up at him I said, "Yeah, what about it?"

"Well, do you know that each of the four leaves represents something?"

"What?"

"Faith, hope, love, and luck. I think I'm doing pretty good in all four of those areas."

"I'm working on the faith part but the rest, I've got covered."

"Yes, you do." Joel kissed me again.

I propped myself on Joel's chest and kissed him back. "Love you." Laying my cheek over his heart, I closed my eyes. Faith, hope, love, and luck. My whole life I'd never considered myself lucky. Always running from death, on borrowed time with a damaged heart and a weakened soul. Grief brought us all to our knees and held us prisoner. Now, with help from the four-leaf clover and all its parts, contentment, joy, and imperishable love were finally found.

# Acknowledgments

Four years ago I sat down with my father and told him I wanted to write a book. His response: "Fine, but make sure it's a good one." This book has been my catharsis and I am thrilled to share it with you all.

I want to thank all the nurses and patients that have come into my life over the last fifteen years. My ICU nurses (and you know who you are) mean the world to me and I miss our time together very much. There was always comraderie, support, and strength among us. You guys are the best! There are some patients that change us, make us want to be better, make us grow, and to those people, I say thank you. Nurses are selfless human beings filled with compassion for others and I am truly proud to be a part of this wonderful profession.

To my editors, Lynne Cannon Menges and E.L. Felder, I thank you for your patience and understanding with my early manuscript. Lynne, your honesty and delicate way of telling me to fix something are much appreciated. You stuck with me and I am thankful for all you have done.

To Brooke Warner who is the beacon to us writers fighting for a spot on the shelves. On the path to publication, you are the light at the end of a long, dark tunnel, and for that, I truly thank you. To Crystal Patriarche and the entire SparkPress team, I thank you for the continued encouragement, support, and collaboration. I'm glad we are on this adventure together.

To my most awesome, supportive, and wonderful critique group, Pam Hait and Sheila Grinell. This book would be nowhere near what it is without the expertise of you both. I am grateful and honored to be among writers such as yourselves. Pam, ever since you came into my parents' lives, I have been the lucky one. I call you my aunt because you feel like family and your support, encouragement, and faith in me has never wavered. I am so appreciative of our relationship.

To my brother and sister, thanks for all the experiences, memories, and love. To my sister-in-law, Alma: you've never let grief steal your warm smile and your giving heart. Your ability to see the good in people, and in life, always amazes me. I'm proud to call you *mi familia*. To my parents, the best model of marriage I know! Thank you, Dad, for giving me your writing trait and for encouraging me to always go for the gold. I am proud to be your daughter and am thankful for the example you've set for us. To my mom whose friendship and unconditional love have stood steady throughout my rollercoaster of life. I don't know what I'd do without you.

To my husband, Glenn, without him my story could not be told, without Claire and Troy, our family would not be complete, and without our little guy Nate, my heart would not know such joy. Claire, you are all the daughter I need and I'm happy to have raised you into such a strong, beautiful woman. Troy, your intellect and humor keep our house on its toes and I have no doubt you will do great things. And lastly, Glenn, you are my strength, my light, my love. I wouldn't be who I am today without you.

Finally, to my readers, thank you for allowing me to share Natalie's story with you. I hope I took you on a fun ride and made you believe. And should you ever find yourself lost on this journey of life, I wish you strength, hope, and love along the way.

# About the Author

photo credit: Jeff Noble

Emily Brett received her first bachelor's degree from the University of Colorado Boulder in Kinesiology, after which she went on to Arizona State University to receive a bachelor's degree in nursing. While working as an ICU nurse, she earned a master's degree in nursing at Arizona State. She is board-certified as an Adult Nurse Practitioner and has been in the nursing profession for over ten years. Presently she serves on the Advanced Practice Committee with the Arizona State Board of Nursing, and shares a medical practice with her husband, a physician. She has been published in a number of medical journals, including *The Journal for Nurse Practitioners* and the *Online Journal of Nursing Scholarship*. She is also a member of the Women's Fiction Writers Association.

# Selected Titles from SparkPress

SparkPress is an independent boutique publisher delivering high-quality, entertaining, and engaging content that enhances readers' lives, with a special focus on female-driven work.
Visit us at **www.gosparkpress.com**

*Tracing the Bones*, by Elise A. Miller. $17, 978-1-940716-48-0. Eve Myer becomes consumed with the world of healing arts—and conflicted emotions—when new neighbors/instructors Anna and Billy move in. Shortly after sessions for her chronic back pain begin with Billy, Anna and her small son drown in the bathtub. As Eve's life unravels, her sessions with Billy culminate in an experimental trip into the freezing woods, threatening the remaining bonds of Eve's marriage and finally uncovering the reason for Anna's death.

*The Year of Necessary Lies*, by Kris Radish. $17, 978-1-94071-651-0. A great-granddaughter discovers her ancestor's secrets—inspirational forays into forbidden love and the Florida Everglades at the turn of the last century.

*So Close*, by Emma McLaughlin and Nicola Kraus. $17, 978-1-940716-76-3. A story about a girl from the trailer parks of Florida and the two powerful men who shape her life—one of whom will raise her up to places she never imagined, the other who will threaten to destroy her. Can a girl like her make it to the White House? When her loyalty is tested will she save the only family member she's ever known—even if it means keeping a terrible secret from the American people?

*Hostile Takeover*, by Phyllis Piano, $16.95, 978-1940716824. Long-lost love, a hostile corporate takeover, and the death of her beloved husband turn attorney Molly Parr's life into a tailspin that threatens to ruin everything she has worked for. Molly's all-consuming job is to take over other companies, but when her first love, a man who she feels betrayed her, appears out of nowhere to try and acquire her business, long-hidden passions and secrets are exposed.

# About SparkPress

SparkPress is an independent, hybrid imprint focused on merging the best of the traditional publishing model with new and innovative strategies. We deliver high-quality, entertaining, and engaging content that enhances readers' lives. We are proud to bring to market a list of *New York Times* best-selling, award-winning, and debut authors who represent a wide array of genres, as well as our established, industry-wide reputation for creative, results-driven success in working with authors. SparkPress, a BookSparks imprint, is a division of SparkPoint Studio LLC.

Learn more at
**GoSparkPress.com**